MEMORIES

OF A

LOST AGE

MEMORIES
OF A
LOST AGE

JAIME ACOSTA ALLEN

TRANSLATED BY MARIANA CASSIDY

First published in 2022 by Mariana Cassidy

ISBN 978-1-915036-02-5

Also available as an ebook
ISBN 978-1-915036-03-2

Typeset by seagulls.net
Cover design by Emma Ewbank
Project management by whitefox
Printed and bound by IngramSpark

I would like to give a special thank you to my dear friend Beatriz Rosales, today resting in peace, who carried out the research for my book. To my sister and tireless translator, Mariana. To Monica for her fortitude, and to my sons Simon and Nicky.

I dedicate this book to my precious grandson, Benjamin, with all my love.

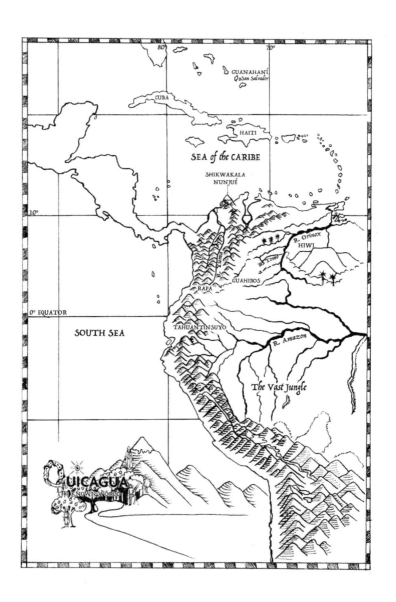

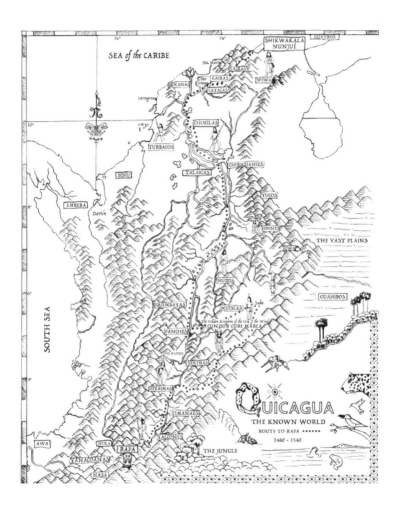

SEA of the CARIBE

GUAHIROS

SHIKWAKALA
NUNJUÉ

Sta. Marta

TAIRAS

MOCANAS

Ciba Cinais

GAIRAS

WIWA

Cartagena

CATACAS

TURBACOS

CHIMILAS

SINU

TALAIGAS

CHIRIGUANIES

EMBERA

Darién

YUCOS

OPONIS

THE VAST PLAINS

UWA

MUZOS

QUIMBAYAS

MUISCAS

Suba

GUAHIBOS

The Golden Kingdom of the God of the Wind

PANCHES

CUNDUR CURI MARCA

SOUTH SEA

THE RAPIDS

COLIMAS

COYAIMAS

TIMANAES

QUICAGUA

THE KNOWN WORLD

ROUTE TO RAPA ••••••

1480 · 1540

AWA

NIXA

RAPA

YALCONES

THE JUNGLE

YANACOANAS

NASA

PROLOGUE

I n 2003, I was asked to take part in the renovation of the cathedral in Santa Marta, the oldest city built by the Spaniards on the continent some 500 years ago. On a hot day, shortly after midday the workers had gone to lunch and I was alone in the cathedral. For some strange reason I was drawn to a section at the base of the north wall that had just been uncovered by the workers. Though the present-day cathedral dates back to the 18th century, it was built on top of the ruins of other, more ancient buildings that had been successively destroyed by fires and pirate attacks. The same urge drove me forward, and I cautiously approached what looked like a small opening set in the ancient foundations. It looked as if it had been built a long time ago to hold something valuable.

All of a sudden, out of nowhere, an old man appeared silently at my side. Clearly of indigenous origin, he was sturdy-looking despite his advanced age. When I recovered from my astonishment, the first thing I thought was that he was from the Sierra Nevada of Santa Marta, but it was becoming hazy all around; the heat, or so it seemed. He addressed me slowly in the Spanish that is characteristic of non-native speakers and common to the indigenous people of the Sierra. Selecting his words carefully, he said in a deep voice, 'We have chosen you to receive a manuscript that is of great importance to our people. Read it, make the necessary modifications to put it into modern Spanish, and publish it.'

He was silent for a moment before continuing, 'You must not change any of the content; it was written by our brother in ancient times.'

He said nothing further and I stood there, bewildered and speechless. He bent over and, using a surprising amount of force, tore away the remaining old bricks. A casket was revealed that was not only well preserved but looked as if it had been specifically made to hold the manuscript. He reverently presented it to me as if he were making a precious offering. My arms and legs trembled as I accepted it. I was so deeply moved that the words froze in my mouth; all I could do was stare at it. When I looked up, his unfathomable eyes were watching me, full of wisdom and kindness. The haze was lifting and my gaze shifted slightly. When I again tried to say something (I do not even remember what) I realized he was no longer there. It was lunchtime. I was alone in the cathedral, in the midday heat, with this treasure in my hands.

The man was the last guardian of the manuscript. Over the past three years I have read, re-read and corrected the language of this 500-year-old document. I have done nothing other than work on this manuscript, which a man from the

Sierra entrusted to me in an unparalleled show of faith. I have not changed anything. I have simply updated the language.

I hope that I have been equal to my assignment.

The Proof-reader
Barranco de Loba
Departamento de Bolivar
Colombia 2006

CHAPTER ONE

Dawn was breaking; I knew it immediately because of the racket the first risers in the village were making. The pair of macaws perched on their favourite roost were squawking and scratching the palm leaf roof of the young people's *maloca*,* impatient for their breakfast. I had become accustomed to their calls after seven enchanting days of passion at Mina's side. I remember at some point my childhood friend Zalab trying to shake me awake, probably because we had to go; we had agreed to leave at dawn as the rainy season had already begun. Furthermore, for three days we would have the company of the travelling musicians and traders who were leaving after last night's festival of 'Welcome and Thank you to the Rains'.

However, Mina's warm body against mine in the hammock, the softness of her skin and her quiet breathing proved an insurmountable obstacle. I carried on sleeping with

---

* Large communal hut

the contentment of a satisfied lover until much later, when I woke with a start.

What a predicament! I shifted Mina, kissed her shoulder and climbed out of the hammock. I hurriedly put on my tunic to protect me from the cold mountain air.

With one hand, I grabbed hold of my *mochilas** and with the other the *poporo.*† I slipped my feet into my *alpargatas*‡ and rushed out. The macaws protested, as they always did when someone entered or left the maloca. I tried to shorten my route by jumping from the terrace, which was about the height of a man's shoulder, and landed on the stone path. At that moment Aluna Jaba, our Mother Earth, not only spared my life but taught me a silent lesson that to this day as an old man I remember in every detail. On the path leading down to the river, I had frequently seen Ulukukwi, the serpent with the lance head that lived among the dried leaves of the forest floor. On this occasion, she was so startled to have someone land unexpectedly at her side that she dug her venomous fangs into what she thought was an intruder's body. When I felt the sharp tug of her fangs tangled in one of my *mochilas*, I understood that Aluna Jaba was giving me another chance to fulfil the destiny for which I had been chosen by the Grand Mama Kwishbagwi, 'the Guardian of the Forests', my teacher and adopted father. Nonetheless, with all the vulnerability of a young lover, I had allowed my love for Mina, the sweet-est and most beautiful woman I had ever met, to divert me.

---

* Woven bags made from cotton or goats' wool

† Small gourds to grind sea shells and coca leaves

‡ Espadrilles made of vegetable fibre

I had missed the opportunity of travelling safely with fellow travellers on what was to be such an important mission for the future of the Taira Nation. Of course, Zalab and I knew the significance of this mission though no one else did. (Aside, that is, from my Master Kwishbagwi, my mother and the other *Mamas** of the Jarlekja, the Council of the Mamas.) But my youth impeded me from grasping the meaning of my destiny. I had only recently been made an apprentice after the coming-of-age ceremony at sixteen.

We, the Taira of the Hummingbird Clan, plus those of the Jaguar Clan and the Toucan Clan, live in the Shikwakala Nunjué Sierra. This mountain range is covered by a vast, abundant forest, which extends down to the ocean and up into the glaciers. We are all children of Gualcovang, the mother of all the Taira since the beginning of days. Our Sierra is separate from the other mountain ranges, the closest is in the south-east, and our customs are different from those of our neighbours. The three clans represent a healthy forest: the Hummingbird symbolizes permanence, the Jaguar, control and the Toucan disperses the seed. We are a people who have a profound respect for and knowledge of the forests that we inhabit. Our lives are adapted to the interests of Aluna Jaba, our Mother Earth. The villages were designed by our elders to preserve the soil and prevent it from being washed away by the rain. The huts are constructed on raised terraces, surrounded by retaining walls built with flagstones similar to the ones with which we make our paths. The terraces are created on different levels to

_____
* A Shaman in Northern Colombia

accommodate the mountainous terrain; each terrace can hold one, two or even three dwellings. The terraces prevent the rain from eroding the soil, and the stone-lined ditches and channels collect the rainwater. It was from one of these terraces that I jumped in my haste to catch up with Zalab.

Our customs are such that we are in harmony with the forests and the mountains. We use wood and clay to make the walls of the dwellings, which not only makes them solid but also durable. The roofs are covered with palm thatching that has to be changed every four or five years when they start to harbour bugs that can irritate the inhabitants! However, this is a gradual process and no two roofs are replaced at the same time, giving the palm trees time to regenerate and produce new leaves. Some of the terraces are used for cultivation because if this is carried out on the slopes, the roots will loosen the soil making landslides inevitable. This way of life was established by the Mamas, allowing us to live in harmony with the Spirits of the Earth.

Among our people, families live in individual huts, but from the age of fourteen, the young live together in the young people's maloca, a very large hut, where I shared my hammock with Mina. What we call the young people's maloca is not only for the young; sometimes older men and women live there if they are alone or have no place of their own; travellers, who are frequent, stay there as well.

If the serpent had bitten me instead of my mochila and judging by the amount of venom that poisoned a large amount of the food necessary for my journey, I would surely have died. That would have happened in spite of the incomparable skills of my mother, the healer of our clan.

I set out on my long journey, alone and frightened by the encounter with Aluna Jaba's messenger and my heart weighed down with love for Mina. The sun had already been up for a while as I walked along the stone path that encircles the Sierra and connects the remote villages before descending into the Gran Cienaga in the west.

The plan we had discussed, with Zalab and the Mama Kwishbagwi, was to get to the Gran Cienaga, a large, calm lagoon separated from the turbulent sea in the north by a narrow strip of beach and mangrove. Here, we were to look for some Caribe fishermen to take us either across the cienaga or all the way to the River Yuma, our Mother River. We would then embark in one of the large boats with many oarsmen, who, depending on the currents of the River, either rowed or made use of long poles to make their way upstream. These boats are used by traders from the different nations that live along the length of the River. Naively, I thought all we had to do was travel upstream until we reached our destination near the source of the River. Once there, we could begin our retreat and train in the grand spiritual centre of our world and become Mamas. Never could I have imagined that the 'lengthy journey' the Mama Kwishbagwi spoke of was going to be such a prolonged one, with so many different and challenging experiences.

My long and solitary route was now through the forests and paths that had been made by the collective effort of the different villages. Substantial stretches were covered with stone slabs that had been cut and laid by the men. Nevertheless, there were sections still unfinished and mud made my progress difficult. In places, I encountered old landslides, where the nearest community had re-laid stones or thrown up little hanging bridges. The more recent landslides were a problem; they were particularly dangerous for the lone traveller – even for one experienced in walking through the mountains on the long trails that unite the different Taira people. Due to my late departure, I was unlikely to reach the next village before the afternoon rains and I would have to overcome any obstacles on the way by myself. I would not even get there before night-fall. The thought of spending the night alone in the forest filled me with anguish. Not only could I not see my way, but I might have to confront prowling wild animals and who knows what other crawling threats. I should have set off early as had been agreed!

However, Mina, a Taira of the Toucan Clan, had arrived in our village whilst Zalab and I were preparing for our journey in the isolated cave of the Mama Kwishbagwi. On my return, my mother introduced me to her. Mina was the daughter of Zhiwé, the powerful healer from the village four days' journey down the mountain by the sea. Mina had come to learn from my mother about the medicinal plants of the high mountains as part of her apprenticeship as a healer. I fell in love with her in the time it takes to look at a beautiful woman and think, 'She has to be mine.' I believe she felt the same about me. For seven days I put off my departure, in spite of Zalab's impatience and, to some extent, encouraged by my mother's mysterious silence. She looked at me in a hopeful, enigmatic way without any reproach. She knew of my mission because of her old friendship with the Mama Kwishbagwi but it was as if she expected something from us. She observed our love without saying a word, waiting for it to develop, patiently biding her time. We each have our destiny, but it is the force of Serankwa, present in every mountain, every creature, every drop of water, that weaves the fabric that interlaces our lives.

All I had on me was the cotton tunic I was wearing and underneath, a loin cloth for when the weather was hot. On my head I wore the cotton cap characteristic of the Taira of the Shikwakala Nunjué Sierra, as well as the alpargatas on my feet, the poporo and the two mochilas. One held the food: the *arepas** (rendered inedible by the poison), a few corn wraps, several strips of smoked venison and various nuts. The other contained my coca leaves and some seashells to mix in the poporo; the necklace with three gold hummingbird figurines symbolizing my Clan; and two sacred Nuaxtashi stones as protection from wild animals. My only weapon was the sling tied round my waist. I would be able to find food on the verges of the paths and the trails in the forest. Plenty of fruit grew there from seeds dropped by generations of travellers for this purpose. If I was assiduous, I could find myself a supper of beans and fruit.

Well, as was to be expected, I did not catch up with the others. I was not making much headway, walking with my heart swollen with love, the parting still so heavy on my mind. I was lagging, and by the middle of the afternoon, when it

––––––––
* Maize patties

started to rain, I was only halfway and the others had probably already arrived at the next Hummingbird village, where they would spend the night. I must have slipped countless times; I was soaked, bruised and frozen to the bone. By nightfall it was clear I could go no further, so I made myself as comfortable as possible between the sinewy roots of an enormous tree not far from the path. I cut some branches and found a few large leaves to make a temporary roof, which would at least give me some protection from the unremitting rain. After eating, I prepared to face a long and dangerous night. At some point a flash of lightning allowed me the glimpse of a coati eyeing me, suspiciously but safely, from the branch of a fallen tree. The sight of it was reassuring, for if the coati appeared undisturbed there was apparently no danger stalking... What you can make yourself believe!

I probably slept a while with the sacred stones of Nuaxtashi clutched tightly in my hand, with Mina in my heart and a chill in my body. But a sudden instinct woke me – or it could have been a protective message from Mama Kwishbagwi. I kept so still that I could hear a leaf fall and then I heard the small, hurried steps of a herd of peccaries.* They had obviously picked up my scent in spite of the rain, as they have a very keen sense of smell. I did not know what to do. I could never protect myself from the sharp teeth of who knows how many peccaries, and if I tried to run, I would easily fall prey to them. Besides, in what direction could I run among the trees in the dark? The best I could hope for was to slay one with my sling,

---

* Aggressive pig-like animal

that is assuming I could see it. I saw no other way but to stand and fight, however futile that was going to be. I was prepared. It was always possible that an aggressive defence might deter them – highly unlikely, but I had no alternative. 'By the force of Arwa-Viku, the giver of life and light, if you want me to carry out my mission, please help me though I am unworthy; it is my own fault for endangering myself in this useless way.'

All of a sudden, I remembered the fallen tree in which I had seen the wide-eyed coati. I stood up, leaving my belongings scattered, and made to run. I hoped I could remember all the multiple obstacles on the uneven ground that could trip me, as well as the exact location of the tree, so as not to crash into it and knock myself out. Just as I took my first blind steps in the dark and the peccaries spotted me, we all heard the noise of a jaguar that had placed itself between me and the peccaries. Then, a leaden silence.

The peccary has a natural fear of the jaguar and in one breath they were gone, leaving behind in the stillness the deep, powerful breathing of the jaguar. Gradually a total calmness invaded me and I sensed the presence of the Mama Kwishbagwi, who, as 'the Guardian of the Forests', had sent the jaguar to protect me, or perhaps he himself had done so. After that, I heard the firm steps of the jaguar receding through the mud and the dead leaves.

Nothing else happened that night. Feeling death so close, then suddenly to be safe, had sharpened my senses and cleared my mind. I was acutely aware of every sound: drops of water falling on the leaves, splashes in the mud and the scuttling of the insects… I had to take several deep breaths before I was able to move and return to where I had abandoned my possessions. I lay down again between the gnarled roots of the tree and as sleep gradually overcame me, I thought I saw my comforting little friend, the coati. But the cold was so intense that by dawn I was on the road again.

CHAPTER TWO

The Hummingbird village where my mother was born is on the bank of the River Guachaca next to where it flows into the sea. It is also the first of the villages of my Clan that you come across when approaching from the west. It had always been like a second home to me. When I arrived and my grandmother and my aunts saw the state I was in, no questions were asked as they hastily came to my aid. They had been worrying about me since the previous day, when Zalab told them I was probably on the way. They fussed over me, fed me, washed my tunic and the rest of my belongings. I managed to talk briefly to my grandmother about my mother and other people she knew before exhaustion got the better of me. I excused myself and went to lie down in a hammock where I slept for the rest of the afternoon and all through the night.

Apparently, Zalab and the other travellers had left that morning at dawn; they had a full day's lead on me. I therefore resigned myself to travelling alone. Even so, I still harboured the hope that I might meet up with Zalab in the Gran Cienaga or on the great River Yuma.

The next morning, I bade a fond farewell to my grandmother and my aunts and set off with renewed vigour. I was carrying a new stock of coca leaves to chew on and give me strength for the journey, fresh food, clean clothes, and a long stick to help me walk and defend myself. For two days I followed a similar pattern, setting off at dawn and walking to the next village, now in the lands of the Jaguar Clan, where I would arrive with the first rains of the afternoon and spend the night.

We, the Taira, are very familiar with the other communities that make up the clans of our nation and frequently travel from one to the other. In this way, we strengthen the bonds that unite us and marriages are often arranged among the young. It was rare not to find a friend or relative in one of the villages. In the evenings I chatted to my friends and acquaintances, exchanging news and remembering anecdotes. Later, I hung a hammock in the big maloca and spent the night with one of the girls I had made friends with. By dawn I was on my way, with fresh provisions. Travelling alone with the memory of Mina on my mind was like a weight on my shoulders and even walking was an effort. I was invaded by memories of her dancing during the celebrations for the 'Welcome and Thank you to the Rains', her beautiful eyes glowing with love by the light of the bonfires. The burdens of love are more arduous than any we carry. They are at the very least more demanding and disheartening. The path was now downhill, and though I slipped a few times, there were no further incidents.

However, meeting up with Zalab was not meant to be. Aluna Jaba had prepared a different destiny and a different route for me. When I arrived at the Gran Cienaga, there was nobody to take me across to the west shore to get to the River. I waited for two days under a small canopy built by Cataca fishermen, with whom I shared food and stories when they occasionally passed by in their small *cayucos*.*

After that, the only people I encountered were the Caribe, who spoke a different language from our Chibcha. I was fluent in Caribe, which I had learnt from my father and my grandparents. A number of them had seen Zalab arrive with traders. Some of them had apparently gone south in search of the Chimila, the nomadic hunters who had the reputation of being shrewd traders. The others headed north, to the Mocana on the coast. Zalab, who seemed to have the good fortune of Serankwa, the Sacred Force of the Earth, embarked in a boat with twelve Chiriguaní rowers. These were leaving the next day for their lands far to the south. They would be travelling up the River Yuma and through the region where the River turns into hundreds of channels and wetlands, a land inhabited by a mysterious amphibious people called the Talaiga, the Turtles. I had absolutely no idea by what means or, even less, how long it was going to take me to get to the land of the Chiriguaní – a journey that Zalab had apparently undertaken in a single boat and would take him approximately three moons.

I did not like the idea of having to wait for days. The heat was unbearable, though when it rained it was a bit cooler. But

---

* Dugout canoes

when it got dark there were mosquitoes buzzing everywhere and we had to light bonfires to ward them off with the smoke. I was impatient to continue on my journey but nothing was working out.

On the third day I met a young fisherman by the name of Tamo who offered to take me to the River. His cayuco was small, and we would have to remain close to the bank and the mangroves to shelter from the rain and find somewhere to spend the nights. It is dangerous to cross the cienaga at this time of year because of the winds, even if Tamo carried the sacred shells of Mesuxse Asigui as protection. I found it interesting that he had these shells, sacred to the Taira, though I suppose it is easy enough to adopt the customs and beliefs of one's neighbours. I have to confess that once I resigned myself to the idea of travelling without Zalab, I was able to enjoy this stretch of the crossing. My companion was the same age as me and we got along well from the start. He was a Caribe from the Gaira Nation. Nearly all his family fished in the sea but he and his father loved the tranquillity of the Gran Cienaga, although it has its dangers; namely, the caimans and the inhabitants of the region, the Cataca, who do not like strangers fishing in their waters. It seemed that Tamo and his father had struck up a friendship with them and obtained their permission.

Tamo showed me how to row and fish, both of which were new to me, as well as the difference between fishing in the sea, in a marsh or in a river. If Tamo was not talking while we rowed, he was singing, sometimes at the top of his voice. When occasionally he sang softly, he reminded me of my father, who was also musical. As the days went by, I become more and more familiar with the Caribe, who live on the coast all around the Shikwakala Nunjué and on the Great River Yuma. These people, who were so cheerful and kind to their friends, can be equally as ferocious with their enemies.

I also learnt to avoid the caimans. When we saw a particularly large one approaching, Tamo, singing in a low voice, would steer us in among the mangroves, where the creatures do not like to go. We drove them away by throwing anything at hand at them. After a number of rather alarming episodes – I was a novice in all that had to do with water – we discovered I could ward them off with my sling. A well-placed stone on the snout was enough for them to leave us alone, even if they had only approached out of curiosity.

At nightfall we would search the trees for a raised wooden platform, built by Cataca fishermen for the purpose of spending the night. Other times, when we came across a beach, we placed branches crosswise to deter the caimans; a bonfire would have sufficed, but any additional defences made me feel safer.

The sling was new to Tamo, and after setting up our camps, I taught him how to use it. We managed to practise a great deal when we found stones on the small beaches among the mangroves or we used pips from fruit. It was great fun and it reminded me of my childhood, when I trained and had target competitions with my friends.

I found out that the Gaira, the Mocana, the Calamarí, the Turbaco, the Wiwa and the Cataca all belong to the Grand Caribe Nation. Several generations ago they were one single nation but because they are scattered over a wide area, they now think of themselves as different nations. The Gaira live at the foot of the Shikwakala Nunjué Sierra by the sea, north of the Gran Cienaga; the Wiwa live on the south side of the Sierra; the Mocana live in the west by the estuary of the Great River Yuma; the Turbaco live in the region further west, in a bay enclosed by an island where fishing is abundant; the Calamarí are the neighbours of the Turbaco in the north and live mostly in the mangrove swamps; the Cataca live in the region of the Gran Cienaga, where we were travelling. The Caribe who live in the desert to the north of the Sierra and in the gulf east of the desert are known as the Guajiro. Tamo also told me that there were Caribe who live on the Islands in the sea north of our coast and are great travellers. It is possible to reach these islands in large vessels, but it is also a region of violent hurricanes. I told Tamo that Caribe blood ran through my veins because my deceased father was a Wiwa and this was why I spoke his language.

One afternoon, after it had stopped raining, we found a sheltered beach in the middle of the mangrove. It was probably a route where generations of female caimans had emerged from the water to lay their eggs during the nesting season. We settled down to await nightfall, having blocked the entrance to prevent any hungry predators from visiting us during the night. Tamo and I had just lit a bonfire and were getting ready to eat when a swarm of angry ants attacked us, sending us scampering into the water. With it up to our waists, we could not stop laughing as we recalled each other's faces and reactions as we tried to gather our belongings before sprinting into the water. Nevertheless, the ants were not giving up. My mochilas and my tunic were covered in them and the only way we could get rid of those tough little assailants was to wash everything thoroughly in the water. Their bite is so fierce it hurts for the rest of the day. Subsequently, we painfully got back into our little cayuco and went in search of somewhere else to spend the rest of the night.

It took us much longer than usual to make the crossing because we played about and had a good time. We were two boys being silly and enjoying ourselves. At night, we told each other stories and talked about our adventures. I told him about Mina and he told me about his romances. We spent our days laughing and practising with the sling, looking out for caimans, fishing and swimming. If we saw any fishermen, we pretended to be very serious and purposeful and when they were gone, we would burst into laughter and continue our games. Now, so many years later, I remember those days with a big smile.

We had another entertaining adventure, though it could have had more serious consequences. We were passing below some low branches in the mangrove when on approaching a platform, a lone serpent dropped into our cayuco sending us fleeing into the water. We had to use all sorts of tricks with a stick to make it go away without biting us. In the end the angry serpent swam off and we had another laughing fit as we got back into our cayuco.

One evening we experienced one of the most magnificent sunsets I had ever seen. The setting sun had turned the sky the colour of gold whilst in the south swirling dark clouds lingered after the recent downpour. The splendid scene was reflected on the clear water all around us and on the waters of the marsh in the east. I found the spectacle so deeply moving that my eyes filled with tears. Tamo must have also felt the magic Aluna Jaba was displaying because he was silent. We were both in a state of harmony or *yuluca*, as the Taira call it. Later, in the semi-darkness we reached a new platform where we prepared to spend the night. As a sign of gratitude to Aluna Jaba, we cleansed ourselves in the water and in silence prepared a little catfish for our evening meal. That night it took me a while to get to sleep and I think Tamo was having the same problem for I heard him sigh several times. Finally, I drifted off, thinking that my journey with Tamo was coming to an end. Rowing was becoming harder and more tiring due to the underwater currents where the cienaga merges with the River.

It had taken us over twenty days to do a journey that usually takes three or four, but I have no regrets. Those were the last days of my life when I did all the things boys usually do. Now, as an adult, I recall those days with pleasure. These were the memories that I evoked during the times of intense physical activity – the extensive rowing and walking – that I would undertake later.

I never saw Tamo again but I still remember him fondly and with great joy. We had promised to meet on my return, to continue our friendship, and I invited him to travel to the Sierra, to meet my friends and to visit my father's clan, the Wiwa. However, Serankwa never crossed our paths again. I can but hope that Aluna Jaba offered him a happy life.

CHAPTER THREE

Before continuing with my story, it would be fitting to relate a bit more about myself. My name when I was young was Kuktu, in memory of the offering in silver my parents made to Aluna Jaba, whom they hoped would always protect me. My parents came from different origins. My mother, Zhi'nita, was descended from an ancient line of women healers of the Hummingbird Clan. She was familiar with the plants and minerals that cured illnesses among her own people and was often asked to do so by other clans. The healers pass down their accumulated knowledge from one generation to the next, which made my mother a person of great wisdom and respect in our nation. Even the Mamas frequently consulted her about the uses and properties of plants. She was a tall, beautiful woman with a strong character. When she was angry everyone, including the Mamas, avoided her. Likewise, when she loved someone, she did so deeply. This was felt by both my father and me, her only son.

My father was not a Taira, he was a Wiwa from a small village near the desert in the west, at the foot of our Sierra. His name was Aru Maku and he was a musician, who, with a group of companions, roamed the different regions, performing their wonderful music. He played the pipes and sang with a voice that captivated all who heard it. My mother was one of the many women he charmed, except that in her case he fell deeply in love with her on his first visit to our people. It is customary in our Hummingbird Clan for the women to remain in their own villages and for the men to seek women from other villages and live with them. My mother was one of the few to leave her village and she did so to be the healer, since my grandmother was already the healer in her village. Serankwa saw to it that my parents' paths crossed and they lived in his village. I grew up with the joy of seeing how much they loved each other.

My mother was always busy with her plants and healing the sick. Even so, we often went for walks together in the forest; she so full of life and joy, gathering plants while my father and I kept her company with our songs and games. My father, with his lively personality, was an endless source of music and tales of his adventures in the regions he had visited. When I was a bit older, I went with him and his musician friends on several of their journeys. I met my Wiwa grandparents and all of my father's family, in a land so hot that people wear no clothing and where I learnt to speak the language of the Caribe. We visited the desert of the Guajiro and saw how they extract salt from the sea. The salt accumulates in large pools of seawater that the sun dries up. It is hard work and the young men rapidly age in appearance.

The salt is traded for food, textiles and essential items with other nations, including us, the Taira.

It is bewildering to someone like me, who lives amidst cool forests and fresh waterfalls, to see what few resources there are in the desert and how difficult life is there.

My father and I also visited the Mocana, the Caribe who live where the Great River Yuma flows into the sea. On one occasion we even ventured beyond the Great River and further than the region where the Turbaco live, to the land of the Sinu. However, after we had travelled for several moons, my father thought it best to turn back, so as not to provoke my mother's wrath. That was how I spent my childhood: accompanying my father on his tours and my mother in search of her healing plants or just living a happy daily life in our hut.

In my eleventh year my father accepted the invitation of his old musical group to travel to the region of the Cuna, in the far west, the land of the Maya, who according to legend were our ancestors. My mother was against the journey from the start, let alone that I should go as well. Eventually she gave in but very reluctantly because the journey was by sea. She had every reason to feel this way, for we never saw my father again. The days, the moons, and the years went by, and we both grieved for him. Something in my mother died. The beautiful woman all the men looked at and admired, the cheerful face that so encouraged the sick, the clear, ringing voice I thought was a gift from Arwa-Viku, everything was extinguished. My mother became careless about her appearance. She dedicated herself to her work and I never heard her sing again. Only with me did she remain attentive and loving. The men who tried to woo her gave up discouraged. The friendship she had always had with the Grand Mama Kwishbagwi grew stronger and she often spent all day in discussions with him in his cave. That is how he came into my life and eventually changed its course. Now, I will tell you more about him.

Kwishbagwi is the title given to the Mama who looks after the forests, the waters and the animals: 'the Guardian of the Forests'. If someone needs a trunk or a strong branch to repair a house, the Mama Kwishbagwi indicates the tree that can be cut. Not a tree or a bush in the Shikwakala Nunjué Sierra can be touched without the authorization of the Mama or his equivalent in other areas. It is the same with animals: the Mama authorizes the hunts and chooses the animals that can be hunted. The Mama decides where the seeds are planted and the necessary compensation if any damage is done to the forests. The trees that are special for their size or location are sacred, and the Spirits of the Kasouggui declare them as such. These trees are untouchable as they protect the soil. The Mama invokes Jate Kalashé and Jate Kalawia, the Spirits of the Kasouggui that reside in the plants and in the mountains, and they tell him what can be used. In this way we are at peace with the Spirits and we prosper.

There are other Mamas who look after the different aspects of our lives and of nature and ensure that we all live in harmony. They observe the movement of the Sun and the Moon to determine the seasons for the crops and the festivals to honour the Spirits and the Gods. They care for the glaciers in the mountains and call on Serankwa, the force that regulates the Universe, to repair any damage done to the mountains, the rivers or the glaciers. The Council of the Mamas, the Jarlekja, decides on matters if there is any danger, a threat or a dispute. The Mamas are very powerful men who are deeply involved with the World of the Spirits.

My mother's friendship with the Mama Kwishbagwi was only natural because of her interest in plants. They exchanged knowledge, which I acquired when I was with them. The Mama did not live in our village; he had a remote cave that was spacious and bright, looking out over the length of the valley of the River Buritaca. I do not think there is any other place with such an extraordinary view. Where the Mama Inkimaku lives, near the source of the water of the glaciers, the view is obscured by the surrounding clouds.

The Mama Kwishbagwi was not of the Hummingbird Clan, he was of the Jaguar Clan, though he had lived amongst us for many years. Everyone said the Mama patrolled the forests in the shape of a large male jaguar. I cannot say I ever saw him transformed into a jaguar though there were always many jaguar footprints around the entrance to his cave.

In due course, my closeness to the Mama and my mother led me to discover that I understood the nature of the forests and I could sense the presence of the Kasouggui Spirits. I spent more and more time with the Mama, and he turned into my adoptive father. I was like a son to him, as well as his disciple. He was an imposing man who radiated calmness; his presence was commanding and his authority indisputable. I never met anyone who dared to contradict or disobey him. One look from the Mama Kwishbagwi had the power of all the Mamas in one.

Zalab, one of the sons of Guka, a skilled weaver of baskets and blankets and close to my mother, started to keep us company. We had been friends since we were little and shared all kinds of adventures and pranks. Together, we learnt to use the sling and became very skilful; no one beat us in competitions with the other boys or later with adults. When the Mama started to instruct us, Zalab became very earnest and devoted to what our master said. He did not have the same aptitude that I have to understand things, but his commitment turned him into an enlightened young man. While I gazed at the eagles flying in search of food or watched in wonder as the condors soared through the air, he sat and deliberated about the messages from the Spirits of the mountains. Zalab and I spent the following five years of our lives with the Mama. They were years of extensive learning in which we gained important knowledge about nature and the spirits that protect it. Zalab spent long periods with the Mama Inkimaku close to the glaciers. I was always with my Master or my mother, who taught me a great deal about the properties of plants.

My mother had a pupil by the name of Walashi, who was learning to become a healer and showed great skill in the use of healing plants. I wooed her and we had our first experiences of love and tenderness together. My time with Walashi, although brief because of our respective activities, was important to my understanding of women. My mother taught her to control her cycle, to have children only when the moment was favourable. She learnt with interest, whereas to a Taira it was strange, because we see children as a blessing from Aluna Jaba as well as the continuation of our nation. However, my mother had other considerations that to her were more important.

I spent as many nights as possible with Walashi, in the maloca of the young people, even though Zalab did not approve. He saw it as a distraction from our studies as well as a weakness. The Mama did not mind, provided I had completed my duties, and to my mother it was of no concern. If anything, I think she had even more affection for Walashi, who was so attentive and loving towards me.

One afternoon, not long after we had our coming-of-age ceremony at sixteen, Zalab and I returned to the Mama Kwishbagwi's cave to find that nothing was the same. The Mama Inkimaku, the Mama Sarabata, 'the Guardian of the Animals of the Sea and the Shores', the Mama Shibulata of the Jaguar Clan and nine other Mamas were all in the cave. It was an important meeting of the Jarlekja. All of the Mamas, elderly men of immense wisdom, were gathered together in consternation, talking in low voices. Zalab and I could not enter into a meeting of such importance and remained outside, making every effort to hear what was being said. We overheard something about the Caribe in the Islands observing strange men arriving by sea, in vessels that looked like giant malocas. I did not really understand, but the Mamas were fasting and this meant something significant would take place.

That night, the Mamas left the cave and we followed them to a ridge in the nearby forest, where they held important ceremonies. They sat in a circle around a rock which served as an altar and from underneath his tunic, my Master removed a bowl that contained *ayawasca*,* from which each Mama drank as it was passed around. We remained silently at the back, not wishing to miss a single word or movement. It was the Ceremony of Zhatukúa, to find out what was amiss and to determine if there was an evil force at work. In this ceremony, the Mamas enter into the World of the Spirits to communicate with them and all the Mamas and Shamans from the other nations. It is a dangerous ritual because, initially at least, it generates physical discomfort and vomiting, but above all because the World of the Spirits is deceptive. Someone not suitably prepared can meet their death or lose their mind. Then, his spirit wanders forever in the form of sad, wailing ghost, lost and trapped between this world and the forests. Only a Mama with a strong mind and the appropriate knowledge can find the truth in the Zhatukúa Ceremony.

All that night and the following morning the Mamas were on their quest. Zalab and I looked after their bodies and prepared food and water for their return. One by one, they awoke and in silence returned to the cave to recover from the journey and the ayawasca. The Mamas had explored the Islands in the sea where the Caribe live. They had located the Caribe Shaman, who gave them the information they were seeking. A number of men who smelt dreadful and dressed in strange clothing had arrived by sea in three canoes as large as malocas. They brought with them some savage animals – similar to our dogs, only much bigger. The men were like monkeys with hair on their faces and bodies. Their Shaman

---

* A psychoactive infusion

had no hair on his head and wore dirty clothing that hung down to his feet. He brandished a stick crossed over by another that to all appearances was sacred, since on numerous occasions the men were seen kneeling and muttering in front of it. The men were unpredictable, sometimes friendly, handing out presents, at other times irascible and dangerous. They had killed several Caribe men and youths and raped some of the women. Their Shaman was the most treacherous of all: he did not carry out the attacks himself but ordered others to do so. They could travel very easily from one island to another in their maloca-like canoes. This was the Mamas' account, as related by the Mama Inkimaku.

That night, after they had recovered, one by one they gravely gave their interpretation of what they had seen. The Mamas knew that what was happening was most unusual and they could not recollect anything similar ever having taken place before. The Caribe Shaman of Guahanaí had every reason to be concerned. The Mama Shibulata remembered that the Muisca, a Chibcha nation who live far to the south, speak of a man with hair on his face, called Bochica, 'The Divine Hand of Light'. He was like a God who had shown them how to grow crops many ages ago. The Mama also recalled that there is a Maya God with a lot of hair on his face who is depicted in the form of Ulukukwi, the Serpent. That God had taught them many important skills at the beginning of the eras, saying he would return. The Mamas studied these ancient myths closely and compared them to the recent report. They talked and meditated all night until they reached the following conclusions: the strangers were not Gods from antiquity as their behaviour was not one of goodness but of barbarity; they were not ordinary men because these do not rape women; they were vicious and it would be wise to consider them a threat to all. The Shaman of these men was dangerous; he did not communicate with nature but with a strange God represented by sticks that could be magic. Under no circumstances was this man to be underestimated.

Since these strangers could travel anywhere in their giant canoes, it was to be assumed that they would reach the coasts of our Shikwakala Nunjué Sierra and the neighbouring regions. The Shaman of Guahanaí thought there were many more in some far-off place on the other side of the sea, but he was not exactly sure of the location. The Mamas were to communicate with the Shamans of the neighbouring villages, to warn them.

The Taira would close off the Sierra to all outsiders and all the communities should be prepared to drive away the strangers when they arrived. The Toucan Clan in particular had to be alert and vigilant, as they lived closest to the sea.

The next morning the Mama Kwishbagwi decided to accelerate Zalab's and my training to become Mamas. Accordingly, a few moons later, we were told that we had to make the journey to the Great Spiritual Centre of our World, close to the source of the River Yuma, a long way from our Sierra. The other Mamas thought this was a prudent course of action and all their advanced disciples would make the journey much sooner than was usual. The Mamas of our nation, when preparing to become wise, powerful men, travel to the Spiritual Centre, known as Rapa, where they extend their knowledge and become acquainted with the Shamans from other nations.

Only the Mamas, the Shamans and those chosen by them know about Rapa. To the rest of the population, it remains a mystery of which they prefer to remain ignorant anyway, fearful of anything to do with Mamas.

I began preparing for my journey, but I missed Walashi, who had gone to stay with the renowned healer Zhiwe of the Toucan. In this way, in an exchange, Zhiwe's daughter Mina came to spend a season with my mother, upsetting the preparations for my journey.

The entire village was getting ready for 'the Ceremony of the Frogs', the festival of 'Welcome and Thank you to the Rains', which takes place over the days prior to their onset. It is called 'the Ceremony of the Frogs' because for days in advance of the rain, these little creatures forecast its arrival. Each night beforehand, there is music and dancing with plentiful quantities of enthusiasm. We drink strong *chicha** and eat specially prepared tasty dishes. The young men make the most of it by courting girls, especially if they are visitors. These celebrations held many happy memories for me, but also sad ones. They reminded me of my father, whose music moved everyone. At the start of the festivities, when my father struck up the first chords and sang in his beautiful voice, I saw many eyes fill with tears. I was among them, only that night I cried because I missed him so much. When I was a small boy, my mother was the most beautiful of the women who danced; my father and I were so proud of her. Subsequently, she sought pretexts to leave the village and spent the evenings with the

---

* Alcoholic drink made from fermented corn

Mama Kwishbagwi to take her mind off the pain caused by my father's absence.

However, at this particular festival, I was with Mina, and how passionately we felt about each other. My lovely Mina, who was dancing with the other women to the sound of the harmonious, rhythmical music. All the men desired her, but she danced for me alone and her eyes told me so. When the celebrations were over, we made love on the bank of the river until the mosquitoes chased us away to my hut or her hammock in the young people's maloca. The days went by between love and festivities and I delayed my journey until, on the last day before the rains arrived, Zalab gave me an ultimatum. He was leaving the next day before daybreak with or without me: he would wait no longer. Fortunately, our master the Mama Kwishbagwi never attended those celebrations or I would never have met Mina and known such complete and fulfilling love. I will say no more about all of this, other than how much I miss her. The pain I felt whenever I thought of her was so disturbing that I even considered unwise actions like abandoning my mission, which of course was impossible, but such is love.

That last night was the most special for she was like an ocelot on heat.

We did not go to the dances or any of the other activities. We made love all night in the midst of a passion that today, so many years later, still surprises and excites me. When finally, we fell asleep still embracing, we were happy, satisfied and exhausted. The night was very advanced or rather dawn was breaking. Now do you understand, dear reader, why I found it so hard to leave?

CHAPTER FOUR

The Great River Yuma or Mother River greeted us in all her magnificence. The distance across from one bank to the other is enormous and the current is very strong; I saw a big tree being swept along as if it were a little branch. We who dwell in the Sierra are not used to rivers this size. I had not seen it since the journey I made with my father and I had forgotten just how splendid it is. It was a pleasure to see the dense, luxuriant forest all along its banks and its waterways; this is what I would see during the whole of my journey.

On the final leg of our crossing, Tamo and I came across a tiny fishing settlement on the channel connecting the cienaga with the River. It consisted of three covered platforms on stilts above the level of the water to prevent them from being flooded At that moment, they were empty. When we disembarked, the first thing we did after selecting the most welcoming platform, was to make sure there were no serpents lurking. We made ourselves comfortable, lit the sand stove* to prepare our meal

---

* Small area of sand and stones used for cooking

and settled down to attempt a good night's sleep, after several entertaining but uncomfortable nights.

My plan now was simply to wait for a boat that would take me upstream.

Tamo hoped it would be a traveller to keep me company as he had to return to his family before they began to worry, if they were not already doing so. I had made a good friend and I was lucky. I could not imagine that I would find someone else with whom I could get on so well. I would miss his company, his songs and his stories. We visualized his mother in a temper because he had disappeared without leaving a message. I teased him by imitating her supposedly shaking a wooden spoon at him. Tamo enjoyed the joke and played along with me, giving extraordinary justifications for his long absence. It made us laugh until we fell asleep.

The following evening, four fishermen arrived, meaning that much to my regret, Tamo would leave at dawn. The fishermen had bad news: because the rains had started, they did not think many boats would venture upstream, against the strong current and with the water level so high. It is usual when the River is low for men to walk along the banks dragging the boats upstream with ropes. In places where the vegetation is too thick, the boats are propelled using long poles; rowing requires a great deal of strength and skill. The fishermen did not think anyone would take me, and it might be at least three moons before the conditions were more favourable. I felt everything was crumbling to the point that I even considered turning back, although I knew this was not possible. It would be unacceptable to my master, the Mama Kwishbagwi, and I would be unworthy of ever becoming a Taira Mama. Whatever happened, I had to persevere. I also had a feeling that these hurdles were sent to test me and were a part of my training to become a Mama, and somehow this reassured me. The discussions with the fishermen went on for a while, but eventually I fell asleep. I worked out that Zalab had more than a moon's lead over me.

Early the next morning, Tamo and I said our farewells. I settled down in the company of the fishermen to await some eventuality. That afternoon several more fishermen appeared with their families. There were women and children of all ages and among them two young girls, who from the beginning seemed to find me attractive. We, the Tairas, usually arouse interest because of our reputation of being mysterious; besides our worlds are so different. The fishermen's water world was completely new to me, accustomed as I was to the mountains. I was dressed in a tunic and they wore nothing at all. They found this amusing and teased me accordingly.

'Come on, show us what's underneath your tunic!'

I humoured them by pulling it more tightly around me. The two girls kept me company even after their families left, though they returned a few days later, much to my regret and theirs… I thoroughly enjoyed this time with them, who in their simplicity were so spontaneous and affectionate. Their knowledge of the River was amazing. If I wanted to fish, they would glance at the water saying, 'not yet', and we continued whatever it was we were doing. Then suddenly they would jump up shouting, 'let's go', and we ran and, without fail, caught something. I do not know how they did it, but they were always right. They also showed me what fruit, nuts and roots in the forest were edible. They never stopped talking about everything that came into their heads. Night and day, I enjoyed their affection and intimacy, their laughter, chatter and enthusiasm. Their names were Nisa and her cousin Apixa. I called them 'my Parrots'.

Then I was alone again. Though I knew how to fish, prepare a hook and bait, scale and bone a fish, it was enough to get by, but even so, there were spells when I was hungry. It was not the same to search the forest alone for something to eat, for I did not have their ability. Moreover, I was not used to the hot climate of the River, accustomed as I was to the fresh air of the mountains. On the other hand, I had my rewards as well. I saw a manatee for the first time, or rather a family of them, and observed how gentle they were. The River dwellers say they are the reincarnations of people who have drowned. I do not know about this but they charmed me. I also came across small alligators, black caimans and river crocodiles. They were my rivals when it came to fishing, and on more than one occasion I lost a meal to them. At least I was out of their reach; one of the big ones could have dragged me into the water and swallowed me without any effort! During the day I was busy either fishing or searching for fruit, roots or nuts in the forest. At night, I dreamt of Mina or reminisced about 'my Parrots' and Tamo. One night, I felt the presence of a jaguar, observing me at length with its sacred eyes, which made my hair stand on end. After a while, it was gone. I wondered then if the Mama was verifying my progress, for I did not feel threatened. Rather, I felt the same way I did when I had not finished a task and he fixed me with his gaze.

Near nightfall the following day, I saw a cayuco approaching and inside was a small, slight, elderly man with a wizened face. He was rowing slowly but assuredly. He came to a halt in front of the platform next to mine and climbed up on to it with the help of a walking stick. He acknowledged me with a gesture and without saying a word made to settle for the night. I drew as close as I could, addressing him with the respect due to the elderly.

'Father, may I offer you some of my coca leaves.'

He ignored me so I tried again, this time in Taira in case he had not understood, but with the same result. I was offended and upset as I lay down. He appeared to sleep all night without moving, but I was so troubled that I was unable to do so. Shortly before dawn, I heard him get up and make ready to depart. Then, without any explanation, he looked at me fixedly and spoke to me in Caribe.

'Well, are you coming, then?'

I was speechless and baffled by his behaviour but he had offered to take me and I was alone and desperate. Therefore, collecting my belongings, I muttered a thank you and climbed into his minute cayuco. That was the beginning of the most singular and interesting journey anyone could possibly undertake.

Without uttering a word, he made his way to the other side of the River, and all the time I was paralyzed by fear. The River was flowing fast and we were small in the midst of all the rushing water, but his skill was incomparable. He rowed in the constant rain, without once allowing the current to sweep us away. When we reached the opposite bank and I turned to look at our point of departure, I saw that we had made some progress. Further on I would come to realize that he had a technique to cut the bends in the River and shorten the laps. More than strength, though he was not lacking in this, was his in-depth knowledge of the River. He knew where the currents were and changed direction accordingly. I did not help in any way, and this made me uncomfortable. Later, I became more skilful at rowing and did my share, though he never asked this of me or reproached any clumsiness on my part. That first night, he pointed with his paddle to a platform made out of some branches in a tree that I had not even noticed. 'We can sleep there.'

He said remarkably little. As the days went by, it became obvious that not having much contact with others, he was not used to talking. He was quiet, but through the gestures and expressions on his face, we communicated without the need for words. There were times when he did tell me things, though briefly. Occasionally, he seemed to withdraw as if in meditation and it was not possible to reach him. When we became better acquainted, I understood that he was a person of importance. Probably in those moments, his mind was elsewhere, scouring the River, in the World of the Spirits or communicating with others. He could do this without the need for concoctions such as ayawasca. I began to suspect that he was a Shaman or the like but I dared not ask him.

Fishing with him was amazing; he seemed to know exactly where to find a fish and even the right size for the two of us. He did not waste or want for anything. He had an absolute regard for anything that concerned the River: the water, the animals, the forests and its climate. In due course, as I got used to the silence, I became more observant of my surroundings and my apprehension turned into respect. I started to think of him as Jawi, in honour of the seashells with which the Taira make their offerings to the rivers. Unwittingly, I used this name out loud, which he seemed to find interesting, because the first time I did, he smiled as if it amused him.

The first moon was rainy and lonely as we encountered no one and I became sick with a fever. One afternoon I was shivering, and on arriving at the place to spend the night I felt very unwell. I tried to tell Jawi it was due to the rain, but he knew otherwise. My illness was caused by the mosquitoes during the rainy season and I was very ill. My skin turned yellow, which frightened me on the rare occasions I was conscious between the bouts of fever. He told me later when I was getting better, that I had been sick for more than twenty days. I had been close to death but, with the help of the Spirits, I got better, though nevertheless it was a terrifying experience. At some stage during the fever, I had a vision that I had died, but I also saw the Mamas, including my Master, coming to my aid. I saw my mother preparing medicines with Jawi; she told me that Mina was carrying my child and was almost in her fourth moon. This news gave me the hope to live and my body recovered with renewed vigour. I was unaware that my mother could make trips with ayawasca. My recovery, quite apart from the physical side, was a revelation for I saw that I was not alone. The Mamas and my mother were always with me. I also came to the realization that Jawi was a wise man, a Shaman of the River. What was perfectly obvious was that my encounter with Jawi had not been by chance, but through the involvement of the Mama Kwishbagwi.

A few days later, I saw some Fishermen and their families address Jawi in a reverent manner, to which he responded by placing his hands on their heads. Without saying a word, he directed them to keep me company while he went away for a few days into the forest to meditate and be alone. I think that my illness and the care I needed, but above all the responsibility, had exhausted him and he needed solitude to recover.

The Fishermen, twelve in all, took good care of me. I was someone notable, probably because I was travelling with Jawi. At first no one spoke to me, until three children approached, and in spite of feeling exhausted, I played with them, trying to catch and tickle them. This made the adults laugh and put them at ease. I had many questions and I saw they were also curious about me. That night around the bonfire, we talked in a different dialect of Caribe from mine, which was Wiwa, but we all understood each other and had a lively conversation. I found out that these Fishermen of the River were a nomadic people who roam the River in family groups, fishing and living off the forest. During the rainy seasons they do not travel much and gather instead in large groups, in settlements similar to the one I stayed in with Jawi. These occasions are important for them to exchange news, arrange marriages among the young and talk about the River. Nothing happens on it that they do not know about, and that included me, though they thought I was still in the settlement.

They did not understand what a Taira was and even less a mountain, but the fact that I was with Jawi made me worthy of respect. In their eyes, he was a holy man and it was a special honour to be with him. Apparently, they are afflicted by the same fevers I had and many perish. They have lost half their families to this yellow skin fever, but if they survive, they do not get it again, which was a relief to me. With so many deaths, it is important for their women to have many children, and from different fathers to regenerate their bloodlines. This was the reason they had left Nisa and Apixa, 'my Parrots', with me and whose company I had so appreciated. It is a difficult way of life which they cling to as best they can.

They offered me one of the women, which I had to decline because I was so weak after my illness and having not eaten much. When I asked them about their nation, they did not understand my question. They are a nomadic river people and have no concept of what it is to live in a permanent settlement or, for that matter, that entire nations of people exist. They see many travellers on the River, but to them they are just people going from one place to another, who are different from them, and their interaction is limited. That first night I enquired about Zalab, telling them the little I knew: that he was travelling in a boat with twelve Chiriguaní who traded with the Cataca. They remembered that at the last family reunion someone had mentioned a vessel full of traders that was carrying salt and shells. There was a passenger with them, who, so it seemed, was travelling far, to the source of the River. They could not imagine the River being any different from how they saw it. It made them laugh to think of it being a small stream at its source, and the idea that it flowed down from the mountains was unimaginable. They lead simple lives. They do not own more than they need on a daily basis: their cayucos, their knowledge of the River and their kindness.

Three days later, I was able to swim and go for short walks. In the course of our conversations, I realized they had no concept of age. One was a child, an adolescent, an adult or an old person; that was it. I tried to explain how to calculate age and how the sun moves across the sky daily from east to west and from north to south with the passing of the moons. The Taira year begins when the midday sun is directly overhead and moving north. This we know because of the shadow cast by a rod on the ground at midday; the shadow gets longer as the sun moves north. The sun reaches its furthest point in the north, and on its return it is directly overhead (at midday) before it moves south to its furthest point and then returns to its vertical position once again. This indicates the end of the year and the beginning of the new one. What is interesting is that the journey south is slightly longer than the journey north but altogether, it is what we call a year. All our villages use this sun calendar. This system makes it easier to predict the seasons of the rains and the harvests. I do not think they understood what I was saying for they do not grow crops, living as they do off the forest and fishing. Nonetheless, they listened attentively, nodding their heads. They probably thought my words were some form of magic, and it filled them with admiration, even though the information was useless as well as beyond them.

In the evenings, they prepared my food and entertained me with their chatter, while I played with their children and observed their customs. On the third day, I felt strong enough to be with a woman. This pleased them enormously, as they said she was fertile at that moment. Furthermore, it would be an honour for my seed to remain among them. On these occasions, to be alone, it was usual to go down to the River.

The following afternoon, Jawi returned. All of a sudden, he appeared without uttering a word or making a sound. As soon as the Fishermen saw him, they fell silent and went about their activities. They prepared the food, and at nightfall we all sat round the fire, talking in low voices. Jawi sat away from them, listening, but they were aware of his presence. That night we all went to sleep early.

The next morning, it was time to leave. I had been happy in the company of the Fishermen and their families, and I would miss their simple ways and their kindness towards me. We had obviously lost a lot of time because of my illness and my convalescence. It was an emotional moment when we said our goodbyes. Jawi silently placed his hand on the head of each one and we set off. They all stood on the riverbank, waving until we lost sight of them. What stories they would have to tell at their next big reunion!

My arms were still weak and Jawi had to do all the work, which he did gladly. Gradually, I resumed the rowing, particularly on the days he went on a Journey of the Spirit. When it was my turn, I placed myself in the rear of the cayuco, where I was in control and could avoid a log or a serpent looking for a comfortable ride. I was learning fast that serpents are a serious matter. The trees that float down river inevitably carry one of these venomous creatures. I did not relish the idea of having to jump from a small cayuco into the big river, and then not be able to get back in again, or there was always the risk of it fatally overturning.

I had now become a Taira of the River, which pleased me enormously. Everything I was doing was different from what a Taira usually does, even on the sea; everything was new to me.

CHAPTER FIVE

We travelled for another six moons before we reached the area where the River divides into two. Once I recovered my strength, as I have already mentioned, I was able to row skilfully. I became so familiar with the River and its currents that on occasions Jawi left me alone while he went deep into the forest, telling me where to pick him up a few days later. The serenity I experienced in Jawi's company, and his continual silence, helped me to get to grips with the River. The days went quietly by, and I felt that I was enriching my spirit. We frequently came across families of Fishermen, who were aware of our journey. They were always as respectful and friendly as the family I had been with during my convalescence. From them, I was learning the value of humility and of sharing everything. Meeting up with the Fishermen was a pleasure that contributed in no small measure to my overall feeling of serenity and happiness. The maximum honour I could bestow was to spend the night with one of their women. I felt emotional at the thought of Mina and the child she was carrying; according to my mother, the birth was now imminent. Furthermore, some of the women on the River, including 'my Parrots', might also be with child.

For some reason, Jawi preferred to avoid the travellers, save for the Fishermen of the River, who I thought were his people until later when I found out otherwise.

At first, I longed to hear the news the travellers had from up and down the River but I made do with watching them go by or seeing their encampments. After a while, it ceased to matter. When the rains stopped and the water level subsided, we took it in turns to either row or walk along the riverbanks, dragging our cayuco with the aid of a rope. When we encountered a manatee, we stroked it and carried on with our journey. On the River, Jawi knew how to ward off the caimans. He carried some dried fruit, which he threw at them if they got too close. He said it produced an irritant when mixed with water that made them go away. On occasions when walking, we came across black caimans or a crocodile – the latter were less frequent. Jawi would make a strange sound with his mouth and clap his hands loudly and they rapidly scuttled back into the water, freeing our path. He knew when a female was nesting and we retreated to our cayuco, to leave her alone.

Some animals looked at us suspiciously, others were unperturbed, but they always disappeared as soon as they saw us. We came across tapirs, pumas, ocelots, all kinds of monkeys, small alligators, boas and serpents, peccaries, turtles, coatis, iguanas and a variety of beautiful birds. I frequently observed an eagle and wondered if it was keeping us company. Occasionally, we spied a jaguar, which made us both happy, and it reminded me of my Master. I loved to watch the flocks of macaws flying along the riverbanks to extract minerals from the clay soil with their strong beaks. According to Jawi, they do this to neutralize the poisonous substances found in the fruit of a jungle palm which is their favourite food. I could clearly distinguish the pairs, as the macaws fly in flocks of pairs, which they keep to all their lives. It was a privilege to be observing all the richness that nature has to offer and that I was getting to know and understand. The people who live on the River are all part of it. I noticed they do not seek the permission of their Shaman to cut a tree, as the Taira do. Instead, they choose one with great care, therefore minimizing the effect on the forest. We all respect the greatness of Aluna Jaba that we honour at sunset while we silently contemplate her splendour. Everything that I was learning with Jawi about the River, the forests, the animals, was fascinating.

At the point where the River divides, I saw what looked like a large island between the two branches. We took the west branch on our right, where the current looked less strong, and kept to the left bank. It did not take me long to see that there was no island. In fact, the two branches of the River enclosed a vast area of channels, streams and wetlands, where we were entering the territory of the Talaiga, the Turtle Men. I would have preferred to be on the other side of the River because I had heard all sorts of tales and legends about this nation and thought it best to avoid them. Perhaps they would allow us to pass if we kept to the River or even a small beach, but I was still nervous. We continued in this way for most of the day. I was full of apprehension and foreboding due to the well-earned reputation of mystery and danger surrounding this land. Rash travellers had entered but never emerged, for the Talaiga guard their territory fiercely. At least, this is what was said, because nobody knew anyone who had gone in or, even less, come out. Not even the Fishermen of the River venture into this land; they keep to the main branches and the opposite banks of the River.

Without any explanation, Jawi guided us into a channel covered by thick foliage. I did not know why, but I would find out soon enough. If it had been up to me, I would still be on the River, but Jawi must have known what he was doing. We were in what looked like a long tunnel of trees about the height of four men and easy to navigate, so very different from rowing on the wide River. I could make out the noises of the jungle in the distance, while all around us there was an oppressive silence. I am not sure if it was our presence or something else, for I had the most unpleasant feeling. From time to time, I turned to look at Jawi, who simply smiled; nothing seemed to unsettle him. As the afternoon progressed, I sensed that we were being watched. We continued rowing, each stroke moving us forward, across other channels, small marshes and streams that flowed in and out. Jawi appeared to know the way because it was like being in a labyrinth. As night fell, we reached the edge of a small marsh, where the vegetation was different, consisting of scrubland and rushes in the water. It was then that I saw them: five women beckoning us. At least, that is what I thought they were, because they were wearing trinkets, like the ones worn by the women of the River, only these women were clothed. As we drew close, they muttered something to each other, looked at us again and vanished.

When we disembarked, we came face to face with five warriors I would have preferred never to have encountered. They were the same warriors who had dressed as women to entice us, and now I was facing the most ferocious warriors I had ever seen in my life. They had bows with deadly arrows, no doubt impregnated with curare or some other dreadful poison. The paint on their faces enhanced their hostility, but what frightened me more was that their threats and aggression were directed at me.

One of them, who appeared to be the leader, left the group and, approaching Jawi, bowed his head reverently. Jawi placed his hands on his head and the warrior said a few words, of which I only understood 'Great Father'. I was somewhat reassured, though the other warriors did not take their eyes off me and did not alter their hostile stance. They gestured to me with their bows to accompany them. The chief went ahead, followed by your frightened narrator, three of the warriors and finally Jawi bringing up the rear. The youngest of the men was walking at Jawi's side, speaking to him so rapidly that I did not comprehend anything. We did not have far to go. On the way, I analysed my situation: clearly, they were not happy with my presence but they obviously knew Jawi, for whom they had a great deal of respect. This was a good sign; otherwise, I would undoubtedly be dead. I would make them see that I had the best of intentions. In any case, it had not been my choice to enter their territory; Jawi obviously had his reasons.

We reached a village and I was instructed to remain in the clearing while two serious-looking warriors stayed with me. In the semi-darkness I could barely make out what was happening or what the village looked like. It appeared to be small and consisted of about nine houses on stilts. The River was low since the rains had ceased and there was a stretch of flat land with no vegetation between the houses, where the inhabitants were gathering to receive Jawi. All the children came running to look at me with wide eyes. Clearly, they did not often have visitors and this hamlet was some sort of lookout post on their frontier. I was told to go inside one of the houses and they indicated a corner where I was left to wait. After a while, one of the women brought me a bowl of corn soup, some pieces of sun-dried bocachico fish and water to drink.

After I had eaten and was getting tired of waiting, Jawi arrived with a warrior who appeared to be the chief of the community. He spoke in a language I was familiar with: a form of Caribe, similar to that spoken by the Fishermen of the River. I was told that at dawn they were sending a messenger to the Council of the Elders, so they could decide my fate. The fact that I was with the 'Great Father' had allowed me to get this far because no one entered their territory without permission. Travellers had to remain at one or other of the River Junctions, where there were guards. There, they stated their business and were given or denied entry; to enter without authorization was punishable by death. At this moment I was sentenced to death but because I was with the Great Father, the decision was not theirs. I had to wait. I cannot say I was altogether unconcerned about my fate, though from a little way off Jawi was making gestures for me not to worry. He did not want to look as if he were undermining the chief, who after all, as the guardian of the region was only obeying orders.

I noticed that the adults had a piercing below their lower lip, where they placed a small gold ornament in the shape of a shell. Jawi also had this piercing though it was now an old scar and barely visible. All of a sudden, the realization that Jawi was a Talaiga dawned on me at which he smiled and nodded, making me feel a lot better. At the very least, I was not going to die there.

Several days went by, waiting for news from the Council of Elders. In the meantime, I watched how the families wanted to spend time with Jawi, inviting him for a meal or to stay the night. Jawi complied but I knew he found it difficult as he was not used to living in a community. I was also conscious of how much I had grown to love and understand him. I saw in him the wisdom of the Taira Mamas and why they had to live in isolation. He reminded me of the Guardian of the Glaciers, the Mama Inkimaku. Since the Fishermen of the River were not one organized nation, the elders of the Talaiga had assumed the responsibility for the stretch of River outside their territory, and this was one of Jawi's tasks as the Shaman, Great Guardian of the River.

I tried by every means to communicate with the people of the village, but it was not possible, not even with the children, with whom I usually found it easy to make friends. I was not welcome and this would be the case until my status changed. Only Jawi kept me company whenever he could. Finally, the messenger returned with good news, because from that day onwards I was treated with courtesy and respect, though not in the same manner they treated Jawi. We were able to continue our journey in one of their boats with four rowers and our little cayuco in tow. Now, as I look back, I appreciate what an honour it was for this mysterious people to have participated in my journey. I was after all only a young and insignificant novice on my way to train to be a Mama.

We travelled through a region that was different from anything I had seen before. It was crossed over by hundreds of channels, tributaries of the River and wetlands of different sizes. The fluctuating water levels were reflected in the vegetation that varied in age accordingly. I struck up a friendship with one of the rowers, who was the same age as me, and he pointed out the special features of everything we saw. Apparently, the work of their nation is the conservation of the sites where the River fish spawn and the banks and beaches where the turtles lay their eggs. I did not actually see any of the beaches but they must have been there, if he said so. What an honourable task, to be the guardians of the region where many of the fish of the Great Mother River are spawned. We spent the nights in settlements of all sizes. However, I never got to see the main village and the whereabouts of the Council of Elders. In the villages, it was not easy to overcome the barrier they had against strangers, though they were always courteous. The use of coca leaves is unknown to them, which is very different from all the other peoples I had met. I would have liked to spend more time in this amphibious region, though I don't think it would ever have been possible.

I shall now tell you more about Jawi, and it took me over five years to obtain this information! He was born in the main Talaiga village. I do not remember his name exactly, but it alluded to the gold shells worn by his people on their chins. No wonder he so graciously accepted the name I gave him and that only I used; it was like a childhood memory. His father was the chief guardian of a branch of the River that flows through the biggest wetland in their territory. The main village is located there and it is semi-aquatic, like most of their villages: some of the houses are on dry land but most are constructed on stilts in the middle of the wetland. Their crops are abundant as the land is fertile. When the River subsides and islands emerge, they cultivate maize and a variety of crops such as tomatoes and cotton; life is plentiful. Jawi grew up as an ordinary child in his community, swimming, fishing and playing as children everywhere do. As he grew older, he spent time with his father on the River and had the opportunity to witness the migration of the fish and the places where they spawned. He began to understand all the complexities of the River. When the turtles laid their eggs on the beaches, he monitored them until he saw the babies hatch from the eggs and scurry into the water. He noted which animals fed on the eggs or on the little turtles. He was learning about Mother Earth, about the positive and negative effects that all animals and humans have, not only on each other, but on all other living creatures and plants, even in the smallest ways that would go unnoticed by most.

In his adolescence, this interest incited him to explore the Great River to its furthest limits and to meet the people who lived there. This was most unusual. At first, people were not sure of the intentions of this young Talaiga, who all by himself was investigating everything he saw. The majority had never seen a Talaiga in their lives and had only heard stories of how dangerous they were. Eventually they came to accept that he was only an inquisitive explorer. This is how he came to meet the Shaman of the River, who was intrigued by the young man. Initially, he could not work out what region he was from, as he got on with all the fishermen and paid attention to everything the travellers did on the River. He saw the young man's interests and found it strange because usually the Talaiga never leave their territory. Undetected, the Shaman gave him little tests, to see what he did. For example: one day, as he was sleeping on the beach, the Shaman left the egg of a specific bird nearby. He noted with interest how the young man identified the bird it came from, looked for the nest and wondered how it came to be where he found it. This would have held no interest for anybody else; the egg would have been ignored or consumed without another thought. The young Talaiga had to understand why, and this made an enormous difference. After a while, the Shaman made himself known and they struck up a friendship to the point that the Shaman considered Jawi his successor. Without further delay, he contacted the Council of Elders of the Talaiga, to ask their permission to make him his apprentice. He also sought the approval of the Talaiga Shaman. The Talaiga are different in every aspect from other nations. The Council of Elders is made up of wise men who dedicate their lives to the care of their territory. Each one is an expert in his field: farming, fishing, construction, culture, combat, craftwork (gold or otherwise) and any other activity they might have. The Talaiga Shaman does not participate in the Council but he abides by the results of its decisions. He is a solitary person, who only appears when he has something of consequence to say. Long periods, even years, can go by without anyone seeing him. But as soon as there is a problem, he is there, demanding an explanation.

The Shaman of the Talaiga and the Shaman of the River were in frequent contact, the former having heard about this unusual, solitary young man whom he had also been observing. They thought it was best that the young Talaiga should spend time with each one, then the young man could express his preference. Either way, it was the Master of Rapa who would make the final decision. Thus, he began his apprenticeship, which lasted five years, at the end of which he was sent to Rapa.

All alone, he reached the land of the Yalcón in his little cayuco, which he left in one of the villages and arrived in Rapa on foot. There he spent the next eighteen years of his life, progressing in his studies and developing his skills. At the end of his time, he stood out as a solitary Shaman with an extraordinary talent for dealing with all matters, anticipating problems and finding brilliant solutions. He had the ability, which I had seen, to make Journeys of the Spirit without the aid of ayawasca, by simply sitting to meditate in absolute silence. He did not strike up many friendships because of his solitary nature. At the end of his time in Rapa, he was appointed to be the Shaman of the River Yuma, from the estuary to the land of the Opón, which included the territory of the Talaiga. This was later extended to the estuary of the river of the Muzo, where I would travel with him many years later. On his way back from Rapa, he found his old cayuco, which the Yalcón had looked after with great care, oiling the wood and preserving it all those years. He embarked and set off alone to carry out his new duties.

I do not know how many years ago this all took place, for it was difficult to work out his age by looking at him. He had the body of an old man, an astonishing clarity of mind and the strength and vitality of a young man.

To return to my story, half a moon later we reached the extreme south of the Talaiga territory, where the two large branches of the River Yuma join up again, or to be more precise, where the two branches of the River separate, because they flow north and we were going south. My friend the Talaiga rower explained that a bit further downstream on the west branch, two big rivers from the interior flow into the Great River Yuma. For this reason, the River does not appear as large or as wide at this point. I could even see a few scattered hamlets on the other side, something that would not have been possible further north on the River. Not very far, to our left, was the entrance to a large wetland, an important fishing centre for the Chiriguaní. Where the two branches of the River separate, the bank is high. There, from where I was standing and gazing south, I had the impression of being on an island in the middle of a water world: the east branch was on my left and the west branch on my right and behind me was the wetland that joined up with the east branch. I made out a small Talaiga hamlet, from where they surveyed the southern entrance to their territory. I could not imagine a more ideal place to have a village. That night, with the full moon, the scene was enchanting, and after spending a long while absorbing the magic energy of the scenery, I retired to sleep feeling my spirit was richer and more motivated.

After bidding farewell to our new friends, we returned to our old routine in the little cayuco. We were refreshed, having travelled with the help of others, which is always much easier. As to our journey, we had significantly reduced the time, though it was difficult to say by how much. The distance was probably the same but in terms of speed and effort, it was better to have travelled through the region of the Talaiga.

CHAPTER SIX

I did not know how much longer I would be travelling with Jawi, as I was unsure how far it was to the source of the River. Judging by its current size, the distance still seemed enormous though eventually, as the moons went by, it began to diminish. Jawi said nothing and I did not ask. Altogether, I travelled with him for close to five years.

When we left the territory of the Talaiga, we entered the land of the Chiriguaní, on the east side of the River. At first, I wondered whether to inquire about Zalab, though it did seem pointless, since I could never have caught up with him. Then Jawi took a lesser branch of the River to avoid the strong current and we left the territory of the Chiriguaní. We returned to the routine we had at the beginning: rowing or walking along the banks during the day and looking for a platform to sleep at night. When we started our journey, it never failed to astonish me how Jawi saw these platforms. Eventually, I learnt to see them myself, and in the end, I was surprised if I did not. We sometimes came across families of Fishermen, who always behaved with the same kindness and respect. It was a big occasion to come across a family we knew. They were aware that we had been in the territory of the Talaiga and were amazed that we were still alive; we had to be sacred, powerful persons! I was frequently able to advise them in the use of some of the medicinal plants that I had learnt from my mother. This was usually to worm the children and to show them the benefits of preventative measures. But I was also asked about the properties of certain plants, some of which were unknown to me.

I taught the men how to use and make a sling, varying the length of the string according to individual requests. We discovered that it is not easy to use in a cayuco. It requires considerable balance whilst standing and presents problems whilst seated, especially if there are other occupants, and the range is somewhat limited. On the other hand, on a beach it is a formidable weapon for hunting from afar. I believe the use of this weapon spread very quickly throughout the whole of the River. For their part, the Fishermen taught me where to find fish during the different seasons. They also showed me how to entice the fish by using a log full of termites that is shaken over the water; the fish appear to have their feast, only to fall prey to the waiting fisherman…

I often thought about Mina and now also about my son or daughter living in the cool mountains of the Shikwakala Nunjué. I remembered moments from my childhood: running around with the small dogs; travelling with my father or searching for plants with my mother; picking *mamoncillos** from a tree

---

* Small round green acid fruit

by the big maloca with my friends. Now my life could not have been more different. I was living through a unique learning experience with Jawi. Somehow, my Master Kwishbagwi made it so that our paths crossed and today I understand why. It would have been difficult to find someone so integrated with Aluna Jaba. His silent presence influenced the Fishermen to such an extent that they felt part of the River and its forests, aiding Jawi in his task as guardian.

Many moons went by, the dry and the rainy seasons came and went and our journey progressed slowly but surely. In the distance, I could make out the mountains behind the forests and the valley of the Great River was gradually narrowing. The Fishermen apprised me of the nations through whose lands we were travelling: the Yariguí, the Opón, the Carare, the Samaná, the Arma, the Pacara, and the Caramanta. We watched their boats going about their affairs up and down the River. To them, we were just river folk and they left us alone.

The Caribe spoken by the Fishermen of the River changed the further south we went. This was no doubt due to the influence of the different people living in these new lands, and I started to recognize words from my own Taira language. I knew that many generations ago the Chibcha were one large nation, which included the Taira, the Muisca and other people from the mountains, and we all had a common language. Later, the Caribe arrived by sea, gradually occupying the lower lands. It was a terrible time of wars and death, until the Mamas and the Caribe Shamans agreed on the territories that each should inhabit: the Taira and the Chibcha in the mountains, and the Caribe on the coast and the plains of the large rivers. This settlement brought peace, and the different indigenous peoples organized themselves into the nations, through which we were travelling. This period of wars became a part of the stories which the grown-ups related in the evenings.

As the Mamas and the Shamans shared the common interest of serving Aluna Jaba, they set aside some land in the mountains, not far from the source of the Great Mother River. It is a region where the presence of Serankwa, the power of nature that Aluna Jaba bestows on us, is felt with remarkable force. All those who are chosen to serve Mother Earth are trained here, in what is known as Rapa, the destination of my journey. I knew nothing further, neither what it was like, nor where or with whom I would live. What I did know was that Rapa was having an increasingly powerful draw on me as we progressed south.

It is human nature to want more land or resources and there are no lack of wars, conflicts or resentment among the nations. Human beings are this way inclined and for this reason Shamans are needed to rise above the problems and find solutions. At times even they can create problems by their decisions or having the wrong instinct, as they are only human. Personally, I never encountered any of these Shamans. One of the purposes of Rapa is to train and ensure that the Shamans are good men, with a great deal of power. The apprenticeship serves as a filter, so that only people with the capacity to interpret Aluna Jaba are sent to Rapa. There are some who try to impersonate a Shaman for their own malevolent purposes, but these are hunted down implacably and eliminated. A Shaman has powers that cannot be imagined and there is no place for impostors or for evil.

Apart from the nights spent with a family of Fishermen, Jawi and I usually travelled in silence. Occasionally, the two of us had 'a conversation' in a manner of speaking. I talked or asked questions and he listened attentively, answering with a few words and signs. That was Jawi's teaching method. He asked me a brief question and I had to find my own solution; he would then make a gesture showing if it was correct. If it was not or I did not understand, he patiently guided me in the right direction. One night, I asked him about Rapa and his experience there. It was the first and last time he spoke to me about it, saying a bit more than was usual.

'It happened a long time ago when I was a young man like you. I was there for eighteen years and I left a sentinel at the tomb of the Master Isa-Ni.' He was lost in his own thoughts until he added, 'I met your Master there.'

That was it. I was so overwhelmed to hear that my two Masters knew each other that it distracted me from the other things he said, and for many days I mulled over it. I was thoroughly disheartened at the thought of eighteen years. My son or daughter would be grown up by the time I returned and Mina might even be with another man. I reflected on this for many a long day until I stored it away in a corner of my mind, not to be discouraged and lose my sense of purpose.

Master Isa-Ni was a very important Shaman many generations ago. According to some accounts, he founded Rapa and was the Master of Masters. I had heard stories about him ever since I was a boy; in my mother's house as well as in that of my Wiwa grandparents. But not with reference to Rapa, only that he was a Master long ago. Jawi said he had left a sentinel by his tomb and would not clarify this point. What I realized was that the Shamans and the Mamas do not say much about Rapa. It is one of the subjects that is not discussed with someone who has not trained there. This mystery would eventually be cleared up, but my thoughts were interrupted by the appearance of an individual who disturbed our peace for several days.

One day, we were walking along a beach, which was strangely devoid of all kinds of creatures. The sand was coarse and our footsteps made a loud noise on the quartz-like grains. A short while later we sat down and I was massaging my sore feet, when we saw a tall, middle-aged, muscular man coming towards us, carrying a wooden mallet. The lobes of his ears hung down, as is usual among the Agatá because of their practice of wearing heavy gold earrings for ceremonies. The man was unkempt, his hair dirty and tangled, his body filthy and he had a most disagreeable smell. I sensed he was evil and Jawi did as well, because he became grave and alert.

The man came sidling up to us trying to look respectful and spoke sluggishly. 'Please, Father... young man, can you spare some food for this poor man?'

The rules of courtesy are such that when someone asks for food or assistance, it is always given. Such was our position and I gave him some pieces of dried fish. When we tried to leave while the man was eating, he placed himself between us and the cayuco.

'Father, allow me to go with you!'

As he shifted constantly, we had to make sure we were always out of the reach of his mallet. Besides, we could say nothing to each other without him overhearing. Jawi assented with a nod of his head. We did not really fit into the small cayuco but I insisted he sat in front, not in the middle as he wanted to, since he could have easily killed me and overpowered Jawi. In the end, the man accepted with a sneer. What he did not know, was that because Jawi and I had been travelling together for so long, we communicated wordlessly. Neither did he know that I had a sling and was skilled at using it, even though in the present circumstances it would not be much use. Both Jawi and I had the same thought: that we would eventually overpower him with the help of some of some Fishermen. However, for two days we had not seen any, nor for the days we had to travel with the man. I thought he might jump us at any moment, but the days went by and he seemed content with watching us. The first few nights, I could not sleep in case he attacked us. Jawi, who did not sleep very much anyway, was always on the lookout. However, the man did nothing and with the passing of the days, we entered into a situation of tense calm. I was constantly irritated by his smell, his farts and his coarse manners, but above all his phony smile.

'My pretty boy, take pity on this poor man who only wants to keep you company, tell me how I can help,' he said, while trying to take the oar from me. Only I was too quick for him and did not allow him to do anything other than travel in the front seat of the cayuco. I watched him carefully because I had become good at observing people. I noticed he was looking out for something on the east bank of the River. Perhaps it was some other scoundrels or some place to do us harm. The days went by and though he tried to hide it, we knew he was up to something. Jawi, in an attempt to lower the man's guard, played the role of a helpless old man. Go-Naka, for that was his name, was in effect an Agatá, who did not live with his community but in the wild, as an outlaw (as we would learn later). We were now entering the land of the Muzo in the east, and he talked about the emeralds they extract. These crystalline stones are a deep green and very sought after by the Chibcha and many other nations. They are used by the chiefs, the women and the warriors as ornaments during their ceremonies. We had also reached the southernmost limit of Jawi's territory.

As we passed the mouth of a converging river, Go-Naka must have seen something in the forest because he suddenly became agitated. He insisted we stop by the beach, saying he had reached the end of his journey.

'Father… pretty boy, I want to disembark here on this little beach. Here, here.' He pointed insistently.

But we did not stop despite his irritation; instead we rowed until nightfall and stopped at a beach further along. We were certain something would happen and prepared ourselves. I was not going to allow Jawi or myself to be hurt without putting up a good fight. As it happened, the moment we disembarked, Jawi, with a swift movement of his walking stick, that was as astonishing as it was unexpected, dealt the man a blow to his forearm making him drop his mallet. Moving as fast, I picked it up and threw it far into the River. The man was taken completely by surprise. Never could he have imagined that the old man he thought decrepit could disarm him so easily. In a rage, he lunged at Jawi, who with his walking stick, dealt him two blows: one to the forehead and another to the chest, knocking him into the water. By the time he got up, we were far enough away for me to use my sling. A well-placed stone hit his shoulder and another his leg, and he ran off in pain, bleeding and limping into the forest. We were certain he would remain hidden, waiting for the opportunity to attack us with the accomplices he was no doubt expecting. We prepared to defend ourselves that night. I told Jawi to get some sleep whilst I remained awake, with my sling and a few stones at the ready. I also had Jawi's walking stick in case I had to fight him hand to hand. There was a full moon and I could clearly see the beach. I was hoping to bring down at least two of the assailants before they reached us, though I had no idea how many they were. Go-Naka wanted something from us and I could not imagine what we had that could interest him. It so happened that night that the jaguar killed him and carried his body away; we heard the screams and the noise. Death is sad, only in this case the man was out to harm all he encountered. The River would be a better place without him. Thank you, Mama Kwishbagwi!

We slept better that night, but with one eye open in case Go-Naka's accomplices were somewhere in the forest. At dawn we were approached by six Muzo warriors accompanied by two thin, haggard-looking men and two others with their wrists tied together. One of the warriors drew near and addressed Jawi with respect.

'Father, allow us to warm up by your fire on this cold morning. These are the rogues who were stalking you last night. Greetings, young man,' he said, turning to me.

Whilst we shared our food, they told us all about Go-Naka and his gang. Apparently, the men were Agatá who had been banished from their nation for their antisocial behaviour. They had come to the River Yuma where they terrorized the inhabitants, capturing men, who were taken by river and forced to work in an isolated emerald mine they had discovered. The captives extracted the sacred stones of the Muzo, receiving very little food, and were subjected to terrible beatings and worked to death. For this reason, Go-Naka, their leader, was always searching for unsuspecting victims. But the Muzo discovered them and executed the villains who were guarding the captives in the mine. They impaled their heads on sticks as a warning to all of what befalls felons. Two of the captives told the warriors that several days previously, the leader and two others had gone in search of more unfortunate men.

For two days, the warriors concealed themselves and watched the villains waiting for their leader to return. They saw us arrive and were impressed by the way we disarmed Go-Naka. That night they heard the jaguar, which led them to believe that we had great powers. At dawn the Muzo captured the villains, still paralyzed and terrified by the jaguar. Their fate would be the same as that of the other villains and their heads would be impaled next to the River.

'That is how we, the Muzo, punish those who disregard our ways; beware all who defy us!' the chief warrior concluded.

The two haggard-looking men, the freed slaves, appeared withdrawn and silent. When we stood up to leave, they approached Jawi, bowing reverently, and asked him to bless them, which he did, placing his hands on their heads. They were in fact, two Fishermen of the River. I invited them to remain with us until they were able to fend for themselves. The warriors observed us in silence, having realized that Jawi was a Shaman. On parting as friends, they asked for his blessing and then solemnly withdrew, dragging the wretched men to their fate.

The unfortunate Fishermen were in a deplorable state. They tried to be of assistance but had very little strength. They were with us for a few days, during which we looked after them and fed them until some of their own people appeared. That evening, the men, now somewhat recovered, told the other Fishermen in detail about their ordeal: how they were rescued by the Muzo warriors and how we had eliminated the chief bandit with the help of a jaguar. I could see how easily legends originate and stories become more exaggerated as they are told. Unwittingly, we had significantly increased our fame on the River. The story told by the rescued Fishermen, who knows how many times and with many more additions from their imagination, changed the way people viewed us. We were looked upon with an admiration I found embarrassing. We were to all intents and purposes the ones who had freed the men from the terrible Go-Naka and his gang. We would be remembered for generations. This made me uncomfortable, as it was not my doing; I was a simple onlooker. If it had not been for Jawi's dexterity, the presence of the Muzo warriors and the protection of my Master Kwishbagwi, I would probably have been just one more slave.

CHAPTER SEVEN

My journey with Jawi was gradually reaching its end. When it began, I had no idea how far I would travel with him. I do not think he knew either but he took his responsibility towards me very seriously. I know he saw me as his disciple and I thought of him as my Master. What I learnt about the ecological balance of the Great River was sacrosanct to me. For example: the water of the Great River Yuma is naturally murky as a result of the vegetable tannins from the decomposing vegetation. If one of its hundreds of tributaries conveys sediment clouding the water, the fishermen report this to Jawi, who instructs the Shaman of the community upstream to find the source of the problem and a solution. This happened on one occasion in an isolated region of the Amení, where an unauthorized deforestation to grow corn had taken place. In general, the Shamans supervise their areas and the people's diligence preserves the natural balance of our Mother Aluna Jaba. Human beings are the ones who upset the natural balance to the detriment of all living things. Contamination in a river can kill the fish that keep certain species of insects or water plants in check, leading to their proliferation, which affects life in the whole river. The role of the Shamans is to prevent this from happening. Human activity, whether in agriculture, in the construction of a village or the extraction of minerals or rocks from the mountains, can cause harm that needs to be remedied. These cases are debated in the Jarlekja or individually so that the problem can be monitored and order restored. No one questions the instructions of a Shaman, who is rigorous in exercising the form of payment, in work or in kind, to be at peace with Aluna Jaba. I started learning about the ecological balance of the forests in the mountains with the Mama Kwishbagwi. Later, with my Master Jawi, I saw the effects, good and bad, as eventually everything reaches the Great River. What a responsibility this 'small', great man had.

Each of my masters had a different teaching method. The Mama Kwishbagwi explained a problem to help me understand the different solutions. Jawi presented me with a problem, allowing me to arrive at my own conclusions. This is how I developed an analytical approach that served me well in the Era of Chaos, Disease and War that was to come later.

Everything changed when we crossed into the territory of the Colima, on the east shore of the River, where it narrows considerably, generating a stronger current. The community of the Fishermen of the River disappeared as it was no longer their environment. Now and then I sighted small, isolated Colima and Panche villages on either side of the River, although most of the villages are up in the mountains where the climate is fresher. I missed the friends I had made among the River people. We were strangers to these new communities and though we could not fault their hospitality, it lacked the cordiality we were accustomed to. Besides, they kept a certain distance. They spoke Chibcha mixed with Caribe but it had a different intonation and they found my Taira odd. It was also difficult for them to understand that I had come from so far: I had to be from the nation on the other side of the River.

'Ah, you mean a Panche!' as I tried to explain.

'Ah, you mean a Colima!' when I was among the Panche.

'Ah, you mean a Muzo!' someone more travelled would add.

They treated Jawi with the respect due to an older person and assumed he was my father. We left it at that and I loved the idea. One day I had the distinct feeling that Jawi wanted to tell me something important. I sensed our journey together was coming to an end and I was full of sadness all day. That night we made camp and later by the fireside, he said, 'Son, tomorrow we reach the rapids and I must leave you. Further along you will find the River as challenging as it is now. It will get easier after the Pijáo and you still have a distance to cover.' Looking at me tenderly, he said no more. He had called me son! It was the first time he had ever done so. Obviously, the way in which we were perceived by the people we encountered had its effect. That night I cried myself to sleep.

At dawn we set out on our last lap together, which turned out to be very short. Jawi knew it was only round the next bend in the River where the rapids were visible. We approached, but not all the way to the village on the east side of the River; neither of us wanted to say our farewells in front of strangers. We drew close to the riverbank and disembarked with difficulty, pulling ourselves up with the aid of some roots. There, without words, as they were unnecessary, we embraced, not knowing if we would ever see each other again. He gazed at me lovingly for a while. Then he turned and went back down to his little cayuco and settled into it with his eyes still on me. He steered it round and the current took him rapidly away. My last thoughts were that at least his return journey would be easier.

I had never felt so alone. When I could no longer see him, I braced myself to face the large number of people that were coming and going next to the rapids. I slowly put on the necklace with three gold hummingbirds, symbolizing my Taira Clan, and my cotton cap. It was too hot to wear the tunic, so I threw it across my shoulder instead. I wanted everyone to see that I was a Taira or at the very least a travelling stranger. My clothes were ready to be discarded after five whole years of river water, rain and being used as pillows or blankets on cold nights. There was not much I could do about that and it was not as if it mattered anyhow. When I was ready, with a heavy heart, I headed in the direction of the crowds.

It was a large village, full of people from many nations and the main crossroads of the region. Boats arrived from up and down the River and their loads were removed and carried across the rapids. The people of the village were Colima and this is how they make their living. It is also the starting point of the main route up to the Muisca Nation in the mountains in the east and to the land of the Quimbaya, the Irrua and the Amení in the west. A group of men, who I presumed were Muisca because they were speaking Chibcha, were loading enormous sacks and baskets full of goods on to their backs and shoulders. There were people from other nations as well, although I could not have said which ones. I approached cautiously but no one took any notice of me. I thought it was best to look for the head of the community or one of the elders, to introduce myself and get their help to continue my journey. I was wandering about, looking round, when I heard someone shout, 'Tairona, Tairona, come over here, we don't see many of you around.'

I turned to see if it was me he was addressing. Only those who speak a dialect of Chibcha and the Caribe call us Tairona. I perceived two middle-aged men eating outside a small maloca. Judging by the shine of the trunk where they were sitting, it was a place where many had sat! I tentatively approached and saw that one was a Muisca; the other, who had called out to me, was a Colima. The latter invited me to sit with them, which was not exactly what I wanted to do at that moment, but when I heard what he had to say, he grabbed my attention immediately.

'Sit down, young man. I'll get you something to eat. It's most unusual to see a Tairona in these parts; I've only ever seen two in these last few years: one was wearing a hummingbird like yours, that was about five years ago, the other a jaguar and that was a year ago. Sit down, sit down, young man.'

He stood up and went to the back of the maloca, where some women were cooking in clay pots over a fire.

The Muisca greeted me whilst I sat down and I asked him the polite questions one uses with strangers. He told me that he was the head of a group of porters who transport goods to the diverse communities who live up in the mountains and on the large plateau of the Muisca. This was known by the charming name Cundur-Curi-Marca or 'The Golden Kingdom of the God of the Wind'. I was not quite sure what he meant by the 'plateau', as I had never seen one. These porters apparently carry a variety of goods such as cotton or silk-cotton blankets. The latter are precious due to the difficulty of picking the fluff of silk from the seeds of the *ceiba*.* They also take dried fish, pineapples and other hot-country fruit they collect on the way. The merchandise even includes gold powder and *totumas*† that are already dried and prepared for use as containers and vessels, and salt, which is exceedingly valuable and is brought down from the plateau in enormous baskets, as well as the highly regarded *turbas*,‡ which were unknown to me.

I find trade between nations very interesting, but I was waiting impatiently for the return of the Colima, who was some sort of trade supervisor. When he returned, he was carrying a large totuma with fish soup, some corn and some delicious turbas. He was a friendly, talkative man and I asked him about the two Tairona he had referred to. He said they were both young like me. One of them had to be Zalab because he was described as quiet and serious. It seemed he had arrived in a large Chiriguaní boat, full of marine shells, which are very sought after by all the nations as they are essential to mix with coca leaves. The rowers told the Colima that they had picked up the young man in Chiriguaní

---

* Silk-cotton tree

† Fruit from totumo tree – cut in half and used as container for liquids

‡ Potatoes

territory and he had embarked straight away in a Coyaima boat to continue his journey. It was most certainly Zalab, who seemed to be travelling under the protection of Serankwa, the sacred force of the universe, because everything seemed to be working out for him.

I had no idea who the second Taira of the Jaguar clan was. He could have been an apprentice of the Mama Shibulata on a similar mission. He had then gone up into Muisca territory thus avoiding an outbreak of fever among the Pijáo. The Colima had also advised him against continuing his journey by river. There was unrest among the Panche, the Sutagao and the Muisca because of enmities that had existed for generations. There are several other possible ways of travelling south. One route is through Muisca territory, on a well-used track that goes high up into the *páramos** and descends on the other side into the land of the Coyaima. Jawi had warned me about the unrest in this area and the alternative route seemed very attractive. I would be travelling through a cooler region which would be a welcome change after the heat and the humidity of the River. It would be a long detour, but the idea of getting to know my Muisca cousins appealed to me. Without giving it another thought, as if it had been my plan all along, I asked the Muisca if I could travel with them.

The man who had finished his meal barely waited for me to eat mine before saying, 'We're leaving.'

That is how I found myself with twenty-five Muisca porters, at the start of a seven-day walk up to the plateau.

---

* Moors

After five long years on the River with my beloved Master Jawi, in which I did not really have to use my legs, I now had to do so. The physical effort was unlike anything I had ever made. I felt my lungs would burst trying to keep up with these burly men, who though laden climbed briskly. If I could have walked on my hands, there would have been no problem… for during the years spent on the River, I had developed a strength in my chest, back and arms that few men had. When they paused in the middle of the afternoon to have something to eat, I was on the brink of collapse. The Muisca leader of the group, whose name was Cholmal Guantibón, could see my problem but there was little he could do except order longer pauses for me to try to catch up and have a bit of a rest. For this purpose, the treks from one camp to another were established a long time ago. Each campsite consisted of open huts with a roof and no walls, where hammocks were hung and up to thirty people could be accommodated. The climate changed as we got higher into the mountains. It got colder and the huts had walls to make them less exposed. There was wood for the burners and each traveller was responsible for replacing what he used.

The first night, I reached the campsite when they were all asleep: only the youngest, called Xante Caita, was awake, waiting for me with some hot food. While I ate, he hung a hammock for me and then, unable to do anything else, I collapsed into a deep sleep. At dawn, Xante woke me to have some breakfast and set off. I felt as if I had hardly slept and the muscles in my legs were very painful. The way I hobbled when I went to help myself to a plateful of corn soup turned into the joke of the day. I did not know how to react to these strangers, and I was not sure if they were teasing me or being serious. They were a taciturn bunch who did not say very much, and it was difficult to know what they were thinking. They were so different from the Fishermen of the River who laughed and talked like parrots all day.

'You'll be better in two days,' they told me between laughs.

It was not exactly two days; it took much longer, but I was not going to admit it to them. My legs did eventually get stronger, and in the end, I could keep up with them without too much difficulty.

I made friends with Xante Caita, who, like all of them, carried an enormous basket on his back which was supported underneath by a leather strap that went across his forehead, freeing his hands. Some of the men also carried walking sticks for balance. I learnt a lot about their customs. They use one name followed by a second that denotes the family they come from. For example, if it is Caita, this is the family name which is the same for the whole village. When a woman comes to live with a man in this village her second name would change to Caita. Likewise, when a man goes to live with a woman in another village, he changes his second name to that of her family. It is mandatory for the woman or the man to be from another village. It is not allowed for two persons with the same second name to unite.

I asked him what the others thought of me as I was still uneasy about the jokes that first morning. He said that I should not worry as they thought that people from other nations were weak. I was not sure how to interpret this comment. I am a

Taira of the Hummingbird Clan from the Shikwakala Nunjué Sierra; son of Aru Maku, Master of Music of the Wiwa, and of Zhi'nita, the chief healer among the Hummingbird Clan. I am a disciple of the Great Mama Kwishbagwi of the Jaguar Clan and a disciple of the Shaman Jawi of the Talaiga and the Great Mother River. I had rowed for five years in a cayuco on the great River Yuma to become the Mama of the Taira. I had recovered the strength in my legs that were now as strong as theirs. I was inferior to no one. I am sure my Masters would have severely disapproved of my arrogance but the superior attitude of these Muisca irritated me. I swallowed my pride to keep the peace and because I did not want to sacrifice the newly formed friendship with Xante. If they observed that I was quiet for the following days, I was not trying to be aloof like them. Rather, I was harbouring a silent rage that felt like a stone inside me. I was trying to calm myself with happy memories, with speculations about my journey and by talking to my new friend.

When we reached the plateau, I saw it was an enormous, flat expanse extending into the distance surrounded by green mountains, with a smaller low range that cut across from north to south. As we advanced, I noticed two further parallel mountain chains, one consisting of three elongated hills called Suba, where Xante lived. The first villages we came across were surrounded by wooden palisades for their defence. This was entirely new to me, not having seen these in any other nation I had come across. According to Xante, they were a leftover from the wars of a not-too-distant past, between the Zipa and the Zaque, the governors of the two Muisca territories.

In the east, the plateau, the land they call Cundur-Curi-Marca, comes up against a high mountain range. It is a substantial area covered mostly by a lake with abundant long reeds. Scattered about on the dry areas are villages with green and yellow fields of corn and turbas. It took me a while to realize that turbas grow in the root of the plant and I had not wanted to ask and show my ignorance. The Taira do not grow turbas but it would be innovative to do so in the cooler regions above the forest, where, as in the high plateau, it is fresh during the day and cold at night.

As soon as we reached the top of the mountains that enclosed the plateau in the west, we split into three groups. I remained with Xante, who invited me to his village in Suba, and two of the others who were going in the same direction. Cholmal Guantibon and fourteen other porters were going further north to the territory of their supreme chief, who they called the Zipa. The other seven porters were going east, to the foot of the mountain range, to the village of the *Cacique** of Bacatá. It was said this cacique was a strong contender to become the next Zipa because of his leadership skills. We said our farewells and I thanked them, though in my heart, I felt little warmth towards them. Nevertheless, they were kind and they had fed me and allowed me to travel with them.

Now I will tell you more about the Muisca Nation. To do the Muisca justice, as a nation they are more developed and advanced than any I have come across; apart from the Taira, that is. The territory in the north is ruled by the Zaque, who at

---

* The head of the village

that time was the Cacique Nemequene, famous for the many laws he passed to help his people coexist peacefully. It seems that even the people in the south abide by these laws. He lives in a large village called Xugamuxi, which is renowned among all the neighbouring nations. The territory in the south is ruled by the Zipa, who is powerful because he manages the production of salt that is needed by all the nations. The Zipa and the Zaque are great rivals, not only in the present but also from past generations; each one tries to be more powerful than the other. They have even resorted to war, though fortunately they try to avoid this extreme, which does not benefit either of them. In the long run, the people benefited from this rivalry, as each cacique sought to improve the conditions of his own people. Necessary routes were made, like the one I had used, and the villages looked thriving and healthy. The Zipa and the Zaque are chosen from among the local caciques, who in turn try to demonstrate that one is better than the other by helping their own communities to be even more prosperous. I found this system rather strange, though it is useful. Among the Taira, the everyday, community decisions are settled in meetings of the elders of the village. Any major decisions are made by the Jarlekja of all the Mamas of the Taira Nation or an individual Mama, if such is the case.

Something that was new to me was that the caciques carry out the functions of a Shaman and a ruler at the same time. This was surprising because I would have thought it difficult to accomplish both roles simultaneously. Very occasionally the son of a cacique, who has special aptitudes, is sent to Rapa to be trained, though most do not have this instruction.

The name the Muisca give to the force of Mother Earth, that we call Serankwa, is Chiminigagua, the male God, represented by the Sun. It is not the same, but what is important is that we all take care of Aluna Jaba, our Mother Earth. Fundamentally, we do share the same beliefs.

CHAPTER EIGHT

Our trek was now through the high plateau on much-used paths. We crossed the lakes and wetlands on rafts made from wood and lined with leather, or bundles of reeds bound tightly together in the shape of a cayuco. The large basket that Xante was carrying on his back contained various rolls of cotton blankets, treated skins and seashells. I helped him carry it, and it did not weigh as much as I had thought. He told me that on his return journey back down to the River Yuma, the basket would be full of turbas, which were heavier. Sometimes, he carried large jars that were full of salt from the mines of the Zipa, which were almost his height and really heavy. He usually exchanged the turbas from his village for whatever his people needed. This was his trade and he made the trip every moon unless another activity prevented it. When the turba harvest was over, he volunteered to carry salt or coal and was given rolls of cotton cloth in exchange. The cloth is used to make tunics, blankets and the *ruanas** that

_____

* Ponchos

are used at night or in the early morning when it is cold. These are like a blanket, covering the upper part of the body down to the knees, with a slit in the middle to put the head through. The Muisca are usually wrapped up, unlike the people from other nations where the climate is hotter.

We travelled rapidly across the plateau and within a day's walk, we crossed over the lakes and the wetlands and arrived in Suba, where Xante's family lived. The village was situated at the end of a little valley, on the west side of a chain of hills. It had about forty inhabitants, who worked the land in the clearings around the hills and a wetland. The slopes of the hills were covered in small trees, slightly taller than the height of two men. What struck me was their similarity to the ones that grow high up in the Shikwakala Nunjué Sierra, where the Mama Inkimaku lives. It was a busy little community that made all kinds of cotton and leather clothing, much in demand in the neighbouring communities, the Mususu, the Subusa and the Cota, the destination of the other two porters who had accompanied us on the last stretch. The Caitas grew an abundance of corn and turbas, of which I was becoming rather fond. There are several varieties and the ones that need to be preserved between harvests are dried out in the sun, which considerably reduces their size. I did not find these as appetizing as the freshly harvested ones.

I was warmly welcomed by the Caitas, which somewhat altered my first impression of the Muisca. As I said previously, they are more powerful and developed than the other nations I crossed. They have considerable advantages as well; one is the lack of illnesses found in hotter climates. Likewise, there are no dangerous wild creatures such as serpents or scorpions nor the mountain beasts that we have to be wary of. Xante told me that there are pumas and bears in the mountains in the east, but according to him, they are not a threat as they shy away from people and do not stray down on to the plateau.

Nevertheless, I thought their system of government had its weaknesses, being subjected as it is, to the whims of the big caciques. Furthermore, there are the petty rivalries existing between the local caciques, which I do not think is healthy. But it is their way of doing things and who am I, a simple traveller, to question them.

Anyway, I stayed in a guest house because they do not have malocas for the young as we do. Instead, families live together in houses made from blocks of sun-dried mud mixed with compact long grass. The roofs are covered with tightly packed reeds, which are abundant in the wetland. The dried grass in the blocks apparently makes them more hard-wearing, though Xante explained that the durability of the houses is more dependent on preventing the uppermost blocks from getting wet in the rain and crumbling. There are some houses made from wood brought from the mountainsides on the other side of the plateau. I mentioned previously that the trees growing on the surrounding hills were not particularly tall or thick. The trees in the valleys of the streams that flow into the wetland are more suitable but the Shamans do not allow these to be cut. If they do give their consent, they themselves select the trees; which I thought was a good thing. A large cedar tree in the centre of all the villages caught my attention. It is a homage to the Goddess Bachué, 'The One with the Naked Breasts', the Mother of all the Muisca.

I was assigned a woman of about my age to keep me company and tend to my needs. Her name was Mixia Caita, a name that reminded me of Mina. She was Xante's cousin, a beautiful woman who had a club foot, and, despite her beauty, her kindness and her intelligence, no man had wanted to marry her. She told me all this during the nights we spent together. She looked after me and cooked my meals but it went further than that. In her, I found a kindred soul, one with whom I could share my feelings. I told her all about my journey and what it meant to me. She listened attentively, asking intelligent questions while she relived all the moments of my story. What she wanted was to become the village healer and she was doing her best to learn all she could. She spent entire days with the Mususú healer, an old woman with a great deal of knowledge. Mixia was excited when she heard I was the son of a healer and from that moment on, we became inseparable.

I remained among these people much longer than I intended, about twenty days in all. During that time, I tried to pass on to Mixia the knowledge about plants that I had acquired from my mother, which I was beginning to realize was not as extensive as I would have liked. At night when we were alone, I told her about our healing practices and she showed so much interest that I regretted not knowing more. No doubt my mother would have found her a remarkable apprentice and I told her so. I also thought that my mother would not have allowed her to grow up with the deformity. I am sure she would have tried to correct it at birth.

I remembered overhearing a conversation between her and Walashi on this subject. Obviously, I said nothing to Mixia as it would have been unkind to do so. I found her to be an intelligent woman so lacking in affection and incentive that I urged her to visit my mother with whom she would surely flourish.

I also happened to attend one of their festivals. The head of the village, the cacique, was celebrating the collective work of the villagers, who had ploughed the fields in readiness for the maize to be sown. During the celebration, known as Biohote, the cacique himself caters to his people. The more food and *fibka** he provides, the greater his prestige and the people's enjoyment. We danced, ate and drank for two endless days. It was fun, though at the end of the second day I had to be carried to my house and I slept all that night and through the following day. We were all in the same state, including Mixia, though not quite as bad as me. It is said of this compelling festival that the God of the farmers, Nemcatacóa, is present. The dances are somewhat singular because everyone present takes part. The idea is that all the movements are carried out at the same time; the more fibka that is drunk, the more difficult and amusing this becomes. It is customary to sit down to eat and drink according to age; the children are last and I, as a visitor, was among the first. It was a great celebration but I admit, dear reader, that I do not think I could do this very often. We ate and drank far too much and it took me days to recover!

When the moment came for me to leave, I believe all Mixia's family thought I would take her with me, though

---

* An intoxicating drink made from maize

sadly it was not something I could do. I dearly hoped that from our time together she would bear my child to brighten her days. In my arms, on our last night, she declared that by whatever means, she intended to travel to the Tairona to find my mother. I was astonished by her determination and I explained as best I could how she should do this; the journey would be considerably easier as it would be downstream. I was aware of the difficulties of travelling alone and I wanted hers to be as simple as possible. I told her how to recognize both Jawi and my friend Tamo should she encounter them and I gave her messages for my mother and my master, the Mama Kwishbagwi. At that moment, she was so resolved that I can tell you, she did indeed make the journey and now, to our good fortune, lives among the Taira. A lucky man found this rare jewel and is her happy husband. She did not have my child but nonetheless she has three children, two girls and a boy. She is a very special woman and though I do not see her often, she will always be my great friend and soul-mate. Our destinies are decided by Arwa-Viku, the force that controls our lives. Zalab travelled swiftly to Rapa, whereas I was fated to encounter Jawi and this remarkable woman. It is as if without knowing it, the only reason for my going to the high plateau was Mixia.

Xante was a good companion and readily told me everything I wanted to know. He was rather cynical though, regarding his leaders. He knew that the head of the village, his grandfather, would never become the new Zipa. There were too many other strong candidates and it seemed that the most probable was the Cacique of Bacatá.

In Xugamuxi, the Zaque of Hunza has a magnificent Temple to the Sun, the God Chiminigagua, 'the Creative Force of Light'. Every year, when the sun reaches its northernmost position, on the day closest to the full moon, the Zipa honours the Sun God by making offerings in a lake called Guatavita, which is sacred to them. Many generations ago, Bachué sent a great ball of fire from the sky that formed a crater which filled up with water. Some believed this happened at the birth of the Muisca Nation, when the first settlers arrived. It is protected by a Chyky or priest, a sort of Shaman. The Zipa covers his body in gold powder, symbolizing the fire that fell from the sky, and plunges into the water from a raft. All the caciques of the Muisca Nation are present, except for the Zaque and the Chykys. All the Shamans and heads of other nations are invited and this ceremony is so renowned that even the Taira have heard of it. All this I learned from Xante and Mixia, who had been told about it by their grandfather, the cacique, the only member of the village to be present. People speculate about it and the mystique surrounding it grows all the time. Today, I can say that the fame of Guatavita has only been a source of sadness.

On my departure, they both gave me the clothes I would need for the páramo. They accompanied me across the plateau to the south, until we reached the road that goes up to the Páramo of Sumapaz, el Nido, in the land of the Usme, a numerous branch of the Muisca. We made the crossing mainly on a raft through the wetlands, rivers and channels until we reached a place called Tunjuelo. From there onwards, the terrain rose gradually and we spent the night in the first of the Usme villages, where we came across a group of men with whom I would travel. Early the next morning, Xante and I said goodbye and embraced. Mixia and I moved slightly apart from the others.

'If we ever see each other again, it will be in your land, for I am leaving today.'

She kissed me quickly and, hiding her tears, ran to where Xante was waiting and they both walked away. I was sad to see them go but pleased to have done a good deed; I had brought hope into Mixia's life. Her final words showed how much anger and frustration she held inside and I knew that it was the best thing she could do. It was then that I realized she was totally prepared for the long journey. I was so wrapped up in my own travel arrangements that I had not noticed. Xante was most certainly going to accompany her as far as the River Yuma.

Feeling somewhat sad, I joined the group of men who were politely waiting for me to finish my goodbyes and we set off. There were ten of them in all. They were nearly all Muisca save for a Guahibo, a Yalcón and myself. Each one had his own reasons for travelling and listening to them while we walked was a distraction, which helped to pass the while and to not notice the distance we covered.

The first of my companions was an old man who was not going very far; only a day's walk to the foot of the páramo, where he lived. He was on his way back from a route he made regularly. He apparently traded a variety of turba he grew himself, which is small and yellowish and when boiled, it disintegrates and makes a thick and tasty soup. He exchanged them for textiles and other articles that his family needed. He did apparently grow other varieties of turba but only for his family. The man with whom he was travelling, of about the same age and likewise a farmer, cultivated *cubios*, also a root plant but with a slightly bitter taste, which the Muisca like to put in their soup. These cubios were unknown to me and he offered to give me some when we reached his house. These two men had been friends for years and had made the trek together on many occasions. They liked to walk with long-distance travellers to hear news about other people. Each led a relatively lonely life, high up in the mountains, where there were not many settlements or ways of finding out what was going on.

Curiosity got the better of me and I asked them if they had encountered any other Tairona. I was thinking of the one from the Jaguar Clan who had apparently taken this very same route. But I was the first Tairona they had ever encountered. I was the centre of attention. A Tairona in the Páramo of Sumapaz is as strange as sighting a Muisca in the desert of the Guajiro. This made conversation much easier and each one waited politely for his turn to speak to me. I told them about our common ancestor and regardless of the distance, we spoke the same language, albeit with some differences. But to them, it was not even comprehensible that someone could live 'five years away'. One of the men, who had travelled through many nations, told us that far to the south, the largest-known nation is called Tahuantinsuyo. According to him, it would take approximately five years to walk to its southernmost limits. This man, an emissary of the Cacique of Bacatá, was visiting all the Muisca caciques to get their support for when the time came to choose the new Zipa, the current one being old and infirm.

He did not state this in as many words; all he said was that he was bearing greetings from his cacique to the others. He was on his way to see the cacique of the village of the two farmers I mentioned previously. I did not like this man and I was pleased when I heard that he would only be with us on that first day. The cacique he sought was of little status as his community was small and isolated, but in times of succession every bit of support helps… I was catching on to Zante's cynicism!

I had never heard of the Guahibo Nation but as the days went by, I found out all about it from another of my fellow travellers. It seems that far to the east, on the other side of the mountain range, there are some hot, extensive grass plains. This is the land of his people, which extends all the way to the edge of the jungle in the distant south. They share this land with the Huitoto to whom they are related. They live in small itinerant family groups with no permanent settlements. At certain times of the year, all the families gather to exchange news and arrange marriages, which reminded me of my friends the Fishermen of the Great Mother River. This Guahibo had a most unusual story. His Shaman had ordered him to seek a woman from another nation, probably to bring new blood into his family. Very obediently he went in search of a woman among the Muisca, but without any success. I can only imagine how difficult it must be for any woman to want to live among the Guahibo, who were in every way more backward than the advanced Muisca. He was advised to go up to the páramo where people lead such hard, isolated lives that perhaps a woman there might be more inclined. We were aware of his quest and continually made suggestions. The walk turned into a merry jaunt to find him a woman, with us all participating with good humour and laughter at his idiosyncrasies and attempts. He was a modest, good-natured lad who always said what was on his mind. He took it all in good grace, seeking the help we readily gave him. In each house or hamlet we came across, we looked for a suitable young woman or widow, so that we could act as intermediaries.

We lost contact with the Muisca on that first day after leaving the region where the two farmers lived. The people we now came across made a living from their sparse crops and the occasional travellers like us. Their mud houses are semi-buried, with roofs fashioned from the stalks of a plant from the páramo called frailejón. The stalks are covered in dried, packed earth topped with loose soil, allowing vegetation to grow. Though this makes them welcoming inside, they are harder to locate and occasionally we only did so when someone fell behind one of them! The interior is cramped and damp in spite of the clay stoves that burn frailejón permanently for heating and cooking. It is necessary to keep these fires burning not only for the cold but also because of the ice on the ground at dawn. Each house can only accommodate about six people. If the families are large, they need more than one house and it is not easy to lodge a group of seven travellers.

At this stage we were unable to find a woman for our Guahibo companion. He was not at all prepared for the intense cold and could not believe his eyes when he saw the mist and the ice on the ground for the first time. This peculiarity distracted him from his mission for a while. What stories he would have to recount when he returned to his own people!

Seven days later, we found him a woman. That day we arrived at a hamlet where there were two families, and straight away we looked for a suitable woman. There happened to be a young widow, whose husband had died in a hunting accident. He had apparently fallen into an abyss whilst trying to retrieve an animal he had killed. She had no children and the possibility of having any was becoming more remote with each passing day. A delegation of us formally approached her father-in-law to ask for her hand, for our companion. We must have presented him as some important chief because the man was so favourable to the proposal that we did not have to insist. Anyhow, from the farmer's point of view, it was one less mouth to feed. The young woman accepted immediately; it was her chance to leave and moreover she now had a future. What joy when she accepted! That same night we improvised a ceremony and they were married.

The next morning, glad to have found him a woman but sad to lose such an amiable fellow traveller, we bade farewell to the happy, unusual couple. I hope all went well for them, especially the woman, who would have to adapt to a nomadic life in the heat of the grass plains. I imagine she did not have the faintest idea of their destination nor the sort of life she was going to lead. But anything was better than a life with no children on the moors where she was a burden on everyone.

Three of my other companions were brothers, who would travel with me for most of the way back down to the River Yuma. The other traveller who would be walking with us was a Yalcón. This pleased me no end, for my concern all along had been about travelling alone. The brothers were born in the nation of the Sutagáo, which is on the east side of the River, near the Yalcón Nation. Their parents were potters. When the three boys were small, the family had gone to live with the Muisca, where their pottery was much in demand. They were brought up as Muisca, doing the same craft as their parents. Now they were on their way to seek the rest of their Sutagáo family: their grandparents, uncles and many cousins spread over the area. They made the enormous clay jars that were used to carry salt from the mine of the Zipa. They explained how the salt is not extracted from inside a mountain, as I initially believed; the Chykys would certainly not have permitted this. Instead, water with high concentrations of salt flows from the subterranean passages of the mountain, which the miners collect in giant jars. These are then heated from underneath and the water boils and evaporates leaving the salt at the bottom. The process is repeated until the jars are full of hard rock salt. This valuable salt is needed everywhere even in the most isolated nations. I tried to describe how the Guajiro extract salt from the sea but they found it hard to understand what the 'sea' was. I depicted it as a big lake but with salty water, not knowing how to explain something as large as the sea to someone who has never seen it. I finally told them that one day they should see it for themselves.

Another of my walking companions was a feather merchant, who was not very talkative and after a few days he went off in the direction of the south-east, heading for the jungle. The man explained that the jungle was so vast that having left the mountains, the jungle covered everything to the south and east and no one knew where it ended. He exchanged the multi-coloured feathers, which the communities living in the jungle brought him, for flutes, ocarinas and drums. He had an ingenious way of transporting the drums; he only carried the dried skins. Upon arrival at his destination, while he waited in previously agreed places to be contacted by the communities (which could take several days), he made the base using balsa wood, which was easily available and light and easy to work. This way he avoided carrying merchandise that was heavy or bulky. The feathers he obtained were much in demand among the Muisca and other nations and were used as decorations.

The last of my companions, as I have already mentioned, was the Yalcón from the family of the Timaná, who lived but a short distance from Rapa. I worked this out based on a comment he had made about the River Yuma. I was politely informed that he could not talk about anything concerning this matter. It is an honour for the Yalcón to be the guardians of Rapa and it makes them wary. He advised me as a visitor to wait at a place called Aipe, where there is a rock that has been used for this purpose from ancient times. There, the visitor is met by a Yalcón to whom he states the reason for his visit and a Shaman authorises or denies entrance into their land. I felt intimidated, but he assured me it is all carried out in a courteous manner. He was on his way back from the Guan, north of the Muisca, to where he had accompanied a Shaman who was returning to his land. He does this whenever it is requested of him, either to carry something or to act simply as a companion. He told me all this on hearing the purpose of my journey; otherwise, he would not have done so.

It was a welcome change to walk down from the páramo through the mountain forest until we reached a semi-desert region. Fortunately, it was not very extensive and in less than a day we reached the River Yuma. The River is wide here, but nothing compared to what it is like where I embarked with Jawi. There were many boats of different sizes going up and down the River and the Yalcón and I decided to wait for one to pick us up. We said goodbye to our companions, who were visiting the Sutagáo, and embarked in a large Yalcón canoe that took us to Aipe in two days. I now bade farewell to my last companion and, following his instructions, I made my way to a small settlement not far from the Aipe rock. There I stayed overnight and informed the Yalcón in charge of my intentions. I was put up in a maloca for visitors and the following day I was taken to the Shaman who lived by the side of the rock. He was a very old man indeed, and as soon as he heard me speak, he exclaimed, 'Ah! The Tairona we have been expecting for a long time; you may enter.'

It was as easy as that. I was assigned a guide to accompany me to the entrance of Rapa. A canoe with eight rowers picked us up on the River and in five long days we reached the nation of the Timaná. I thought I might come across my travelling companion but I did not. It was a two-day walk and I was so full of excitement and apprehension that I hastened my steps to get to Rapa as quickly as possible. My guide obliged me without asking any questions. In that frame of mind, we reached Rapa and I bade him farewell.

It had taken me more than five years in which I had undergone a very extensive learning experience. I had seen for myself how Aluna Jaba, our Mother Earth, weaves the tapestry of life that makes everyone responsible for the care of nature. I perceived the ecological balance that is everywhere and that we, the Mamas, must protect. I observed how the Shamans carry out this work in all the nations. In some, as with the Taira, their labour is more obvious. In others, as with the Muisca, it is more discreet but equally effective. I was no longer the rash, impulsive young man I was when I set out. I was more observant and critical of the actions of men. I felt more akin to nature, as if Serankwa had established a bond between us. I had learnt all about Mother Earth and now I was ready to become a Mama.

CHAPTER NINE

alking into Rapa was unlike anything I had ever done. I was in the mountains, in a valley covered by a mature forest that climbed steadily to the páramo and the glacier that is the source of the Great Mother River. It is hallowed land that only the chosen can enter, guarded by the Yalcón in the north and the Nasa on the southern side of the mountain range. There were no signs of any inhabitants, only an awe-inspiring feeling, daunting to any casual visitor not authorized to enter. It is not frightening; rather I had the overpowering sensation of being in surroundings so obviously sacred. Instantly, I felt the presence of Serankwa and the Kasouggui Spirits that dwell in nature – the Spirit of Jate Kalashé in the trees and the Spirit of Jate Kalawia in the earth. All around me was complete harmony with Aluna Jaba. I took a cobbled path that led up to what seemed to be a clearing among the thick trees. I was not sure what to expect, nor was there anyone to give me any indication. Of one thing I *was* certain: this was my destination, my purpose for the last five years and where I knew I was welcome. Soon I began to encounter solitary stone statues of stern warriors and animals. They had obviously been there for a long time and were green where moss had partially covered them. These were the ancient guardians from the very beginnings of Rapa. It was cool and the paving was so overlain by generations of decomposing leaves, that the yellow-brown stones were slippery. Huge mature trees bordered the path, and the powerful silence was broken only by the occasional song of a bird and the sighing of the wind. In the middle of the morning, I reached a glade where an elderly man was sitting by the side of the stream I had been following. What astonished me was the sight of his forehead and the back of his head. They were strangely flat. Nonetheless, I attempted to hide my reaction. He was seated on a tree trunk next to a large rock. Its surface was covered with numerous hollow spaces through which water from the stream was cascading into a pond that flowed back into the stream. Each movement of the water generated its own clear, melodious sound which was delightful and soothing. The man waited for me to draw close and take in the beauty of the rock pool.

'Welcome Tairona, we were expecting you; please follow me.'

Slowly and silently, we walked up to an arbour where the glade ended and the trees appeared again. There sat another elderly man who seemed part of the forest itself. While the blanket draped around his shoulders made him look very old, what I found striking was the depth of his eyes. They glowed with life and wisdom, set in a face as lined as the bark of a tree. The man I was following introduced him.

'This is our Great Father Tarminaki, the Master of Rapa; I am An Yupami of Tahuantinsuyo and I will be your tutor.'

I knelt at the feet of the Grand Master with my forehead to the ground.

'Great Father, my master the Mama Kwishbagwi of the Taira has sent me to learn the wisdom of the ancients; I am but a grain of sand at your feet; I am unworthy of this honour.'

Still prostrate, I turned my head to address An Yupami. 'Master, I will try to be a devoted learner.'

I was conscious of the Great Father's intense gaze assessing me, searching my spirit. Never before had I felt someone read my thoughts. I was so overwhelmed that I remained on my knees, staring at his hands, not knowing what else to do. After what seemed like an age, apparently satisfied, he spoke slowly in a deep, gentle, voice.

'I like the Tairona; they are not only strong and intuitive, they are also good disciples. We will have time to talk in the future; your training will be short, for difficult times are ahead. As from today, you will be known as Xu, "The Wind that Scatters the Dead Leaves". Go with An Yupami and open your mind to Serankwa; allow the spirits to show you the other world we live in. You will be "The Messenger of the Future". Observe everything, assimilate everything and question everything. I know you have already learnt a great deal from my brothers, your Great Mama and the Talaiga Shaman of the River. They were both disciples of mine whom I dearly love and admire. I am pleased you benefited from the journey that has enriched your spirit; you have made a great deal of progress.'

He made a gesture with his head and An Yupami and I quietly withdrew, after I had picked up my scant and well-travelled belongings. Silence is one of the main features of Rapa. I would later see how everyone who lives here, at all stages of learning, does so in silence and isolation. I was neither surprised nor troubled by this aspect, having been trained by Jawi. Along the way An Yupami talked about himself.

'I still have some time left here in Rapa before I have to return to Tahuantinsuyo. I am one of the younger sons of the Inca Topa Yupanqui, the former ruling cacique, who died six years ago, leaving one hundred and fifty children he had with various wives. This is why at birth my head was made into this shape, which surprises all who see it, not least of all you! My older brother, our reigning cacique, the Inca Huayna Capac, has asked me to return to be the Huillaq Uma of Machu Piqchu, my mother's village north of Cuzco, where I grew up. I have been here so long, I do not know if I can adapt to being a supreme priest, though Master Tarminaki thinks it's important for the protection of my people.' He paused briefly before continuing, 'In the meantime, I will be your tutor as the Grand Master has ordered. Here we all build our own shelters and lead solitary lives. I will take you to a place not far from mine.'

And I, who thought I had been able to hide my reaction at the sight his head… no such thing. An Yupami's perception was well known, as I would find out. A short while later, we took a narrow path to the left, running alongside a stream. I was instructed to build a temporary shelter whilst I found a place my spirit could call its own; An Yupami's was higher up.

'I will come back down in five days to talk to you about your duties.'

The location An Yupami showed me was shady and fresh with a stream running through it. Even if it was somewhat insignificant now, the vegetation told me that in the rainy season, the stream swelled and any construction would be washed away. This was not a good place. Further along, there was an outcrop of rocks that acted as a barrier, guiding the stream. Straight away, I noticed that the upper part was more or less flat and wide enough for a small shelter; this might be the ideal location. I climbed up on to the rocks and sure enough the canopy of the forest spread out in front of me. Without giving it a second thought, I knew I had found my place. In the distance, I observed the mountains that rose from the valley of the River Yuma and the thick forest that expanded and stretched far up into the páramos before disappearing into the clouds. My heart knew this would be my dwelling place for the next few years, until the Grand Master decided otherwise or Aluna Jaba called me. Mind you, if it had been up to me, I would have spent the rest of my life there.

After eating some dried fish and maize, I settled for the night on a bed of leaves, covering myself with my worn tunic. I lay looking at the stars and absorbing the magic of Rapa that was already invading my spirit. It made me happy to think that both the Mama Kwishbagwi and Jawi had been here for so many years. Although everything was new to me, I knew I belonged, no matter what destiny awaited me in the future.

Over the following days, I made my chosen place habitable and explored the forest all around as well as the nearby stream. Painstakingly, I searched for suitable stones to make a support wall for a terrace on which to erect my dwelling. I used the flat surface of the outcrop as the floor, which I levelled with compacted soil and sand from the stream. The rocks would retain the soil and serve as steps down to the water. Eventually, I managed to build a tiny dwelling place using logs, mud and branches, with poles to hang a hammock and a roof of palm leaves. From its entrance and facing north, I could sit and meditate, inspired by the beauty of the scenery in front of me. To the east and west, on clear days, the two large mountain ranges that enclosed the valley of the River Yuma were visible. Later, I learnt that in the south-west, there is a dormant volcano and a glacier close to the source of the Great River Yuma and other major rivers unknown to me. I think there is no other place like it in our known world; Quicagua, 'the Range of Mountains, Valleys and Rivers'.

After five days, An Yupami returned to find my terrace ready with a relatively comfortable little hut. It appealed to him because he came from a nation that dwell in the mountains with major stone constructions and terraces on which they live and farm. He apprised me of the daily routine, duties and teachings for all the Shamans in training. Every ten days or so, we had a gathering with the Grand Master, which all at Rapa were expected to attend. This was the opportunity for everyone to meet, irrespective of the stage they had reached in their training, and the new arrivals were introduced. There were discussions about outside events of interest to everyone, as well as regional matters. Zhatukúa, the Journeys of the Spirit, for the more advanced, took place at night. Among our daily activities were exercises to quiet the spirit and seek inner peace. We learnt how to transfer our spirit into the body of an animal in the same manner as the Mama Kwishbagwi had done, when he sought the jaguars that protected me during my journey. Of course, it was the Grand Master who decided which animal we had an affinity with, but only after he had got to know each novice. Our instructors set us themes on which to reflect and we carried out exercises to explore the characteristics of the senses and the abilities of the mind. We learnt how to call on the Spirits of the Kasouggui in the forest, to find the illnesses that afflict the human body... I could go on, but it would not be appropriate.

We each had to take up a craft that would engage us physically while leaving our minds free to reflect on spiritual matters or on a theme suggested by the Master. Many took up carving stone statues to stand as guardians; there are hundreds everywhere. Now I understood what Jawi meant when he said he had left a guardian at the tomb of the Master Iza-Ni, the founder of Rapa in ancient times. In fact, I saw the fierce-looking statue he had placed on the left-hand side, in front of the tomb. He carved this statue to replace another that was cracked by the weight and passing of the years. It recalled the deep affection I felt for this great 'small' man of the River. I chose as my pursuit to find, select and prepare medicinal plants and roots which were always needed, and not an activity that many carried out. In this way, I got to know a few of my male and female companions when they were unwell or had an accident. Those who wanted to carve stone statues had to be helped to move and stand the chosen rock in the location their spirit had selected; this could take up to several days. Others grew vegetables that were periodically distributed to the whole community. The Yalcón provided us with fish and meat and the Nasa who lived up in the moors supplied us with turbas, maize and millet.

Our pursuits never impeded us from attending the gatherings with the Grand Master that happened two or three times every moon. I remember the first gathering with the Grand Master very well; it took place in the clearing in the forest where he lived and where I had met him on that first day. Everyone was there, about seventy people in all, including instructors and novices, gathered about him in his arbour. They were mostly men but there were a few women. It is unusual for a woman to want to be a Shaman. She would have to choose not to have children, which must be a difficult decision for a woman to make. The life of a Shaman is isolated and solitary with rituals that take the body close to death, hardly suited to raising children. On that day, I counted fourteen women, one of them an old, revered teacher. The Grand Master spoke to us in a surprisingly strong voice and introduced me to all present.

'Today, Xu, of the Tairona, is amongst us after his special training with the Master Talaiga of the River Yuma. He is your brother from whom we will be expecting a great deal in the future.'

I was seated at the back and feeling rather shy. I stood and walked to the front, saying with all the humility I felt,

'Brothers, the Grand Master honours me, by allowing my presence among you. I am your faithful servant.'

I heard many voices of welcome, among them that of my friend and fellow brother Zalab, who made signs that we would speak later.

What followed was a discussion on one of the issues the Grand Master put forward.

'The nations that live in the vast jungle on the other side of the mountains in the east, believe that it is only necessary to have one Shaman for every four or five of their nomadic communities.'

Thus, a big debate ensued, which lasted all day, in which all present participated with many different points of view. The purpose was for everyone to voice their ideas and exchange experiences that would broaden their judgements and increase their knowledge; everyone listened attentively. Wisdom does not only consist of knowledge, but also the capacity to understand what is around us and to accept the ideas of others. There was generally a consensus on certain topics, such as the balance of Aluna Jaba and the care of the forests and the rivers. However, any issue touching on people or communities is more complex, and opinions varied according to individual experiences and the characteristics of each one's nation. The Grand Master guided the discussions with a wisdom that was mesmerizing, paying attention to the different opinions and ensuring that everyone joined in and expressed what was in their heart. Everyone in Rapa took part in these discussions, including those in charge of providing the meals. Sometimes the debates continued well into the night, and when this happened, we slept round our fires. We then returned to our dwelling places to reflect on the theme over the following days. At the next gathering, if necessary, the discussion was brought up again until Master Tarminaki saw that there was clarity on the subject. The purpose was not that we should all agree; rather that each person should express his own point of view, but above all recognize that of the others.

On that first occasion, I told them about my years with the Shaman who watched over the length of the River Yuma, from the estuary to the rapids. I explained how it was in fact the Fishermen who kept him informed of everything that happened. Even if he was far away from a problem, he was aware of it and could find solutions through the Fishermen themselves. I told them of Jawi's amazing insight and how this unique way helped him to watch over such a vast area. Of course, he also relied on the Shamans of the nations bordering the River, to resolve matters that might arise in any of the tributaries of the River Yuma.

Additionally, the Grand Master Tarminaki had regular discussions with individual pupils. We did not know beforehand what subject he was going to bring up, but they were all interesting. He made us talk about ourselves and our points of view on all sorts of matters.

We discussed our doubts and worries and he only gave his opinion or an explanation when he was sure that we had sufficiently deliberated on the matter. He told us about Rapa and other similar locations in our world, Quicagua. On other times, we discussed our spiritual journeys and on occasions, to increase our awareness, he told us of his own experiences and those of the other Masters. The role of the tutors was to guide us in our learning, and with them we held discussions on all sorts of topics. It was they who also made decisions concerning more mundane matters. The tutors were the Shamans who had effectively completed their training, and among their obligations before returning to their communities was that of guiding newer disciples.

There was no exact duration that each one remained in Rapa; this was determined by the Grand Master. He based his decision mainly on the level reached in the training and their role in the Centre. There were other underlying factors, for example: the ability of each one and the needs of the communities they came from. Only the Master made this decision and it was irrefutable. The tutors were fundamental and for this reason some stayed on for many years. This was the case of An Yupami, who had been there for more than twenty-five years. He was seen as a serious candidate to succeed the Grand Master, though as he explained, he would not be remaining for much longer.

Tahuantinsuyo is a vast nation that exists on the mountain range far to the south. It is an advanced, organized and large nation, ruled by an Inca. For generations, it had expanded by conquering neighbours and taking over their land, which had caused a great deal of turmoil. The Inca has to delegate due to the size of the territory and he has to trust that those he appoints to govern the provinces are wise and upright. As we know, men have all sorts of conflicting personal interests and are not always wise and just. This is where the Shamans try to redress the stability and intervene if a governor has to be removed by the Inca, whose power is absolute. The Shamans also have to restore the balance of Aluna Jaba or Pacha Mama as she is known to them. To this end, the Grand Master was sending An Yupami back to Tahuantinsuyo.

There was now an additional concern that had us all in a state of alert, regarding the strangers who had settled on the Islands of the Caribe. They seemed to be obsessed with the gold metal that was driving them insane and they were making continuous incursions to the mainland searching for it. The Grand Master, while seeking council with the Jarlekja of the Shamans, was particularly anxious about the consequences of the presence of these hairy strangers, who showed every intention of staying and conquering new lands. He was prepared to lose his best disciples to resist them.

It brought me great joy to see my dear friend Zalab, who was already an advanced disciple. His dwelling place was nowhere near mine. His tutor was a Shaman called Berich, who came from a small nation not far from the Muisca, called the U'wa. We found time to talk about the very different journeys that Aluna Jaba had reserved for us. My journey was unhurried with much learning, in a new environment, whilst his was swift, without delays and had taken him a total of ten moons. Zalab had given me up for lost until he reached Rapa and the Grand Master informed him of my progress. It never failed to amaze us, how the Grand Master Tarminaki knew everything about each one of us, even before we arrived in Rapa. This man of such an advanced age is the wisest man I have ever known and, most certainly, everyone thought the same. The fact that he had been the Mama Kwishbagwi's and

Jawi's tutor was of great significance and filled me with the deepest respect. One day, when I had already been in Rapa for over four years, in the course of one of our discussions, I asked the Grand Master a question that had been on my mind.

'Great Father, on the day of my arrival in Rapa, you told me I was "the Messenger of the Future". I have thought long and hard about this and I still do not understand what you meant.'

He looked at me in silence for a while whilst he searched my spirit, then in a soft, deliberate voice he said, 'We all leave something for the future: our children, our customs, even guardians in our beloved Rapa, but we run the risk of losing the real meaning. If a father or a mother fails to teach their children our history and the reasons why we have certain customs and ceremonies, the child will still grow up, but he will do so cut off from his origins. This is how a people become weak and the Gods are forsaken. A people with no memory can forget Aluna Jaba, though her labour never ceases. If she is not taken care of, she will lose her equilibrium and chaos will ensue, with everybody wanting everything and giving nothing in return. A person's craving can have no limits but resources are scarce. This is why conflicts exist and the world becomes a nightmare filled with insatiable people.' He paused before continuing. 'A long era of chaos, disease and death is approaching. The hairy men, who have arrived in our world, bear the seeds of many ills that will afflict our nations; all have been alerted to the danger. Some, better than others, will be able to defend themselves from the ideas and the death that will follow. I have seen that they bring illnesses that will decimate many of our nations. The few who survive will not have the strength to resist the conquest that will follow.' He stopped for a while.

'But I have also observed them from the World of the Spirits, and I have seen they have something that can be useful to us. They have the ability to paint a word on what looks like the large leaf of a tree, only it is thin and used specifically for this purpose. In this way others can look at these paintings and know what has been spoken. This is how ideas can be preserved for the future.' His gaze rested on me.

'I have seen you will survive the illnesses due to the skills of your mother, the healer of the Tairona. You will learn from these hairy men how to paint ideas and you will be "the Messenger of the Future". This is why we have taken special care of you above the others, for this is your mission. Reflect on this and prepare your mind for what is to come. I was not going to tell you now, but I see you are ready. We will speak further about this. Now, go and deliberate on all I have said.'

That day was the most important of my life. The Grand Master Tarminaki had assigned my mission for the future. I was filled with doubt and apprehension but I was prepared to accept what was being asked of me, though I had no idea how I was going to proceed. That night and the following days, I thought about what he had said, and I talked to An Yupami, who had known of my assignment all along. My attention was now focused on studying these hairy men and on making my spirit stronger to be 'the Messenger of the Future'.

We promptly initiated my training to enter the World of the Spirits. At the beginning, I took ayawasca but eventually, all I needed was to be in the right state of mind. This was a considerable ability, a gift from Aluna Jaba that Jawi and the Grand Master had, among others in Rapa. In this way, I was able to see my master the Mama Kwishbagwi and Jawi again.

We do not talk about the experiences of Zhatukúa with those not initiated or who do not have the strength of mind not to get lost in this dangerous world. Without going into too much detail, I will tell you about a significant journey I made with the Grand Master and An Yupami, who were always with me.

After fasting all day in preparation, An Yupami and I took doses of ayawasca, which was as traumatic as usual, producing a great deal of physical discomfort. When finally, we went into a trance, we could see our bodies prostrate where we had left them in An Yupami's dwelling. Without too much difficulty, we came across the Grand Master, who made a gesture for us to follow him.

It is so bitterly cold in the World of the Spirits that it invades the spirit. We found ourselves enveloped in a pale blue haze where the lost spirits of bad men were wandering and wailing, waiting for the Gods to decide their fate. The spirits that are passing through are seen in a soft golden light. If there is any hesitation, any fear, the spirit turns grey and others have to come to its aid and encourage it to overcome the danger. It is easier to communicate here than in the physical world, which is seen as a vague, distant shadow. The Grand Master guided us to the occupied Islands, to see the hairy men who were such a threat; he wanted me to witness for myself the depiction of ideas and words. That day, I surveyed their settlements and saw the strange animals they use to get around on, as well as the ones from which they obtain milk. I also sighted their large dwellings and their gigantic canoes.

Finally, we reached the place where some of their Shamans lived. These had no hair on their heads, only on their faces and they wore long clothing that covered them from head to foot. I saw the implements they use to paint words and, what is more, I had the good fortune of watching one of them making small symbols on some sort of white leaves, by the light of a fire. There was no obvious reason for the authority they seem to have over the other men and the few women I saw. They had no evident powers, as our Shamans do; more exactly, they looked ignorant and dirty. However, the Grand Master was very emphatic; under no circumstances were we to underestimate these men. After each one of us had observed what he wanted, we returned to our bodies and, on recovering, discussed what we had seen and reached a few conclusions. Thus were our journeys to the World of the Spirits.

For the following four years, I had a new routine. Every four or five days, An Yupami and I would travel through Quicagua. An Yupami reported any failings he saw in the communities to the Master so that these could be resolved. Nearly all the communities were on high alert, having closed their borders and isolated themselves to improve their defences. However, it was not easy. There were some that had conflicts with their neighbours. Others were not taking the threat seriously because they thought the invaders could be repelled easily. Some were being careless and weakened by having Shamans who were not sufficiently prepared. But one thing I can tell you: the Jarlekja of the Shamans did everything in their power to resist these new men, with greater or lesser success depending on the communities.

In the course of one of my Journeys of the Spirit, the Mama Kwishbagwi informed me that in spite of all my mother's efforts, Mina had died while giving birth to my son. This was hard to bear because being so hopelessly in love, I had only left her out of obedience to my elders. That was one of the most difficult decisions that I had ever made.

After nine years in Rapa, the Mama Kwishbagwi informed us that the hairy men had finally reached the shores of the desert, north-east of my Shikwakala Nunjué. The Wayu Caribe had seen them, and though they were only there for a few days, they had repeatedly raped some young girls. In the end the girls had taken their own lives because of the revulsion and despair they felt. A young warrior by the name of Carajay had had his head blown off by the explosion of one of the invader's thunder-like weapons. The invaders then embarked and sailed on up the coast.

The threat was now near my home and my days in Rapa had drawn to a close.

CHAPTER TEN

The history of Rapa was about to be radically altered, something that had never happened since the Grand Master Isa-Ni founded it many generations ago. The Mama Inkimaku informed us of the terrible battle that had taken place between the invaders and the Toucan Clan of the Taira. They were unable to defeat the aggressors because of the attire they wore: a sort of metallic garment that repelled arrows or another where the arrows became embedded and did not reach the skin. On the other hand, many of our people had been killed, victims of the unfamiliar weapons, one of which sounded like thunderclap but produced smoke and fire that discharged death. Very few of the enemy had fallen but we had lost many, among them the Mama Kwishbagwi, my Master and adoptive father. He had not taken part in the battle as a warrior but wanted to observe the enemy at close range. Towards the end of the battle, he was detected and knocked over by one of the enemy who, mounted on one of their gigantic animals, had run him through with a lance.

Zalab and I were devastated. We grieved for many days until the Grand Master Tarminaki sent for us. It was a harsh blow, and I tried my best to ease the pain and anger I felt in my spirit. For many days, I found it almost impossible to enter a state of meditation to come to terms with what had happened.

Several of my companions were already with the Grand Master when I arrived, among them Zalab and his instructor Berich. An Yupami was present with another of his disciples, a Muisca called Zyo, whose face was scarred by a burn he had as a boy. He and I became good friends during my last years at Rapa. He was the son of the Zaque of Xugamuxi, of the Muisca, and would later be known as Quemuenchatocha, 'the Grand Lord of the Heights'. In all, eleven of us had been summoned.

The Grand Master began by pointing out the gravity of the situation, and then proceeded to assign responsibilities. Zalab would not be returning to our nation. Instead, he was to go to the Emberá and the Cuna, where he would coordinate their defences. The communities there, who like us were of Chibcha origin, inhabited the strip of land between the two seas, known as Darien, located west of the Sinú, on the way to the Maya. Berich was to go back to his people and coordinate the resistance of the fierce Yuco. These hunters live in Cata Tumbo, the mountain forests in the north. Zyo was to use his status to guide his people. I was to be the new Mama Kwishbagwi of the Taira, the Guardian Mama of the Forests, in the mountains of my beloved Shikwakala Nunjué Sierra. Additionally, I was to assist Jawi on the estuary of the River. I eagerly accepted my new duties, being fully aware of the urgency. The Jaguar Taira, who had come to Rapa, was to reorganize the Toucan Clan, decimated by the enemy. Moreover, he was to oversee the coastal region of our mountain range, all the way to the desert of the Guajiro or Wayu Caribe in the far north. The others were to go to the Coyaima, the Yalcón, the Guahibo, and the Amení. A young Muisca by the name of Sagesagipa, only recently arrived, was likewise the son of a cacique of the Muisca, in his case the Zipa. He could remain no longer and was to go with Zyo as his disciple, to his own village. We were, nearly all of us, the youngest Mamas and Shamans in the history of our nations. It was a big concern to all of us, to have all these new responsibilities but to lack the training and the confidence that goes with it. The Grand Master asked us to seek new disciples, but with a difference; it was to be carried out in secrecy. He informed us that his successor would be a distinguished and respected Yalcón by the name of Chubaquín, a hermit from a remote region at the foot of the great western volcano known for its subterranean tombs.

Over the next few days, whilst we prepared to leave, the Grand Master ordered everyone else in Rapa to return to their nations: to the plains and the jungles in the east; to the mountains in the south, where my friend and teacher An Yupami would be going; others would return to the jungles by the sea in the west and to the neighbouring mountains. Only two Shamans, Chubaquín, his successor, and a Nasa were to remain with him to conceal our spiritual centre from the enemy.

During those last days, I kept the Grand Master company as often as I could. I sensed that behind his great strength of spirit, his heart was full of sadness. He had dedicated his life to Rapa and he knew full well that the end of an era was approaching. All the Shamans and Mamas that existed in Quicagua, the known world, had been his disciples. No other living being possessed the knowledge he had of this and other worlds. From the small, humble abode where, due to his age, he spent most of his time, he had visited every single community of our world. On one occasion, he spoke to me of another Rapa, far away on an island, south of the west sea. Of this I know nothing more than what he told me that day.

Before proceeding with my story, I will tell you more about my Master, the Shaman Tarminaki, the Ninth Grand Master of Rapa. The story of his life, I heard partly from him and partly from An, who knew him better than anyone.

His name as a boy was O'tomo, 'Son of the River Tomo'. He was born in a very small nomad community, the Hiwi of Arawac origin. They live on the eastern plains where O'tomo spent his childhood wandering about on both sides of an enormous river, known as the Orinox. During the rainy seasons, they travel even further east to the ancient, sacred Flat Top Mountains. There, in the summits, dwell the Benevolent Spirits alongside the Malevolent Spirits that are shrouded in mist. Every year, they make the journey to summon the Benevolent Spirits to come down in the form of cascading waterfalls. Likewise, they make offerings to appease the Malevolent Spirits to prevent them from sending forth punishments such as floods, sicknesses or a big snake, the Guio that devours children. From the moment he could walk, he had to learn to keep up with the others on their daily treks, for which he developed the great strength in his legs that all his people have. His father taught him to hunt and be guided by the stars on the vast plains. His mother was a spiritual woman, who transmitted the knowledge he would later use to change the course of his life. The Hiwi live in small family groups on the plain they share with the Guahibo and the Saliva who speak a different language. Every year, during one of the rainy seasons, all the Hiwi gather in the region of the Flat Top Mountains. They arrange marriages, exchange stories, hold dance festivals and drink quantities of *picquigui*, a type of chicha, an alcoholic drink made from the fruit *chontaduro*.*

From a very early age, O'tomo discovered he had the ability to see the future in his dreams. He guided his father when he went hunting and could predict any eventuality; he was always right about what he saw. At the onset of puberty, an old Shaman who lived like a hermit in the Flat Top Mountains began nurturing O'tomo's aptitudes. When each year he returned, the old man was amazed at the progress the boy had made. However, by the time he suggested that he should train to be a Shaman, O'tomo was in love with a young woman and their marriage had been arranged.

The life of a nomad is hard and even on reaching adult-hood there is always the risk of sudden death due to an accident, illness, hunger, being bitten by a serpent, drowning or even falling victim to a wild animal. O'tomo had to live through all of this. By the age of eight, all his brothers had died, some of starvation, others due to illnesses. His little sister disappeared one night, probably seized by a jaguar, and though

---

* Species of palm native to tropical forests

her body was never found, animal tracks were seen nearby. When he was twelve, his father died from a rattlesnake bite. When he was fifteen, the year of his marriage, his mother died from an infected fracture of her leg. For these reasons, his little nation appreciate life to the full; it is something that has to be conquered daily. The families with adults go to great lengths to seek others so that their sons and daughters can unite and perpetuate. Two years later, crocodiles killed his wife and baby daughter whilst they were attempting to cross a river swollen by floods. After so much grief, O'tomo was ready to accept the Shaman's invitation. He rapidly discovered he could make spiritual journeys without any aid and that he possessed an instinctive understanding of the balance of Great Mother Earth. Without any hesitation, the Shaman now sent him to Rapa, though getting there was not an easy task for a little nomad from the plains.

It took him a very long time; even he does not know how long. He travelled alone or with families going west until he reached and crossed the mighty River Orinox. When there was no one to travel with, he ran or walked alone and covered the length of the plains reading the stars as his father had taught him. He passed through the small forest on the edge of the River Tomo, where his mother had given birth to him and from whence his name came. There, wanting to pay tribute to his parents, he gathered up some metallic stones that covered the ground like a scab and made a pile on a mound, to prevent them from being washed away in the rainy seasons. As time went by, the heap increased as each traveller that went by added more stones.

He was a strong, attractive young man who received many offers of marriage from young women along the way. But apart from sowing his seed, he declined the nomadic way of life of his people to reach his objective. Running through plains, swimming across dangerous rivers full of crocodiles and piranhas, sometimes alone, other times accompanied, after many moons, he finally reached the foot of the mountain range. There he encountered people from other nations, whose lives were an enigma to him. Towering mountains, great forests, lasting settlements, permanent crops, stone paths and unfamiliar animals, everything was new to him.

He was a pleasant, intelligent young man, who readily learnt new languages more complex than the simple one, consisting of short sentences and signs, used by his people. He was welcomed in all the settlements and homes he came across. He climbed mountains and felt the cold for the first time in his life. This did not distress him because he found the advantages instead and was able to appreciate why so many liked it. His mind was like one of the sponges the Caribe find in the sea. He absorbed everything and was not ashamed to ask questions with a big smile and people gave him all the explanations he wanted. He was remembered by the people he met as an attractive, inquisitive young stranger who was always helpful and smiling. He travelled through many nations until he finally reached Rapa, where he was received by the Master Yana Yacu of the Quechua, the Eighth Grand Master, who called him Tarminaki, 'the Merry Flute'.

He spent the rest of his life in Rapa, as a disciple, a tutor, a Shaman and finally as the Grand Master. He had gone from being a simple young nomad from the plains to become the most important person in Quicagua, 'the Range of Mountains, Rivers and Valleys', our known world. No one knows how many years he lived in Rapa. He never forgot his little nomad community, the Hiwi, doing everything within his power to help his people and make their short lives better. I think he lived to be over one hundred, but I am only speculating.

Each Grand Master of Rapa is known for a special characteristic: the Master Iza-Ni, the First, the founder and a visionary; the Second, the peacemaker; the Third, the expander of our way of life into other nations; the Fourth, a deep thinker; the Fifth consolidated the Jarlekja; the Sixth, the promoter of culture and the arts; the Seventh, the organiser of nations; the Eighth, Yana Yacu, the leader of a new expansion; and Tarminaki, the Ninth, and last for now, whom I shall call the Defender.

The Grand Master, at his grand old age, lived in a small arbour. There was no weather or situation that prevented him from carrying out his duties. If it rained, his body generated enough heat to dry his clothes and the water evaporated from his back. This power of mind was sought by all who lived in Rapa. The tutors informed the Grand Master whenever a disciple had attained this level, which was indicative of the stage he had reached in his training. However, what was most remarkable about the Grand Master was the capacity he had to remember everything about each one of his disciples' past and present. He could also correlate each one with the characteristics of their nation. This is an incomparable ability.

Now it was time to say goodbye to my little hut and to my neighbours, the birds that had hatched over generations. I was leaving the pool that I had made with such effort and in which I bathed daily. I was leaving the serpent residing nearby, whose undisturbed behaviour was a sure sign from Aluna Jaba that my presence had not affected the environment. I imagined all the other disciples saying their farewells and having similar thoughts. I climbed up to An's dwelling, near the splendid stone statue of a mighty rat gazing up at the sky for inspiration, which he had carved during his first years at Rapa. He was in deep meditation, so I sat silently outside until he returned to his usual state. We said our goodbyes and he gave me a few assignments to be carried out over the subsequent moons and years. I should have carried them out there, but these were not normal times. It was the end of Rapa, as known to all previous generations.

On the last day, the Grand Master gathered us all together and spoke clearly and decisively. 'My Brothers, we are facing an enemy such as has not been seen before. Even if we survive, our world will have changed to such an extent that it will never be the same again. I have seen great sorrow in the future, but I have also seen major achievements among you. Beware of the new diseases, they will open the door to the enemy. The communities that are protected will survive. Our gods and our beliefs will fall into oblivion. It is up to each one of you to preserve for the future, our faith in the balance of Our Mother Earth. Those who are near, I will see again, others I will encounter only in the World of the Spirits but we will all meet again in the next life. Go and do what is necessary to protect our people.'

Then he called me aside. 'My son, your mission is one of the utmost importance: take great care; learn from the enemy, but do not fall under their influence; study their Shamans, but do not let them know you are one of us; if it is safe, live among them but be prudent and humble to mislead them. The animal that most relates to you is the jaguar, as was the case with your master. I did consider other animals but I think it is the most suited to assist you with the enemy: it is cautious, stealthy and vigilant; it will protect you, as it has always done.'

We said our farewells and set off on our journeys in the groups previously set up by the Grand Master. It was straight-forward for our group. The River Yuma would take each one of us close to our destinations. With our spirits weighed down by sorrow, we arrived in the land of the Yalcón, who were dismayed to see so many Shamans together. They had never seen anything like it and it caused all kinds of specula-tion. Fortunately, their own people provided the explanations, sparing us from having to do so.

Zyo was good company. He knew his people well, having witnessed the decisions his father, the Zaque of Hunza, made from when he was small. His forceful personality made up for his disfigured face, which at first sight made him look somewhat strange. I have seen few men so determined to save his people. We spoke a great deal about this on our walk and subsequently in the boat provided by the Yalcón for us to travel to the rapids of the River Yuma.

I will now tell you more about the journey and some of my companions. We were fortunate to be travelling with Zalab's teacher, Berich, who had been instructed by the Grand Master to look after us until we all went our separate ways. Berich was an elderly man of about forty-five according to Zalab, and one of the permanent tutors at Rapa. Silent and reticent, he was remarkably observant; he missed nothing and analysed everything. As the days went by, I noticed he had a temper and was irritated when he thought someone was not living up to his expectations. Zalab was used to his ways, whereas Zyo and I were accustomed to the calmness of An Yupami and his thoughtful comments, so we found the first days somewhat difficult. We understood Berich's concerns and tried to adapt, though not before a few reprimands when he thought we were distracted. But overall, we gave him few reasons to be annoyed.

In the evenings, after travelling all day and making camp, we told each other more about our lives. Berich's was rather interesting. His father, a Yuco cacique, went out hunting one day very near the territory of the U'wa, where he came across one of their families. A dispute followed as to whose land they were on. They are two fraternal nations and though they did not want to fight about it, they did have a day of arguments and discussions. It happened that Berich's father noticed a young U'wa girl listening on the side, whilst preparing the food. She did not participate in the discussions, leaving these to her father as head of the family. She was to be Berich's mother… From then onwards, Berich changed his tone and tried to persuade the father he wanted the girl to be his wife. The father, after all the heated arguments, would not even consider the offer, which on any other occasion, he would have been honoured to accept. Over the following moons the Yuco cacique wooed her persistently until the two lovers began to meet in the forest at night. Very rapidly, she became pregnant but would not leave her family without the consent of her reluctant father. Eventually, the Yuco, tired of waiting, returned to his people and the baby was born a long way from him. The parents reached an agreement by which the boy spent time with each of the communities. Though he became familiar with both ways of life, it meant that Berich grew up somewhat estranged from his two families. Fortunately, the Shamans of the two nations noticed his spiritual inclination and prepared him to be sent to Rapa. Thirty years went by and he carried out his training whilst being an assistant to the Grand Master Tarminaki. Now he was a Shaman Tutor, a man of great dignity and knowledge. I felt that going back was not going to be easy for him. He had been away from his people for such long time but the orders of the Grand Master are indisputable. Furthermore, he realized the importance of his mission, as we all did.

The Shaman of the Yalcón was only with us for four days. His vital task was to prepare his people to close off all access to Rapa so that only those authorized by the Grand Master could enter. It would never be mentioned by its name again. A village nearby would now be known as Opo-Rapa, 'The Wealth of Rapa', so if the name did come up, it would be assumed that the village was being referred to. He had a great responsibility on his shoulders. That night, sitting around the fire in silence, we united mentally to give him the strength to carry out his task. When we woke at dawn, he had gone.

The five Yalcón rowers were so overwhelmed to have nine Shamans on board that they kept to themselves. We were advancing at great speed, or so it seemed to me, after my long journey upstream with Jawi. Now we had the current in our favour and several strong, expert rowers as well.

Berich set us tasks such as finding out what type of soil was needed to grow a particular plant or to explain the presence of certain animals in the water or on the banks. I was asked to instruct the others about the main features of the River, since Berich knew that few had my knowledge. I enjoyed being able to do so and to share what I had learnt from Jawi.

The River, wide in this area, flows rapidly down from the mountains and does not have the bends that appear later. I taught the others how to entice and catch fish. I was familiar with all kinds of tricks that not even the rowers who lived on the River knew, which made them view me with more respect than I warranted. I showed them how to detect the difference in the speed of the currents and how these erode the banks, creating bends. I made the rowers stop, to the surprise of a family of small *babillas*,* when we came across the first of the lakes in the shape of a quarter moon. I asked everyone to disembark and explained why this feature had occurred.

The days went by, until our Coyaima companion had to leave us on reaching the land of his people. He was a quiet, mature man, who was pleasant and showed a great deal of resolution. He had followed my lessons eagerly, which was very pleasing. On his departure, we carried out the same ceremony to give him strength as we had done for our previous companion.

A few days later, we approached the rapids in Pijáo territory. This seemed to make Zyo and Sagesagipa rather nervous because of an old enmity existing between the Pijáo and the Muisca. Berich was the first to disembark at the big settlement

---

* Colombian reptile smaller than a caiman

near the mouth of a river flowing down from the large Muisca plateau, Cundur-Curi-Marca. As soon as he noticed some hostility towards our Muisca companions, leaving no doubt as to his temper, he put an end to the problem in a thunderous voice I had never imagined he had. The entire village ended up prostrated and trembling with their foreheads in the dust. The local Shaman of the Pijáo hastily arranged a welcome and there were no further incidents. I thought it a sad situation, that these two big, important nations should be in this predicament, because it undermined their union against our common enemy. That night I had a long conversation in Caribe with the Pijáo Shaman, and it was clear the problem was of great concern to him as well. The will of the caciques usually prevails and all he and the other Shamans could do was prevent open warfare but not the antagonism. These grievances were only going to be to the detriment of both nations.

Sagesagipa had turned into a faithful disciple of Zyo and we were sometimes asked to join in their discussions. In this way, we were able to contribute to Sagesagipa's training even though it was evident that he was missing the one he would have received in Rapa: the silence and meditation, the discussions and lessons with the Grand Master Tarminaki, the exercises with a tutor and all the other knowledge I cannot talk about. Berich was concerned about this and asked Sagesagipa to accompany him back to his people for a while. We all agreed it was a good alternative but before going to stay with Berich, he would spend a few moons with Zyo in Cundur-Curi-Marca. In the meantime, Berich would be ready and would make the necessary arrangements between the two nations. This young man with a pure and strong heart knew his limitations better than anyone and was committed to overcoming them. We had no doubts about this, and when we finally reached the rapids, we could see the determination on his face.

It was going to be a sad moment when I said goodbye to my friend and fellow disciple Zyo. I think he knew the destiny that awaited him and Sagesagipa and nonetheless accepted it. He would do everything possible to strengthen his people. What he could not have known was the extent of the viciousness with which the invaders would take over his nation or the bitterness, death and destruction it would bring. Now as an old man, I can no longer see clearly as I write, I weep to think of the torment inflicted on them by the enemy. I know death would have come as a relief. However, more than the physical pain, they died with their spirits full of the anguish of knowing that their people had been defeated and subjugated by the insatiable conquerors.

CHAPTER ELEVEN

Eleven years had gone by since I was last in this bustling Colima village. Not much had changed. People from many nations were coming and going, whilst others were getting ready to travel by land or by river. Our presence put a stop to all activity and everyone silently watched the spectacle in amazement. They had never seen the arrival of so many Shamans at once. We stand out because of the long cotton (or ceiba) capes we wear and the characteristic heavy walking sticks we carry. No one else dresses like us.

We were eight in all, of which three would not be continuing the journey with us on the River: Zyo, Sagesagipa and a Guahibo. The latter, a short man, about as tall as a twelve-year-old boy, was nonetheless endowed with a great deal of personality and a truly commanding presence. He had had an accident as a child that had deformed his arm, rendering it practically useless. A hermit for the last few years in Rapa, he was on the point of leaving, having completed his training. This Guahibo, whose name I am ashamed to admit I cannot remember, was a nomad from the eastern plains on the other side of the mountain range: the same nation as the young man searching for a wife with whom I had travelled up to the moors. They share the plains with the Hiwi, from whence the Grand Master Tarminaki originated. Many think they are the same nation but this particular Shaman informed us otherwise. Though their lifestyle is similar, their languages are not. The Shaman's nation is of Muisca origin and they speak a very simple Chibcha dialect, whereas the Grand Master's people are closer to the Arawac nomads of the vast jungles (found further south of the plains) and the Caribe, who inhabit the coast by the estuary of the River Orinox. This rather modest man was particularly articulate and someone who did not go unnoticed. He would no doubt have complete command over his people.

The rumour of our arrival spread rapidly and everyone in the village gathered to see us. People generally feel nervous in the presence of a Shaman, but eight of us must have been frightening indeed. Although we tried to make it appear that nothing was amiss, it was difficult to dispel their fears and their curiosity. The Yalcón rowers had only conveyed us this far and we gratefully bade them farewell. They walked away, making their way with pomp and show, enjoying their moment of glory. On that night and the following nights before they went back to their land, they would no doubt have a lot of stories to tell – most likely products of their own imagination – and many a young woman would vie for the honour of sleeping with them.

Presently, the man who had made me welcome when I arrived in this village so long ago was brave enough to approach rather nervously to ask if he could assist us. He was now the head of the village and as he did not recognize me, I left it there. Acting as our spokesman, Zyo asked for a place to spend the night. He emphasized that the chief should not put himself to any trouble, as we did not need a dwelling, only a campsite. The man looked visibly relieved. The idea of putting us up must have been frightening and it would have been in his own house due to his rank. He hastened to clear a space behind the village. Once we were settled, with the village people still watching us from afar, we informed him that we would be needing transport. Three of us were going up to the land of the Muisca and the other five had to continue their journey on the River.

As it grew darker, the people gradually went home to discuss an event that would not be forgotten for generations. When we were finally alone, eating the meal the chief had kindly provided, we saw an old man struggling to join us. He was the Shaman of that region, and we were moved by the effort he was making to come and see us. When he was sitting in our midst, next to the fire, he asked after the Grand Master Tarminaki, who had been his tutor. This venerable old Shaman was a contemporary of the Master. Berich immediately remembered the Shaman from Rapa although they had not come into direct contact. Until late in the night, we listened to all he had to say and he never tired of answering our many questions. He proved to be an inexhaustible source of information and was well aware of what was happening. Apparently, he had a young assistant who carried out most of his tasks. Zyo raised the issue concerning the Pijáo and the Muisca. He expressed our same concerns, namely that the enmity between the two nations was a weakness the enemy could use to their advantage. He had tried to seek an accord between the opposing nations without much success. He lingered with us until we were asleep; by dawn he was gone.

The Colima chief arrived early the next morning to tell us a group of Muisca was leaving shortly, should our companions wish to join them. He also informed us there was an Opón boat departing the following day. Our three companions decided to remain with us until we left, considering it unnecessary to have company on their way up to the Muisca. That last day, we discussed our different options and settled on a period when Sagesagipa would go to stay with Berich. The people from the village had gathered again, observing us attentively from a distance. The fact that their revered old Shaman had spent the night with us somewhat allayed their fears but we were still the focus of their interest.

Halfway through the morning, I decided to go for a stroll in the village though I knew I was attracting a lot of attention, which I tried to ignore. On my way down to the River, whenever I saw someone stop their activity, I made signs for them to carry on and take no notice of me. It was difficult at first, though in the end, I managed it and was able to look around with relative ease. Close to the River, I came across a group of children playing the game of 'who can throw a stone the furthest'. I sat on a rock to watch them, much to their delight at having a spectator. There were six of them and, as usually happens, the biggest was the strongest and could throw the furthest. After a while they turned to slings, somewhat more successfully, and I tentatively joined them, since I was out of practice. Quite soon my skill returned and

I could aim at the other side of the River quite accurately. I was enjoying myself and while searching for a stone to throw, I noticed a group of about fourteen people camped outside the village. On closer observation, I realized they were a family of Fishermen of the River. If I had seen them, it was because they wanted me to do so. I continued to play a bit longer, not wishing to draw the attention of the boys to them. Finally, I stopped playing and made my way towards the group. They had noticed me approaching and were preparing to welcome me.

My heart was filled with happiness at the sight of them. They were some of Jawi's Fishermen and it was strange to see them this far south. They usually keep their distance, so there was obviously a reason for their presence. I was expecting to come across them at some stage, but not so soon. I placed my hands on the head of each one and then we sat down to converse. They were one of the families with whom Jawi and I had spent time after the disagreeable incident with Go-Naka. I could not recall their names but there was an old man and a woman, two young men, four young women and six children of varying ages. It is customary when initiating a conversation with them to talk about the River, the weather, relatives and gradually it turns to more personal matters or a message to be delivered.

While I was thus engaged, I observed a pretty young woman making gestures in my direction. She was holding the hand of a nine- or ten-year-old boy. All of a sudden Aluna Jaba enlightened me. She was showing me my son! Everyone noticed I acknowledged him and there was a general rejoicing with plenty of embraces. The boy, who did not understand what was happening, clung to his mother in tears, much to the amusement of all. How special it is to discover a son and at a stage when I was no longer thinking of such matters. It had been stored away in a little recess of my heart and now he was there, in front of me. It made me feel whole again, and I was unable to hold back my tears. Here were the spirits of my mother, Zhi'nita, and of my father, Aru Maku, embodied in the child whom this beautiful woman had given birth to. I have had many joyful moments in my life but this was without doubt one of the most significant. We spent the rest of the day eating and chatting. I tried different ways to ingratiate myself with my son, until in the end he came up to me and I was able to play with him. Everyone was delighted by these advances. There was nothing I would have liked more than to stay with them but the heart wants one thing even though the mind knows it is a delusion. Inevitably at nightfall, Zalab and Zyo came looking for me. They were somewhat concerned because I had been gone all day and I shared my happiness with them. Zalab, who is rather serious about most matters, was pleased for me and played for a while with the children.

The Fishermen were in awe of having three Shamans among them and made every effort to attend to us. This attracted the attention of many in the village. They could not understand why some Fishermen of the River, who they usually ignored, were being honoured in this way. I hope this served as a lesson not to underrate these people who are so cordial, kind and rich in values.

At one stage in the evening, the eldest among them indicated he had something to say. We moved away from the others and when he told me that he had a message from the 'Honourable Father', I understood immediately that he was referring to Jawi, who was in fact north of the Talaiga and hoped to see me there. This was far north indeed but it fitted in with our plans. The Opón could take us a considerable part of the way and I would then find Jawi with the help of the Fishermen. What did not appeal to me about travelling with the Opón was the speed at which they rowed in their large boats. This meant the Fishermen of the River, who I really wanted to see, would be ignored. Anyway, it is not as if I had a choice, so I resigned myself. I thanked the old Fisherman for the message and we both re-joined the group. I went over to my son's mother and offered her one of the three gold hummingbirds that represent my Taira clan. I wanted her to give it to the boy when he grew up. She was deeply touched and put the hummingbird carefully away among her possessions. She said it would protect the boy from fevers and other eventualities, ensuring he would reach adulthood. We chatted for a long time about this and other matters.

Zalab and Zyo were captivated by the hospitality and friendliness of the Fishermen, though they did not speak Caribe very well. Zalab only had the basics because of the contact the Taira have with the neighbouring Caribe. Besides, he knew he would need to practise and improve because of his new duties. Zyo, who did not speak the language at all, was enjoying himself trying to communicate with signs, while Zalab and I translated. Between laughter and gestures, they had a very pleasant evening.

I decided to spend the night with my son's mother. What a delight it was to feel the warmth of a woman's body again and to hear her gentle breathing as she lay sleeping next me. I realized how much I had missed this over the last few years. It is a privilege a Mama loses as he becomes isolated from the communities by constantly moving between the regions in his charge. I knew how important it was for the Fishermen to have new blood in their families. As for me, it was not only pleasurable but I was contributing to their survival as well.

It was still dark, not yet daybreak, when on leaving soundlessly, I invoked the blessing of Serankwa on the little community. The old man watched me go from where he was resting and bade me farewell with a gesture of his head. I walked through the silent village to join my companions. As we had done prior to the departure of the others, we mentally combined our energy for the success of our missions. I would never again see any of these Shamans in person, though I would do so frequently in the World of the Spirits.

I think it is time to tell you about one of my other companions, the Taira Mama of the Jaguar Clan, now known as the Mama Rigawiyún, 'the One who Teaches'. I did not have the opportunity to get to know him before this journey but during the days we spent together, he told me about himself. He was from a Jaguar village distant from where I was born. He had a vague memory of me touring with my father and his musicians, though I was too small to remember him. He was a disciple of the Mama Sarabata, who sent him to Rapa as soon as he came of age. This was four years after I set out. During his journey, he survived three grave incidents, establishing the fact that Aluna Jaba had a specific destiny in mind for him. The first happened two days after setting off, when a highly venomous lance head serpent bit him. As is well known, this type of bite is usually fatal, but a skilful Cataca healer saved his life and two moons later he was able to continue his journey. Further along, he was bathing one morning in the River Yuma when he accidentally stepped on a poisonous river ray that stung him. Once again, he was saved, this time by a Carare healer who also nursed him back to health. A few moons later, he resumed his journey by river in a canoe. While lying back on some sacks of cotton with one leg trailing in the water, an enormous crocodile grabbed him by his leg. Had it not been for the other occupants of the canoe, he would certainly have been dragged into the depths of the river. All he had to show for these three episodes were some horrible scars on his legs. When he reached the rapids, following an outbreak of yellow fever, he decided he had had enough of the River. Without giving it a second thought, he went up to the Muisca in the mountains and took the same route that I would take a year later.

Now there were only five of us from Rapa left. The day before, it had been agreed in a meeting (at which I was not present) that the Amení Shaman would continue his journey to his people by land. He chanced upon some Colima porters who were going in the same direction. They would cross over the western mountain range and descend into the other big River valley. We bade him farewell and the four of us remaining went down to the River to look for the Opón boat that would take us on the next leg of our journey. Only two moons had gone by since leaving Rapa. Already, I felt distant and disconnected from the life I had there because of all that was happening around us.

It was getting light when we embarked as the only travellers with the six Opón oarsmen and one helmsman. We set off swiftly with the current in our favour and the momentum of the rowers. They were nervous and kept trying unnecessarily to ensure our comfort. Berich tried to reassure them by saying that we wanted to be treated like any other traveller. Though they found this difficult, they did try, if only to please us. Before setting off, I noticed the group of Fishermen had disappeared. Further on, I glimpsed them briefly in three tiny cayucos and waved to them. They are difficult to spot on the water and no one else would have done so, given the speed at which we were travelling.

Over the next few days, we travelled in complete silence, in view of all we had to think about. It was the Opón who held long conversations at night, keeping their voices low so as not to disturb us. I spent the days trying to detect the families of the Fishermen of the River or trying to find the platforms they might be occupying. They were my people now and even more so when further downstream they would be in my charge. I was delighted when I sighted them and I could not help waving. I think they all knew who I was and waved back. Some evenings, it was I who indicated an empty platform for us to spend the night. The Opón were always amazed as they could not do so. I imagine they thought I used some sort of magic.

After several days our rowers were more at ease, and the four of us helped with the rowing. We travelled for one-and-a-half moons to the land of the Opón, completing this phase of our journey. In Berich's case it was the end of his journey on the River Yuma. He would continue on one of the tributaries and cross over the eastern mountain range to get to his people. When we arrived at a village on the estuary of the largest river in Opón territory, we disembarked to find new ways to travel.

The village was an important trading centre for the neighbouring nations and those on the mountain ranges on both sides of the River Yuma. There were Carare, Samaná, Guane and Yariguí traders and porters everywhere. It was not difficult to recognize the different nations. Although nobody wore clothes due to the heat, they each had distinctive ornaments: paintings on their skin, headdresses, or jewellery worn in ears and nose or round their necks. As usual, our presence attracted a lot of attention. Fortunately, the Opón rowers dispelled the onlookers and the noise and the bustle rapidly returned to what it had been before we arrived.

The head of the village drew near to invite us to rest in his house. He also told us that his Shaman would see us after we had eaten. We thanked him for his kindness, not wishing to offend him, but said that we wanted to see the Shaman straight away. He and two other men accompanied us into the jungle where the Shaman lived. On the way, the chief informed us that, following instructions from the Shaman, his people were ready to repel the hairy men. They would attack them from the banks of the River to keep out of reach of their thunderous weapons and their animals. We found that the further north we went, the more alert the people were regarding the enemy. They had accepted that sometime in the near future they would have to confront them. Apparently, the lesson of the battle of the Taira had been assimilated.

The Shaman of the Opón was an elderly man, constantly on the move, visiting the different villages. He was waiting for us in one of his temporary shelters, a makeshift canopy of branches and a rush mat on the ground. Our guides bid us a speedy farewell and were gone. It seems that each nation has a different attitude towards a Shaman or a Mama and some people do not like being near a Shaman's abode. This was new to me, for among my people we were close to our Shamans and did not shy away or fear them. It was something we were going to have to get used to. Zalab, who was not familiar with the Emberá or the Cuna, had no idea how they were going to react to him.

This particular Shaman was very imposing, with a piercing gaze that made him look formidable. He wore a cape covered in all kinds of amulets hanging in small leather bags. Though he was old, of an uncertain age, he was full of vitality and could not keep still.

'Welcome, my brothers. I see that our Grand Master accurately described you as a generation of very young brothers. You will need all your youthful energy for the task ahead.' He indicated for us to sit on the mat.

'Our Master Tarminaki has asked me to tell you,' he said, looking in Zalab's direction, 'that the hairy men, whom we have called the *Sué*,* plan to establish a settlement in the land of the Emberá. It will be easier to prevent if you are prepared; the Caribe Sinú will assist you.'

Then addressing the Mama Rigawiyún and me, he said, 'They tried to build a settlement in the village you call Bonda, but they were repelled. Now they make raids in search of gold and women and men to enslave. The ones they capture are submitted to some sort of strange ceremony, in which their Shamans recite words and spray them with so-called sacred water. Be prepared: you will be going right into the heart of the area where these assaults are taking place.'

That night in the World of the Spirits we visited the beleaguered region. I looked for Jawi to find out where we would meet and we determined a course of action. First, I would arrive in Bonda as a Fisherman from the Gran Cienaga to organize the resistance, using the ability that the Fishermen of the River have of making themselves invisible. I would have to brush up on this particular skill. Jawi also said there would be a boat waiting for us in the Talaiga village near the big fork of the River Yuma. Zalab would be taken across the cienagas and smaller rivers north-eastwards, to the land of the Sinú, where he would be near the land of the Emberá.

That afternoon, we returned to the village to prepare for the next stage of the journey. The Shaman of the Opón accompanied us to ensure people knew how important it was to find ways to travel. Berich came across a group of Guan from the mountains who were leaving the next day and invited

---

* The White Birds

him to join them. They would be travelling on the river of the Opón and then across the mountains on a well-used path. I had grown fond of Berich and sadly bade him farewell after performing the ceremony to give each other strength. In this we were aided by the powerful source of energy emanating from our Shaman host. He secured a Chiriguaní boat for us, who after a resounding order from him, had no option other than to leave the following day. Accordingly, we set off to the land of the Talaiga.

Zalab would have to find another means of transport on the second lap of his journey. I was going in search of Jawi and, further on, the Mama Rigawiyún would be going to the Gran Cienaga and subsequently to the Shikwakala Nunjué.

CHAPTER TWELVE

Now our journey had developed a sense of urgency. I did not point out to our rowers the small branch of the River that Jawi and I had used. This was convenient when travelling upstream against the current but now that we were going downstream, it was quicker to stay on the main River. There were eight Chiriguaní rowers and a helmsman, and the boat was larger than the previous one, also much heavier due to the cargo: several jars of rock salt from the Muisca; a large quantity of cotton and cotton-silk fabric; dried fish, pineapples, *guamas*,* passion fruit, and even some *maranones*,† for our consumption. We shared the rowing and thus did not have to stop to rest at midday. The man not rowing put together the frugal meal of dried fish, fruit, a few *envueltos*‡ or some hard, tasteless arepas. Zalab was improving his rudimentary knowledge of Caribe with his characteristic

---

* Sweet fruit in long pods

† Small fruit with nutty taste (cashew fruit)

‡ Maize or corn wraps

diligence. He started practising with the rowers when we set out from the Colima village by the rapids. He was making good progress and we also lent a hand and taught him the new vocabulary used by the Caribe on the coast.

In the evenings, we only stopped at the Fishermen's platforms if I managed to find one that was empty. The Fishermen recognized me as we went past and waved. I waved back, but we kept our distance, respecting their custom of avoiding large vessels. I was aware that my companions did not see them. I had not given further thought to this ability of making oneself invisible until now that I would use it as a weapon against the Sué.

When we paused for the night, I fished for our meal. The men looked on me as a River Shaman because of my knowledge of the River and the ability I had to fish. In a similar manner, I knew where the sandbanks were likely to be so they could be avoided. I showed them how to counter the waves and the wind to make rowing easier. After a few days, the rowers did not hesitate to follow my suggestions though they themselves were experienced on the River. The water level was low enough for me to have walked on the riverbanks, but this was out of the question. Given that it was not raining, we rowed all day, and although the men were tired due to our pace, they never once protested.

In less than one moon, we reached the village that marked the border of the mysterious Talaiga territory. The Chiriguaní were terrified of approaching, and I had to order them to do so. Even then, they dropped us off as far as possible from the village and hastened to get away. We barely had time to say goodbye and thank them.

The three of us made our way towards the village, located in a magnificent strategic place on the large embankment where the River splits in two. A large delegation of Talaiga was awaiting us. Some of their rowers would convey Zalab, now known as the Shaman Kaku, to the Emberá and others would take the Mama Rigawiyún and me across their land. That night was the last time I would be with my childhood friend. I would only ever see him again in the World of the Spirits. We conversed until late and then, as was usual, carried out the ceremony to give each other strength. He asked me to deliver some messages to his mother, Guka, and to everyone else he knew in our village, since he was not going back to our people. Master Tarminaki had decided that he should organize the defence on the coast and the forests in the nations where the Shamans were too old to do so. The Sué had invaded those regions, searching for wood to construct their large boats and for supplies of fresh water and meat. We were certain they would try to settle in the area, to hunt for the gold that was plentiful there, especially in the adjoining nation of the Sinú. Their craftsmen make the gold figurines representing the Caribe and the Taira clans which they exchange for other goods. Altogether, the Taira have fourteen Mamas, including Zalab (the Shaman Kaku) and myself, which meant that I was not needed in the Sierra and at the present, my obligation was to assist Jawi on the River.

I was excited about travelling through Talaiga territory again, this time as their honoured guest. We embarked in a canoe that was smaller than we were accustomed to with six rowers: four rowed, two rested and there was no cargo. I made sure my companion, the Mama Rigawiyún, knew what an honour it was to be travelling through the most mysterious land in the whole of Quicagua. I described what usually happens when they see a stranger: how dressed up as women they lure the intruder and put him to death without any qualms. In my case, because I was with Jawi, I was only made a prisoner until I was given the authorisation to enter.

We were enthralled by the beauty of the region, travelling all day from dawn to dusk for six days, with the rowers taking it in turns to rest. I was aware that even though we stopped in small villages for the night, we never approached any of their larger ones; these would remain clouded in mystery. One day I casually enquired about this and I got my short answer.

'We can't stop for visits.'

Although he was polite, I realized there was not a chance this would happen and I left it at that. On the sixth morning I saw the rowers loading supplies and I also refrained from making any comment. When we were back on the River, I assumed we were going to be transferred, with the supplies, to a boat belonging to another nation but this was not the case. It was really surprising that the Talaiga were leaving their territory and for two journeys: to take Zalab west and the Mama Rigawiyún and me north, but these were strange times indeed.

Three days later we came across Jawi. We were nearing a beach when I saw him, though no one else did. I instructed the rowers to stop and approach. At first, they were disconcerted by the suddenness of my order but nonetheless they took the boat up on to the sand. Two of them jumped out and secured it to a large, semi-buried trunk. The expression on my face told them I had seen something and although they looked in all directions, they did not spot Jawi until he came up to us with a big smile. After their initial surprise, the remaining Talaiga got out of the boat and ran towards him, falling to their knees in the sand at his feet. Jawi greeted them with his usual modesty and blessed each one. He and I embraced with all the affection that we had for each other. I introduced him to the Mama Rigawiyún, who reverently bowed his head. Jawi, as expected, did not say a word, much to my companion's surprise. But on sensing the bond that existed between Jawi and me, he smiled and said nothing.

We were going to settle down for the night and were stretching our legs, when Jawi detected a movement in the water. Without another word, with a swift movement of a harpoon, he speared a large catfish that we all ran to catch and drag to the shore. That night we ate very well. The Talaiga grilled the fish in large leaves to keep it from drying out. Everyone was happy and relaxed on full stomachs. During the past few moons, ever since leaving the rapids, we had not eaten very well and were all skin and bones.

After eating, the three of us made our own fire to one side. Jawi and the Mama Rigawiyún had only ever seen each other in the World of the Spirits. This was another of those happy moments in my life. This dear old man was like a father to me, even more so now that my Master, the Mama Kwishbagwi, was no longer there. Despite his reticence, I could nonetheless feel how pleased he was to see me. He had not changed. He was the same small man of an unspecified age, with a noiseless gait and an aura of calmness and wisdom. Further on, he allowed me to do more of the rowing as he tired easily, though we did not speak of this. But I am getting ahead of myself! I had only just met up with Jawi and I could not have been happier.

That night we decided that I would remain with Jawi and the Talaiga would take the Mama Rigawiyún to the Gran Cienaga. As Jawi had already foreseen, the Fishermen there would show him the way. Our task over the next moons was to get to know the families of the Fishermen that roam the stretch of the Mother River until it flows into the sea. I would also have the difficult task of becoming familiar with the enormous region of the estuary, which we had not even reached. This huge complex delta is strategically important, for it is the access route to the whole of the interior of Quicagua. As a child I had travelled through this area with my father but all I remember now is him. Only the Fishermen are familiar with this aquatic region and I was relying on them to help me. I was already acquainted with a certain number of the families, though they all seemed to know me. Further north, I would see about the others.

That night we performed the ceremony to give each other strength, and the following morning we bade farewell to my young brother, the Mama Rigawiyún, and the Talaiga rowers who had brought us this far. I stood for a while on the beach watching them depart and it struck me as I lost sight of them that we were on the threshold of a new era, unknown and uncertain, but waiting. I could not even have imagined what the future had in store.

To be travelling with Jawi again was like going home and we got back into our old routine very easily. Once the others were out of sight, we embarked and set off, except that now we travelled much faster than we used to. The downstream current did most of the work and we only needed to row hard when crossing from one bank to the other. We frequently encountered families of Fishermen in whose company we spent the night. We warned them about the invaders though they were evidently aware of what was happening. Nevertheless, they listened and passed our warning on to other families. My idea was that the Fishermen would be my eyes and ears throughout the region. When I put it to them, they readily accepted.

During those days, Jawi spoke more than was usual for him. I was able to ask what he thought of using the Fishermen as an attack force, should the Sué try to gain access inland via the River. Jawi did not think they would be effective on the offensive because they are peaceful, few and rather scattered. On the other hand, they could observe, keep us informed and harass the enemy. We agreed this would be the best course of action and started to prime them. It was essential that the Fishermen have more contact with the nations bordering the River than they usually do. It was our task to ensure these nations listened to the information they were provided with. We were alerted that some Fishermen had on two occasions sighted enemy vessels in the region where the main branches of the River Yuma flow into the estuary. It was obvious that they had been unable to find their way onto the main River.

While we travelled, with Jawi's help, I practised the skill of seeming invisible to any person other than a Fisherman. We tried it out when we came across another canoe or boat or went past a village. The result was that in broad daylight I could be a few feet from someone without them seeing me.

Though it was amusing and it felt like child's play, it was vital that I perfect this ability that was to serve me well in the future.

As the days went by and the rainy season returned, we were obliged to slow down and spend more time in any one place. This meant that we could get to know more families and renew old acquaintances. I came across another son and a daughter and I gave the two remaining gold hummingbirds of my clan to each of the mothers. To them, they were powerful amulets, whereas my intention was rather that my children should have something to remember me by in the future. These encounters and my acknowledging the children were always cause for celebration. I also found out that many, among them other children of mine, had died during the periodic outbreaks of the river fever. Thus was life on the River, unpredictable and difficult, but full of conviviality. It was usually expected of me to make one of their women pregnant and it would have been an offence not to have done so. I must confess this made travelling more agreeable, though sometimes it was exhausting and I did not always feel up to it.

I was hoping that at some point I would come across the pair of cousins I had met fifteen years previously, when I first encountered a family of Fishermen. What happy memories I had of 'my Two Parrots', Nisa and Apixa, who had kept me company on the River before I embarked on my journey with Jawi. I did indeed happen upon Nisa a few days later and I will tell you about this major event.

One afternoon in the middle of a tremendous downpour, we were on the southern edge of the estuary of the River Yuma. We were cold and soaked through. I was rowing and

Jawi was baling. We had no visibility; the wind was against us and the waves so strong that we were going to capsize if we remained on the main River any longer. We were hugging the east bank almost inside the vegetation when I stumbled across a small stream. The change was instant: the wind and the waves ceased and though it was still raining heavily, it became easier to row. A short distance away, I saw a platform and some Fishermen making signs to us. As soon as we reached it, they got down and helped us to tie up our cayuco. In next to no time, we were seated and warming by a fire, with the very welcome offer of some food. The family consisted of an old couple, an adolescent boy and a good-looking mature woman who I recognized immediately, as she did me: it was Nisa, one of my 'Parrots'. Life had been hard on her and this is the story she told me that night.

After they had left all those years ago, both she and her cousin Apixa found they were with child. This was a moment of great happiness for all. Their lives continued as normal during the following moons whilst the babies grew in their wombs. They travelled, fished, picked fruit and nuts and prepared food for the family. When they met up with the other families, there was much rejoicing at the sight of them both so heavily pregnant and close to giving birth. Indeed, they were both delivered of girls within two days of each other, first Apixa then Nisa. The girls were nearing their first birthdays, when there was an outbreak of yellow fever that took the lives of the two little girls, of Apixa, her mother and two of Nisa's younger brothers. Nisa, along with her uncle's son, the boy who was with her now, had survived the illness and she had looked after him ever since. This had not only been a catastrophe for the family but for the whole community because so many died that year. From one moment to the next, a growing family, with several young people to ensure its continued existence, was on the verge of extinction.

Nisa turned down several offers of marriage to stay with her parents and bring up her young cousin, who was just three years old when the outbreak happened. She had no more pregnancies and gradually all the joyfulness she had in abundance when I met her, faded away. She was now a beautiful woman of about thirty but with the sadness in her heart clearly reflected in her eyes. She had dedicated her life to looking after her small family. Now they were awaiting the arrival of another family, with a young girl promised to her cousin. At least what was left of her family had a chance of surviving. It also relieved her of the responsibility. That night when everyone was sleeping and I was holding her in my arms, we were looking at the fire when she said, 'Kuktu, take me with you; I will be your woman and take care of you whilst you carry out your work.'

Many Shamans choose to lead solitary lives; others like me need the company of a woman. The idea was more than appealing because I did not have Mina. Here was a woman who was prepared to share my new life on the estuary of the River Yuma. She knew the River and all the secrets that are only known to someone who has spent their life on it. What is more, we had an affection for each other. Not the passion I had for Mina but rather the contentment of having someone you want to share the future with. Aluna Jaba gives us the opportunity of having a companion for life but it is up to each one of us. Today I have no regrets about the decision we made all those years ago in front of that fire. I told her of my plans of reaching the sea with Jawi and of going on to Bonda, a village particularly harassed by the Sué. Afterwards, I wanted to go up into the mountains, to my beloved Shikwakala Nunjué, to see my family and take part in a Jarlekja of Mamas that was planned for when I arrived. I suggested she should continue north with her family. We would then meet in a Mocana village of her choice on the main River. In the meantime, she would procure a vessel and anything else we would need for our new life on the estuary.

The following morning, we informed her family of our decision. They took it well and were glad for us even if they had some misgivings. It was especially hard for the young boy for whom Nisa had been a mother. There was also the matter of his forthcoming marriage. He was about to become the head of the little family with a new bride and his grandparents in his care. It was a challenge he regarded with mixed feelings but which he dolefully accepted. Nisa comforted him, saying her departure was not imminent but when she did leave, they would surely meet up frequently on the River. Jawi, as usual, did not say a word but I felt he had no objections. Nisa would be an asset with her knowledge of the region and this took a weight off his shoulders. Moreover, because of her strength of character, her advice would be helpful when I had to make important decisions.

We waited for two more days until the other family arrived, and in a little ceremony, they handed over their shy young daughter. Our presence was seen as a sign of good luck for the two families. Few could claim they had two Shamans present at their wedding and had been blessed by both! We left the next day and when I said goodbye to Nisa, her eyes were again full of joy. We would see each other ten moons later in the Mocana village or find a way of getting a message to each other if there was an impediment.

Now, navigating on the main River was more complicated than I had anticipated. The estuary opens into many branches that all flow into the sea; the setback is that many are interconnected. It is essential to know which one to take and it is easy to make a mistake and end up somewhere other than intended. This only confirmed I had made the right decision by accepting Nisa as my companion; her knowledge would be indispensable. The complexity of the delta is a deterrent that had thus far prevented the Sué from entering our world, but I was under no illusion. It was only a matter of time before they worked it out or forced someone to guide them.

Jawi and I were back to our usual routine. We had a word with all the Fishermen we met and with many of the Mocana communities who lived on the delta. They were expecting us and Jawi introduced me, making it much easier. The Mocana, but particularly the Turbaco in the west, and the Gaira and the Guajiro in the east, had all been attacked by the Sué. These were now making more frequent raids in their big boats to kidnap men and women who, it was said, were taken to work as slaves on the Islands. It appeared that the Caribe who lived there had been annihilated. At the same time, they were seeking the gold articles that for some reason they valued so highly or avenging the deaths of any we had managed to kill.

The Guajiro, who lived in the desert and the gulf in the east, had been the most affected by these attacks.

Every night we held long discussions about how best to thwart the Sué and be vigilant. We came to several conclusions. There would be permanent lookouts and a warning system consisting of continuous sounds emitted by shells. On hearing this sound, everyone was to take refuge in the jungle. The warriors would prepare surprise attacks from a distance because at close range the Sué had strange, deadly weapons. Our warriors had found that poisoned arrows were only effective when aimed at the legs, arms and necks of the enemy or when they were not wearing their metallic or thick cotton attire. In addition, it was suggested that the animals should be targeted as well, particularly the large ones the Sué were mounted on and their ferocious dogs, that were much bigger than ours and trained to attack. This seemed to demoralize the enemy, who were visibly shaken when this happened. Initially these animals terrified our people and accounted for many defeats and deaths. We were only now starting to realize that the animals were not gods, that they were as mortal as the men themselves.

Our mallets were not suitable because when our warriors raised their arms to strike the blow, the enemy stabbed them with long, thin knives. We could inflict injuries with a sling, but it was only fatal if the head was unprotected. Their larger thunderclap-sounding weapons discharged hard, round metallic stones that travelled a considerable distance and were deadly. But these weapons only performed once and needed some sort of preparation before they could be used again. Many of their men had bows shaped like crosses that shot arrows with great force and speed and could be reloaded swiftly. The wounds these inflicted were terrible, if not fatal, due to the speed with which they struck. Some of the Sué, usually the chiefs, used smaller smoking weapons which, in close combat, were also lethal. Their ships were armed with gigantic weapons that smoked and hurled immense metal balls that caused a lot of death and destruction. Some of the boats they used for landing had smaller versions of these weapons on their bows. We would, therefore, not gain very much by attacking their ships or boats. Many of our warriors had learnt all of this at the cost of their lives or suffered wounds from the metallic stones that wedged in their bodies and got horribly infected. The strategy with the best results was to entice the enemy into an ambush when we could use our poison arrows. The Sué were terrified of our arrows and the *cerbatanas** with which we blew the poison darts. However, with this tactic alone, we could not prevent them from landing and attacking our people. When they pursued us mounted on their large animals, it was practically impossible to outrun them. I remembered how a Sué mounted on one of these had slain the Mama Kwishbagwi. All this I had viewed in the World of the Spirits, but I had yet to see all this armament used in combat.

The Gaira had a few arrows as well as some of the metallic stones. They had even managed to get hold of one of the bows and two long knives. I wanted to see everything for myself when I arrived in Bonda. I thanked all the brave warriors who had faced the enemy for their accounts. As we

---

* Blowpipes

drew nearer to the sea, it became obvious the inhabitants were in a war situation and felt threatened. I began to think that I was not well placed to guide them. Besides, I was not even sure how I was going to infiltrate the invaders and learn the symbols they used to describe ideas. This was, after all, the very important task the Mama Tarminaki had entrusted to me. What I needed to do was keep my ears and eyes open. Something would come up. Whilst Jawi agreed with me, I saw the pain this gentle, peace-loving man was enduring as he listened to all that was going on. But we do not choose our destinies and now our peaceful nations were confronting a new and bewildering enemy.

When we finally reached the sea, the two of us said our farewells. We were on a little beach by the side of a minor channel, in the large delta that is the mouth of the River Yuma. It was not the last time we would see each other in the flesh but we did not know that then. We would certainly see each other during the Zhatukúa ritual but that is not the same. By the fireside, we gave each other all the advice we could think of. He disclosed to me that the animal with which his spirit had its affinity was the eagle. So that was how he travelled the length of the River and why he could cover such a vast area. All the years I had spent with him without realizing this. Now I understood his occasional disappearances, his trances while I was rowing and his ability to watch over the entire River from his little cayuco. A Shaman never reveals the animal with which he has an affinity. That he had done so was his way of expressing his love for me as a father, as my teacher and now as a brother Shaman. Before I could say anything, he said, 'The jaguar will give you the freedom you need and it will protect you; be cautious; do not let them find you out.'

This wise man knew everything about me without me even telling him. He had the most extraordinary insight and understanding. I could only aspire to have his wisdom someday.

The next morning, under a beautiful clear sky, we warmly embraced. Without a word he got into his little cayuco and made his way onto the River in the middle of the dense jungle. I watched him until he vanished from sight. All my love went with him and I think he sensed it because his last gesture before disappearing into the vegetation was to raise his arm without turning his head.

I picked up my walking stick and my belongings, put on my Shaman cloak and headed north-east along the beach towards the Shikwakala Nunjué Sierra in search of whatever the future had in store for me.

CHAPTER THIRTEEN

I was going to have to build up the muscles in my legs, yet again!

Eleven moons had gone by since I left Rapa and I had spent most of it in a boat. Now it was essential to recover my strength to walk. Fortunately, I did not have to keep up with anybody, unlike all those years ago when I walked up to Cundur-Curi-Marca with the porters. I was glad no one could see me now, walking in such a pathetic way. My strength gradually returned after several days but what I found surprising was that I did not encounter anyone. On the other hand, I was pleased that the communities seemed to be taking the threat seriously and had moved their villages away from the coast. Eventually, on the fourth day I was approached by three Cataca warriors who, emerging from the forest, bowed reverently and asked for my blessing. That evening, as I sat with them, they told me that they were the guards of the narrow stretch of land that separates the sea from the Gran Cienaga, where they lived. Further inland there were more Cataca and Mocana lookouts to whom they would relay a warning if any Sué boats were sighted. They were anxious for my safety, though they did not dare interfere directly with any matter concerning a Shaman. Whilst endeavouring not to be disrespectful, they advised me to conceal myself in the thicket should I see anything suspicious on land or sea. I thanked them for their concern and the following day I was on my way again.

The scenery was lovely and, in the distance, I could already make out my Shikwakala Nunjué Sierra. The beach that stretched out in front of me was broken only by small streams weaving their way down into the sea, where I cooled down and found fresh water. I saw turtles that would return at night to lay their eggs in holes they had already made in the sand. A few coral snakes were warming in the morning sun and several iguanas were hunting for fallen fruit. Whole families of gannets were diving into the sea where they had spotted shoals of fish. Further along I was delighted when I identified jaguar footprints that I felt were keeping me company. Occasionally I met groups of lookouts who greeted me politely. As I got closer to the Sierra, the lookouts were no longer Cataca but Gaira. They recounted in detail their confrontations with the Sué, whose raids they had been enduring for the last few years. One of the men was holding a few of the intriguing metallic stones from the smoking thunderclap-sounding weapons. They had been dug out from tree trunks where they had lodged during the attacks. Likewise, they had some arrows that were short with tips made from a metal similar to that of the stones, only much lighter. I was shown a tree where an arrow, clearly delivered with force, had stuck and could not be removed; such an arrow would go right through a person. I found it sickening that someone could invent a device designed to cause so much harm to another human being. It made me very sad to think that my people were victims of such wicked weapons.

At last, I arrived in Bonda, or what was left of it. Once a prosperous village, it was now deserted, inhabited only by a few Gaira warriors who acted as lookouts. The rest of the population had fallen victim to the new weapons or had been carried away as slaves to the Islands. The survivors had gone up into the Sierra, to the Taira of the Toucan Clan. Furthermore, the warriors told me that the Sué were now turning up by land, probably attempting to outmanoeuvre the lookouts who were proving so successful at sighting their ships. They were landing at night, at a distance, and making their way through the forests to carry out surprise assaults, even up in the Sierra. Sometimes it was possible to ambush or harass them without getting too close, although they could not be driven back. We found the night attacks disconcerting since our people would not do such a thing. It was not our way, but we were learning fast.

When the Sué saw anyone wearing gold jewellery, they became even more dangerous and violent. This brought to mind the inhabitants of Darien where Zalab, the Shaman Kaku, had gone. The men wear gold shells to protect their penises from insect bites; it was an invitation to be attacked. Gold is eye-catching and we call it 'Tears of the Sun'. Our elaborate ornaments and jewellery are made from gold and are distinctive to each of our nations and clans; we wear them for ceremonies and solemn occasions. However, gold cannot be eaten nor made into tools; it has no medicinal purpose nor is it used for trading. The craftsmen who make the figurines exchange them for food. We failed to understand why the strangers found it so valuable. A clay pot is more functional and has many uses – to store grain from a harvest, to hold water or to keep salt that preserves food.

One of the ways the Sué behaved when they captured someone was to torture them in plain sight, to make sure they were seen by the family. They only ceased when provided with enough gold. Where women were concerned, they were gang raped by the men, who went crazy with lust at the sight of them with no clothes on. The sexual favours a woman grants a man who pleases her is something that is mutually satisfying. It should be by consent and pleasurable to both, and to force it is contrary to nature. The Sué were like demons rather than humans. Our women were now taking part in the battles and were as ferocious as the men. I am glad I was not one of the enemy.

One of the things we found most disconcerting was that on occasions the Sué were friendly. They offered presents such as short metal knives or coloured beads in exchange for gold or food, showing no signs of violence. I was able to take a good look at the strange bow they used to shoot their arrows with such force. In the shape of a cross, it was made of wood and metal but we were unable to make it work. I also examined their long, sharp metal knives that, I have to admit, would be an effective weapon. They could be secured to our lances that were after all only sticks with sharp ends, hardened in a fire. We debated with the warriors whether to utilize the Sué's weapons against them. Unless we could use them correctly, it would be detrimental, though we did not really like the idea. Personally, I found it unacceptable to use anything belonging to those men, and several of the warriors thought the same. We concluded it was better to observe how the weapons worked in order to better protect ourselves but to keep to what we knew. If we did learn how to use them, we might then reconsider. Many of our people chose death if they were captured, much to the anger and frustration of the Sué. All these stories were most distressing and I still did not know how I was going to infiltrate them. With all this in mind, I said goodbye to the Gaira and set off for the Sierra to reunite with my family and to organize the Jarlekja of all the Taira Mamas. I had a lot of information in my head and I needed to sort out my ideas. Everything was new and very worrying and I had to work out a plan.

Usually, walking up to the Sierra would have given me great pleasure, but these were different times. The villages of the Taira were full of Caribe displaced by the hostilities, and there was none of the usual cheerfulness. I had a long conversation with Zhiwé, Mina's mother, who was a great friend of my mother's. It was so sad to see that now one of her occupations was to make great quantities of poison for the warriors' arrows and cerbatanas. The concoction consisted of poison from the green fruit of a tree that grows by the beaches; the poison of venomous worms, fierce ants and scorpions; the sweat of some coloured frogs and the sap extracted from various trees. Altogether, there were more than twenty poisonous ingredients. They were added slowly and boiled for ten days, in a well-ventilated area because of the lethal fumes. Even the vegetation around the fire withered! The end product was a dark tobacco-coloured tarry substance that had an immediate effect. It terrified those who came into contact with it and they died in agony. We had never used such a poison before, not for hunting or even long ago when there were wars between us, but, as I have already said, these were different times. It was heart-breaking to see these women who had devoted their lives to healing and saving others, now preparing death for the enemy.

The son that Mina had borne me had become an adolescent who lived with my mother. He had spent long periods with Zhiwé, though not recently since it was safer up in the Sierra. I was so filled with anticipation that it was painful to listen to her talking about him, and I was eager to reach my village. He had been named Nuaxtashi, in honour of the protection the Taira sought from the sacred stones and because Serankwa, the force of life, watched over him. I was full of apprehension, not knowing what he thought of me or how he would react. I could only hope my mother had told him all about me.

I was in good spirits as I walked for three days to my village amidst the quiet mountain forest. I paused from time to time to drink in the streams that ran down the mountainsides or to greet the occasional traveller. I spent the nights in small villages where everyone was pleased to see me. They must have thought it strange that someone they had watched grow up had now become a Mama. In this way, I found out that my entire village had prepared a big welcome for me. All the members of my family from other villages would be present, including my beloved grandmother, who despite her age wanted to be there when I arrived. It was not exactly what I would have chosen but there was no getting in the way of their rejoicing or their good intentions. What was even more difficult was being called the Mama Kwishbagwi, the name I associated with my old Master. I was apparently expected to settle where my old Master had lived. In this time of war, I did not see myself having much of a role as the Mama, Guardian of the Forests. Besides, my absences were undoubtedly going to be more prolonged than we had anticipated in Rapa. I would be spending longer spells on the River than with my own people but it was not the moment to say anything and cause unnecessary grief.

The last stretch was the most exhilarating. I remembered the places where I played with my friends as a boy and the ones where we hid to playfully harass the travellers. The big, old trees with their shadows brought back memories of my first amorous encounters with Walashi. When at last I saw my village in the distance, I was so excited that I started to run. I could just make out the heads of the people who had probably been alerted by a lookout I had not even seen. Finally, I arrived in my village and the people were all lining the way. As I went past, they reached for my arms, my head, my back, shouting greetings and words that were unintelligible. I recognized my childhood friends and their parents and lots of children I had never seen before. Then at last I caught sight of my family. My mother, as beautiful as ever, was looking very dignified. My aunts and my grandmother almost tripped in their rush to hug me and then, there was Nuaxtashi.

The sight of him was the most powerful, emotional feeling I have ever experienced in my long life. He was shyly standing next to my mother, watching me, not knowing what to expect. He was the image of his mother and as beautiful as a god among men. I could not stop myself from crying like I had never done before. I tried to edge my way towards him and my mother, surrounded by relatives and friends embracing me. When I finally reached them, we hugged, amid sobs and tears. I was speechless as I held them tightly in my arms, expressing all the love in my heart. Meanwhile, the happy crowd around us patted me, said incoherent words, sang and played instruments I had not even noticed they had. These are the moments that make life worth living.

That night, when the welcome parties were over, and I had only let go of Nuaxtashi's hand briefly while I ate, the three of us were alone. I could hardly believe this handsome young man was the fruit of my passion for Mina. Furthermore, I found out that my mother had arranged it so that Mina would be fertile during those days before I left and I could make her pregnant. What women can do! That night we had so much to tell each other that we talked until we fell asleep near dawn.

My mother and the Mama Kwishbagwi had feared for my life when I contracted yellow fever on the River. They were in daily contact with Jawi until I recovered. She told him which plants to look for to bring down my temperature and prevent me from having convulsions, and which ones would build up my strength to fight the illness. Further along, in spite of all my mother's efforts, Mina died in childbirth, though she saw our son briefly before joining Serankwa. It was my mother and Zhiwé who chose the name Nuaxtashi for the boy who grew into a tall, strong, intelligent young man protected by the Forces of Nature. He had many friends because of his kind nature and excelled at games because of his strength and ability. He was so handsome that now he was at courting age all the girls chased after him. After overcoming his initial shyness, Nuaxtashi was more comfortable with me, listening attentively to all I said. He gave his views when required and joined in my mother's stories, making me proud as I listened to him. I would have so much liked to be a part of the early stages of his life. Though he had grown up with neither Mina nor me, he was nevertheless the fruit of our great love and his grandmothers had given him everything that we had not been able to. The following days were shared between family and friends, as they all wanted to hear about me and talk about themselves. I renewed relationships and strengthened others. Exhausting? Yes, but very enriching for the spirit.

It was a real pleasure to see Mixia Caita, my kindred spirit from Cundur-Curi-Marca, now the mother of two delightful little girls and pregnant with her third child. She had been my mother's apprentice and was now a healer in the nearby Hummingbird village in the north-east, where she first encountered her husband. I met him, a big strong man, who was kind but rather shy with me. I thanked him from my heart and congratulated him on obtaining such a rare and exquisite jewel.

I saw Guka, Zalab's mother, who was pleased to see me but full of sadness because she would not see her son again. I told her all about him, his journey, our reunion, our years in Rapa, his responsibilities and his new destiny. She was grateful and bade me farewell, trying to hold back her tears. I promised to keep her informed if there was any news from him, as would be the case in the years to come.

The reunion with Walashi was full of warmth and affection. She had been waiting all this time after the death of Mina and had been a second mother to Nuaxtashi. With her usual shrewdness, she grasped immediately how different my life was now. She was the first to realize that I would not be spending much time among my people. I told her about Nisa and Jawi and my new responsibilities on the estuary. Her response was to say she would be my woman whilst I was among them and would continue to be a mother to my son. She added that, Aluna Jaba willing, she would bear me children. What a generous, strong woman she was. She had been living with my mother and Nuaxtashi making a family of three. With the arrival of Mixia Caita, it became a family of four, until the latter left to be the healer in the Hummingbird village. It made me happy to see how much my son loved her and that she was like a daughter to my mother. She had also been her apprentice and was now a healer in her own right and a very capable one too.

The days went by and my grandmother and aunts went back to their own village and ours returned to normal. We began by sorting out my old Master's cave, which would be my dwelling place. It was in a good state, as my mother, who had been so close to him, had looked after it and sometimes stayed there on her way back from her healing tours. Nevertheless, we had to make sure that neither snakes nor bats had moved in! Aside from this, it was fresh and dry with a magnificent view over a large section of our Sierra. So began my life as the new Mama Kwishbagwi, alternating between my cave and my mother's house.

I was waiting for the Jarlekja of all the Taira Mamas to take place in my cave because it was so central and convenient. I think everyone liked the location. Straight away, Nuaxtashi and Walashi set about making arrangements and preparations for this event. A few of the Mamas were to be lodged in houses as the cave was not big enough. Meanwhile, I communicated with Master Tarminaki, Zalab, Jawi and all those known to me, informing them of the state of affairs in my region. With my spirit in a jaguar, I inspected the forests, the rivers and the animals and visited the beaches of the Gaira and the Mocana, where all was quiet at present. I encountered the Mama Rigawiyún in the form of a condor and together we surveyed the estuary of the River all the way to the Turbaco.

Finally, the big day of the Jarlekja of the Mamas of the Sierra arrived. There was an atmosphere of expectation in the village and everyone was ready to help. But, as is usual with us Mamas, we do not require very much: just a quiet place to sleep, eat and meditate. Consequently, when everyone had arrived, they made it clear without being discourteous that all they needed were the basics and no formalities. Most of the time, they would be in my cave having discussions and dealing with matters concerning the Mamas and the World of the Spirits. We were fourteen in all, including my brothers the Mama Shibulata, the Mama Inkimaku, the Mama Sarabata and the Mama Rigawiyún. We would come across all the other Mamas of Quicagua during the Zhatukúa Ceremony. It had been a very long time since such a reunion had taken place. Nuaxtashi, who was present assisting us, was the only one who was not a Mama.

The Jarlekja lasted for six days. We began by invoking: Serankwa, to give us wisdom; Aluna Jaba so that our knowledge and decisions were for the good of the Sierra and all the Taira people; and finally, the Spirits of the Kasouggui present in the mountains and forests, to transmit their harmony. We did this prior to fasting in preparation for Zhatukúa. The following day, during the course of our journey, we encountered the Grand Master Tarminaki and gave him our reports. They varied in length, according to the imminent danger in each region. It was probably the longest journey we had ever made. It lasted for two days, at the end of which we were all exhausted. On the fourth day we rested, to recover, especially the Mamas who had taken ayawasca.

The Shamans on the Islands apprised us of what their people were enduring. Not only were they being enslaved but strange, deadly illnesses were afflicting them. One affected the lungs and another, which we had already been told about, produced a rash all over the body. Even the few who tried to conceal themselves in the jungle were hunted down by huge dogs from whom they could not escape. The Shamans feared that within a short time there would be no Caribe left on the Islands. Now the boats were sailing to all the coasts – north, south and west – seeking new slaves. Besides, the Sué were continuously searching for gold that was melted down into bars, to be sent to their grand chief on the other side of the sea. It seemed that one of the characteristics of these men was the bad faith and intrigue that existed among their own. They schemed and used every possible way of cheating each other, incapable of working together in solidarity. Each man was out to get what he could for himself, including their Shamans. On the Island of the Cuba, there was a chief, who was like their cacique, appointed by their supreme chief across the sea. However, there were other minor chiefs who were constantly deceiving him, giving him reduced amounts of the gold they had stolen from us. The commander, in turn, unscrupulously sent his supreme chief far less than he should have done. Given their way of thinking, each boat that landed on our shores had multiple interests. This somewhat explained the different ways in which they behaved. The Caribe were able to observe all that went on whilst they worked as slaves. Since the Sué did not even consider they were human, it made no difference to them that they witnessed all their scheming.

But the ill-fated Caribe did report all they saw to their own Shamans. We had a long discussion about whether this benefited us or not. We finally reached the conclusion that greed was never a good thing and it made men behave insanely, to the detriment of their victims. We were warned about one of them in particular. A man called Ojeda, or some such name, who was preparing four boats and around two hundred men to go in search of gold in the land of the Turbaco, once the hurricane season was over. The Shaman of the Island of the Cuba considered that in a matter of three moons, this man would be heading our way. I was responsible for the Caribe Nation he was planning to attack. This meant I would be in the centre of it all and would have to act accordingly.

A seabird, the gannet, would warn me when they set sail. Zalab, the Shaman Kaku, informed us that a few moons previously, two boats had entered the gulf of the Atrato estuary. They had been warded off without casualties on either side. He thought that one of the Sué chiefs was the one that the Shaman of the Cuba had mentioned.

Once we had recovered, the Mama Inkimaku, the wisest of those present owing to his age and experience, brought up the question of my replacement as Guardian of the Forests. It was clear that I would be engaged elsewhere. Since everyone else had already been assigned their duties, it fell to the Mama Rigawiyún to carry out my functions. It was arranged and the different communities would be duly informed since it was vital for the preservation of the forests of the Sierra.

By the end of the Jarlekja, we all knew our roles for the near future. We upheld the decision to close the Shikwakala Nunjué to all excepting the Caribe-Gaira who were being displaced by the Sué. They would be assigned specific areas to settle under the supervision of the Mama Shibulata. The sites needed to have fresh water and arable soils, as well as being defensible. The land would have to be prepared to prevent the harmful effects of the partial deforestation. The Mama Shibulata knew of such locations of dry forest on the south side of the Sierra and he would immediately inform the Gaira and the Taira who lived close by. It was a major change of life for the Caribe, to be far from the sea, but at least they would be safe. After their exodus, the defence of the coastal area of the Sierra would be almost exclusively in the hands of the Toucan Clan of the Taira and the Gaira warriors who remained.

The last days of the Jarlekja were reserved for matters relating to us Mamas which are not relevant to my story. When it was time to leave, two of them accompanied the frail, old Mama Inkimaku, who walked slowly and cautiously back up to where he lived near the glacier. The two apprentices he had arrived with had been sent to carry out the duties he had assigned them. The large cave, where generations of Mamas and their apprentices had dwelt, was in a splendid location, cold because of the high altitude, with no vegetation. It was nevertheless comfortable and sheltered from the wind and the rain.

It was time to inform my family that my departure was imminent. My biggest worry was Nuaxtashi with whom I was building up a relationship that I did not want to disrupt. In the end it was Walashi, with her usual practical sense, who suggested I take him with me. Nuaxtashi was delighted to be part of what he saw as an adventure and we began making preparations. I spent those last days in my cave with him and occasionally with Walashi. My son guarded my body while I travelled the length of the River as a jaguar, in search of Nisa and making certain that everything was safe. I was exhausted by the Jarlekja and the days I had spent watching over the estuary. Both the fasting and the activities of the spirit had been physically demanding. I spent my last day resting and eating, to recover and be prepared to return to the River Yuma.

We left at dawn that morning and went west, taking the same route I had taken when I had set off for Rapa all those years ago. Only now we would turn off after the cienaga. We planned to go down to the Gran Cienaga and ask some Cataca fishermen to take us to where I would meet up with Nisa. From there we would travel to the bay where most of the Turbaco lived. On the way, Nuaxtashi and I talked at length. We were getting to know each other better and consolidating our relationship. I wanted him to know how difficult it had been to leave his mother, and I told him all about my subsequent adventures, one of which was my encounter with the peccaries. We visited my aunts, and it was the last time I saw my grandmother alive as she died a few moons later. She was so full of knowledge, energy and love for her family and all who had needed her care. My last memory was of her happiness on seeing Nuaxtashi and me together. That night she gave us a lot of advice such as the old are wont to do.

CHAPTER FOURTEEN

s soon as we arrived in the Gran Cienaga, we came across one of the large Cataca boats with six rowers, who respectfully took us to the other side of the cienaga. I only gave them a rough idea of the location of the Mocana village where Nisa and her family were waiting. I did not want them to take us all the way there; I preferred to leave it to the Fishermen. We set off in the direction of the River and the Cataca rowed all day and night. On reaching the west side of the cienaga, they took the boat through a small waterway where one of the large branches of the River flowing into the estuary was barely visible. I asked them to drop us there. They would have taken us wherever I requested but I also wanted Nuaxtashi to have a few days, training in a cayuco in preparation for the next stage of our journey. I also wished to talk to him about Nisa, our future travelling companion. I knew the Cataca were uneasy about dropping us in such an isolated place, on a tiny little beach in the middle of the dense forest. However, out of respect, they did not dare say anything that might be seen as interfering with a Shaman. They probably reasoned that I had my own obscure reasons for wanting to be left there. Already, I could see a small group of Fishermen and three cayucos on a platform above the location. We said our goodbyes and after blessing them, we watched them as they rowed away. For certain, in a day or two all the Cataca would know of the return of the Shaman.

Nuaxtashi's initiation into life on the River was about to begin. He was enjoying himself immensely. Everything was new to him and the way in which I was treated made him feel important. I pointed through the trees to the wooden platform where the Fishermen were and at first, he could not see them. We were practically underneath them before he finally did. They hastened to greet us and Nuaxtashi was the centre of attention when they heard he was my son. The children wanted to play with him, the women wanted to look at him, touch him and spend the night with him and the men congratulated me on having such a grown-up, strong son. This is their custom. There is no greater source of conversation and admiration than children and relatives. More specially among the young, probably because their mortality rate is so high. From the onset of our journey, I had been working on Nuaxtashi's rudimentary knowledge of the Caribe language. He had the basics, acquired during the period he had spent with his grandmother, Zhiwé, near the Gaira. He was making an effort to speak it and to understand the Fishermen's dialect, which was not as clear as that of the neighbouring Caribe – it was also more basic, with less vocabulary. That night, I talked about my plans and asked the Fishermen to take me to where Nisa was waiting. I also requested their help in instructing Nuaxtashi, or Nua, as they had taken to calling him, since they found it hard to pronounce his name. No sooner had I spoken, than they all began arguing about whose cayuco he would go in, who was going to instruct him and what he would be taught. They all wanted to be with him and teach him. In the end the elder of the family took matters in hand and assigned responsibilities and turns to be with Nua (even I had taken to using this name). I watched without saying a word, content to see their enthusiasm and my son happy to be part of their hospitality. Thank you, Jawi, for introducing me to these wonderful people.

We travelled for ten days until we met up with Nisa, during which time Nua's training was taken very seriously indeed. They made him row; they taught him to fish; to bathe without attracting alligators; to cook while travelling and the upkeep and care of a cayuco. They even taught him how to go to the toilet in motion! In the evenings, he learnt to prepare baits and to cook without making smoke. They taught him how to look for food in the forest and to extract oil from fish or fruit, as well as to hunt with a cerbatana. They even showed him how to make himself invisible to other travellers. At night, as they massaged the muscles in his arms and back, they told him stories and anecdotes in preparation for the following day. The elder among them made everyone laugh by imitating how Nua walked when he got out of the cayuco in the evenings and even Nua had to laugh at himself. They introduced him to other families, who welcomed him with equal warmth. My poor Nua was exhausted every night but he slept with a smile on his face. On the occasions when I travelled as a spirit or as a jaguar, on my return I always found that someone had put a shade over me and made me comfortable. Moreover, I had the certainty that Nua was in good hands.

One day whilst I was listening to their conversations, I overheard them say something that sounded like 'Mamakwish'. On asking them what it meant, there was total silence. No one answered or even looked at me; they simply carried on with whatever they were doing. In the end, it was Nua who came close and quietly said, 'Father, don't be silly, that's what they call you!'

Apparently, ever since my return from Rapa, this is what the Fishermen had been calling me, because they found it hard to say Mama Kwishbagwi. Jawi had told them it was all right to do so. I had no idea, as I was always addressed as 'Sir' or 'Shaman'. I thought it charming and told them so, much to their relief. They turned it into a joke that was not shared with me and again it was Nua who told me of it. I imagined the entire community was not only having a laugh at my expense but they were mimicking me as well. If it was the elder who was doing this, it must have been very funny.

By the time we reached the Mocana village where Nisa was waiting, Nua was strong and confident in his new abilities. Besides, he was completely at ease among the Fishermen. As we drew near the village, I saw Nisa and her family waiting for us on a raised wooden platform on the opposite side of the River. I imagine this platform had been used for generations, to the complete ignorance of the Mocana on the other bank. It happened to be a large village with a good deal of trading but we were not going there. It was a happy reunion and, as usual, Nua was the centre of attention. I was pleased that Nisa took to him so favourably and very soon they were chatting as if they had always known each other. I saw her nephew's new wife, at whose wedding Jawi and I had been witnesses. She was heavily pregnant and about to give birth judging by her size and the attention she was receiving from the other women. How resilient these fishermen are and how quickly they recover from all the blows that life deals them. We did not waste any time and the next day, the three of us set off in the new cayuco Nisa had acquired. I told her we were heading for the Bay of the Turbaco and after a brief discussion with the others, Nisa knew exactly which direction to take. When we left, it was gratifying to see Nua embracing all the members of the family we had come with. Everyone looked genuinely sad to see us go.

Our new course would take us crosswise over the forks of the River, in a south-westerly direction. It was exhausting to row each day against the current and to cross over the very large branches of the River. Fortunately, almost every evening we encountered Fishermen with whom we spent the night and they helped us with directions. Eventually, we reached an area devoid of all forestation where there was a cienaga with islands made from the sediment of the River that changed from one year to the next. It required all Nisa's concentration to find the way. Besides, it was not safe to disembark because the grass was so high that it was not possible to see where to walk. There was always the risk of getting stuck in mud where the ground was too soft, and sinking up to the waist or, even more alarming, coming across a hungry caiman looking for food or, worse still, a startled poisonous snake. We were in this cienaga for three days and two nights. The nights were harder because there was nowhere safe to rest for the night. We opted instead for stopping in narrow waterways whilst trying to avoid all contact with the vegetation on either side for fear of drawing a serpent into our cayuco. We took it in turns to stand watch in case a black caiman or an alligator should make us keel over. On the second night, a startled Nua woke us hastily saying that he had seen something very large alongside us. It was with great relief that we discovered a family of manatees observing us with curiosity.

Nisa gently caressed them whilst uttering some charming words. 'My friends, may the peace of the River be with you in your new lives; thank you for being here.' Turning to us, she said, 'These gentle creatures are the reincarnations of our drowned brothers. They have come to reassure us and to tell us there are no caimans nearby.'

We slept peacefully for the remainder of that night and whoever was on watch stroked the manatees. I took advantage of the peace and went to look at the Turbaco villages as a jaguar, to check they were being vigilant. That day a gannet flew overhead and landed on the water next to us. The Shaman of the Cuba was letting me know the enemy had set sail.

The following morning, Nisa sighted the small channel she was looking for that led to the Bay of the Turbaco. It never ceased to amaze me how well these fishermen knew the River! We carried on for two days, propelled by the force of the current, until we arrived at the sea. We walked to the nearest village, which was the largest of the Turbaco Nation. As usual, our sudden and unexpected appearance provoked the aston-ishment that always followed me as a Shaman, thanks to the ability unique to the Fishermen.

The initial confusion allowed for a speedy summons of all the Cacique and elders of the Turbaco in the area of the bay. Throughout the evening and into the night they promptly arrived, compelled by the haste with which I summoned them and the sense of urgency I had conveyed. When at last even the furthest away had arrived, I told them the Shaman of the Cuba had warned me of an imminent attack by the Sué, almost certainly prompted by greed. The enemy were proba-bly after the gold they, the Turbaco, were reputed to possess to decorate their bodies. They accepted what I said without question; besides they had already had small skirmishes with the Sué. This time though, it was going to be a major confron-tation. I also had to reprimand them because I had noticed when reviewing the villages that the lookouts were not being altogether vigilant. They had become complacent and were not carrying out their duties properly. I heard them say that they had seen jaguar prints near their villages which frightened them. All the better. I hoped it served as a warning! Apparently, they had a good supply of lances, arrows for their bows and darts for their cerbatanas with quantities of the deadly poison. Some of the young were being taught to use a sling. All this had created a sense of security which I quickly demolished.

The bay has two entrances, one on either side of the big island in the middle, and we placed our main lookouts on both. We also positioned them on an island in the south and in the cienagas in the north, should the Sué come by land to take us by surprise. I emphasized that the strategy was to ambush and attack them with arrows and darts while keeping our distance. The warriors should also be prepared to move quickly when the enemy landed.

We did not have long to wait. Eight days later, four Sué boats sailed through the larger of the two entrances of the bay. At last, we knew where to concentrate our forces. At dawn the men disembarked in a leisurely way and followed two of our people to the main village. We had suitably adorned the pair with gold ornaments to act as bait, and from a distance they looked innocent enough. There were about one hundred and fifty soldiers, some better armed than others. We had narrowed the paths by placing trunks and rocks in such a way that no more than two or three men could walk abreast at a time. They were ambushed and attacked from both sides of the forest. Never having suffered such an attack before, they panicked, and we were able to kill most of them without suffering a single loss. Three or four escaped though and hid in the forest or buried themselves in the sand on the beach. Unfortunately for us, one of those was their leader, Ojeda, who managed to reach his boat the next morning. We estimated that there were still some sixty men left on the boats that swiftly set sail for the open sea.

We were overjoyed by our victory. I had never taken part in an act of war before but it was pleasing that our plan had been such a success. As a Shaman, I did not participate in the battle but Nua did with his sling. Nisa and I witnessed the attack from the trees. We left the bodies of the enemy to the birds of prey and collected the weapons with the hope that in the future we could learn to use them. For now, only the long knives would be attached to our lances. Not wishing to take part in the celebrations of the warriors when they returned to their villages, Nua, Nisa and I went to an isolated beach to happily discuss the day's events.

Except that we severely underestimated the Sué leader, Ojeda.

Two days after his escape, in the dead of night, he returned with his men and creeping stealthily over the stinking, decomposing bodies of their fallen comrades, they made their way to the largest Turbaco village. They surrounded it and set fire to the roofs, whilst everyone slept. Every one of the inhabitants perished, over seven hundred men, women, children and babies; anyone trying to escape was slain. Nothing like this had ever been seen. We attacked them in a legitimate battle but they burnt the people of the village alive. In the morning, they scavenged among the ashes and the charred bodies, finishing off anyone who was still alive, tearing and severing parts of the bodies to strip the gold from the dead. Then, to our utter revulsion they did the same to their fallen comrades, the ones we had killed in battle. They ripped off rings and ornaments and anything else they could find among their clothing. It was their turn for jubilation as they calmly returned to their ships and this time, set sail for the Island of the Cuba.

That morning, we awoke with a feeling of unease, as if something bad had happened. We arrived at the village mid-morning to be confronted by the full horror. The enemy had only just left, after scavenging among their own dead. But one remained, overcome by greed, hunting for gold among the smouldering bodies. Using every ounce of my strength, I aimed a stone with my sling that cracked his skull and he fell among our dead with an expression of surprise frozen on his face. I had never killed a human being before but it was impossible to contain the fury and the feeling of utter abomination I felt. I would have preferred someone as young as Nua not to have seen all those massacred people. As it was, we stood in the middle of the devastation with tears running down our faces. Eventually, one by one other Turbaco arrived.

I summoned all the Caciques and the elders to a meeting on the beach. Even a delegation from the neighbouring nation of the Calamarí arrived. That night, I vented my outrage against the Sué. I told them it was the duty of every Caribe to be ruthless with them. If one amongst us showed any weakness, we all suffered the consequences. I had to get the atrocity I had witnessed out of my system. Amid an enraged silence, we organized the burial of our people, starting at dawn the next day. We knew that never again could this terrible enemy be misjudged, even in defeat. Later, under the stars, in the World of the Spirits, I communicated with Master Tarminaki, Zalab and many other Shamans and Mamas who were waiting to hear from me.

Accounts of the massacre spread rapidly among the regions of the Caribe and eventually to all the peoples of Quicagua, giving rise to an anger that had never been felt before, especially among the Caribe who were at the front of the war against the Sué. I decided to remain longer among the Turbaco to help with the burials and in reorganizing the nation. The chief Cacique had perished in the flames and a new one had to be elected. I wanted to make sure whoever was chosen was a man capable of leading his people wisely in this war. Once this was done, we returned to the River to share our experiences with other Caribe and the Taira. This would occupy me during the following moons.

Life was relatively calm for the next two years until Zalab apprised us of the arrival of two Sué ships in the gulf of the estuary of the River Atrato, in an area we call Darien. Here, they had run aground and sunk at the entrance to the gulf and the men had been trapped on the beach by the Caribe Emberá. They were decimated by hunger and continuous attacks. Out of the initial hundred, only thirty remained, who had barricaded themselves in a sort of fort they had built using the remnants of their ships. The so-called Ojeda was apparently amongst them. The siege of the Sué lasted for several moons until the few who remained were rescued by another ship. They were taken to a location near the mouth of the River Atrato and there for some reason, were abandoned. Only Ojeda was taken to the Island of the Cuba. Zalab kept us informed of what was happening. The men who were left seized an Urabá village and enslaved the population. The women were used as sex slaves and the men forced to work. The Sué were thus able to recover from the moons of hunger they had endured.

In the new settlement they were led by two veterans of the siege, Balboa and Pizarro. It was obvious to Zalab that they were not on friendly terms; there was ill feeling between them. Periodically ships arrived with more men and arms. It became a matter of urgency to expel them before we were wiped out like the Cuba on the Islands.

There was a situation that we had not taken sufficiently into account when we devised our initial plans in Rapa: the discord and strife existing among the many communities and nations. The Sué were using this to their advantage. Much to Zalab's frustration, the Sué who had escaped from the Emberá siege and were transferred to the other location in the gulf were initially welcomed by the community there. To make matters worse, they had even participated in the enslavement of the neighbouring villages with whom they were in conflict. The Cacique of the village, Panquiaco, had organized an expedition of the Sué to the sea in the west and on the way, they had subjugated the communities they came across. This Cacique had even told the Sué about Tahuantinsuyo and the quantity of gold that existed in the mountain called Potosí. They were now obsessed with the idea of this gold and wasted no opportunity to question anyone about it. An expedition to the sea in the west was organized to try to get from there to the land of my tutor, An Yupami. Panquiaco was rewarded with one of the animals the Sué rode, giving him the prestige to impose his authority on his neighbours. Zalab was trying to make him see the great mistake he was making. We were all fully aware of the harm that the enmity among the nations represented to our defence strategy.

Whilst Zalab was preoccupied with these affairs, I continued with my routine on the estuary and in the Sierra. Nua and Nisa accompanied me everywhere except when I went up to the Sierra. On those occasions, Nisa remained among her people and kept me informed of any new events. Nua, now a young man, had come of age and was still attracting all the young girls. The three of us had strengthened our relationships and were unified as a family.

But this state of affairs was about to change. Nua came to me one day whilst we were in the Sierra to tell me he wanted to become a Mama. This gave me great satisfaction, not only because he was my son but also, I had seen the ability he had to understand the balance of Aluna Jaba. Nisa and I had observed how quickly he correlated what he saw in the forests and the rivers with the effect that people and animals had on them. He could not be my pupil because of our kinship but I thought of the Mama Rigawiyún with whom I was in touch. I consulted both him and Master Tarminaki, who decided it was best for Nuaxtashi to spend time with the Mama Rigawiyún, who could make an unbiased assessment. It is unusual for someone so young to be an apprentice. Nevertheless, Nua was used to living with me so he would not find it strange. We all thought it was a sound decision and thus I lost my companion of the last few years, but such is life. Children grow up and choose their own way in Serankwa's design, and parents have to accept the laws of life.

Another matter Zalab and I had discussed was the possibility of infiltrating the Sué in the settlement in his area. He had no difficulty coming and going among them, as they could not distinguish one of us from the other. Then, by the time Master Tarminaki had agreed to my plan, new events changed everything.

I received this information when I was in my cave in the Shikwakala Nunjué. That day, I had explained to my mother and Walashi why Nua had gone to stay with the Mama Rigawiyún and outlined my plan to infiltrate the Sué in Darien. But that night, in the World of the Spirits whilst Walashi watched over my body, the Guajiro Shaman contacted me. The Guajiro had captured a Sué. No one knew why he was alone when he was apprehended. He might have been left behind when a group of them had come ashore and were driven back. He would have been killed had the Shaman not prevented it. He knew of my mission and wisely thought the man might be useful to me. He was now a prisoner in the Guajiro village. This was the opportunity I had been waiting for and I told him I would go immediately. Accordingly, I informed my mother and Walashi, who offered to accompany me to the Guajiro Desert. I agreed, realizing that it would be the first time in our lives we were going to spend some time alone together. We made our preparations and after eating we bade farewell to my mother, who was returning to her village.

The next day we set off, this time in a north-easterly direction. I estimated it would take us about ten days to get to the village where the prisoner was. The first night we stayed with Mixia Caita. That night, we told her all that had happened and I met her third child, the five-year-old boy she was pregnant with when I returned from Rapa. The rest of the journey was uneventful. All I remember was that Walashi was helpful, a good walker and entertaining company; at night she was loving and passionate and during the day an excellent travelling companion. We walked down to the sea and along the beach for the next seven days. This way it would be easier to find the Guajiro village we were looking for near the shore. Besides, the Shaman had arranged for the communities along the way to assist us, as someone not used to the desert can easily get lost and perish through lack of water.

As the journey progressed and the desert conditions intensified, it was a continuing source of worry to find water. The streams that flowed into the sea became rarer, but Walashi, in her resourceful manner, heated some stones on the fire at night and in the morning, collected the condensation that had formed around them. This way at least, we had a very small amount of fresh water to start with, and for the rest of the day we managed to obtain some from the Guajiro, though their water, found in deep wells, had an unpleasant taste. They also provided us with the food we needed. We did not stay in their villages, choosing instead to sleep out under the stars. The Shamans and Mamas have a need for solitude which intensifies with the passing of the years. I found it distracting to be in a village with all the activity going on around me. Fortunately, no one questioned this or insisted on us staying with them.

When we reached the village where the prisoner was, the Shaman and the Cacique were waiting to show him to us. They were holding him in one of their huts, which, to allow the wind to blow through, consisted of a palm roof and branches tied together to make the walls. There were, however, men outside guarding him.

My first impression was of a young man with a shock of black hair and some on his face, though not as much as I had seen on the men in the battle with the Turbaco. His skin was white with red patches on his face and the clothing that concealed his body and most of his legs was in a bad state. In silence, Walashi and I sat and watched him for a while as he slept in a hammock. We then quietly walked out and went in search of the Shaman and the Cacique. Apparently the Sué had appeared one day out of nowhere, hungry and thirsty and desperately begging for water. The Cacique had prevented anyone from killing him before he consulted with the Shaman. It was decided that he was not to be harmed and he was allowed to walk about the village waiting for my arrival. He had learnt a few words in Caribe and it was possible to have a very basic conversation with him.

I realized of course, that if I wanted to learn anything from him, I would have to establish some sort of relationship where he was not afraid of me. I explained to everyone what I intended and asked them to leave him to Walashi and myself. I would let them know if I needed any assistance to subdue him but I did not think this was going to be necessary.

CHAPTER FIFTEEN

This was the beginning of my relationship with the man called Andrés Arias. When he awoke, I was standing close, watching him, and judging by his reaction, it was obvious he did not know what to expect. He knew that his captors were waiting for someone to come for him, that much he had understood. He got out of the hammock and made some sort of a bow that I can only assume was the way he would behave with one of his own chiefs. He started to say something but I made a sign for him to be silent; I wanted to see how different he was from us. His eyes were a strange green colour and he was thin and much taller than us. When I indicated that I wanted him to turn round which he which he complied with apprehensively. He began imploring in his own language mixed with a few Caribe words such as 'friend' and other nonsensical words. My smile somewhat reassured him and I again indicated that I wanted him to turn round, with which he complied apprehensively, allowing me to lift his garment. His skin was much whiter than on his face and neck and his hair was not as thick as ours. His arms and legs were covered in some sort of black fur we had never seen before. I made a gesture for him to follow me outside, which he did uneasily, as if fearing for his life. As I headed towards the hut Walashi and I had been allocated, he followed nervously, glancing about in all directions. He probably thought someone was going to attack him but there was no one around.

On our arrival, Walashi had prepared some fish and I pointed to a bench made from a flattened tree trunk, for him to be seated. I sat opposite to continue my observation. Walashi brought us our food on earthenware plates and I straight away saw that he was embarrassed and refused to look at her, not even when she told him to eat. He glanced at me instead, which I thought was rather odd. I watched him eat with pleasure and I smiled to myself, thinking that the Guajiro had probably not bothered much on this account. When Walashi came back with water in a totuma, he behaved in the same way, keeping his eyes averted when she sat down by my side. Without taking my eyes off him, I addressed Walashi: 'This man must think you're so ugly, he can't even look at you!'

She answered with a smile: 'I don't think that's the problem. It's fairly obvious he hasn't been with a woman for a while; I can see it in his eyes. He's also trying to pretend that he's not interested in another man's woman. You really can be so naive!'

'Then we must find him a girl who doesn't mind being with someone rather strange; I'll leave that up to you.'

I inquired with gestures if he wanted more to eat, to which he answered affirmatively. When Walashi got up, I had another chance to watch his reaction and he did look self-conscious and somewhat confused. I saw the 'I told you so' in her eyes. He attempted to say something in the few Caribe words he knew, but I made him understand that I wanted him to speak in his own language. I certainly did not want him learning ours! I pointed to different things and he told me what they were in his language. I repeated what he said, trying to memorize his words, which he corrected as necessary. When Walashi reappeared, I teased him by pointing to her leg and touching it. He turned bright red, looking uncomfortable while Walashi mouthed, 'Leave him alone!'

'It's a matter of some urgency to find him a woman!' I said to her.

All day, I pressed him for words in his language, which I endeavoured to memorize. I asked him ordinary words and expressions like 'let's go down to the sea', 'pass me the dish' and 'would you like some water'. Walashi learnt along with me and we corrected each other. By the end of the day, he seemed less troubled by Walashi's presence, and I thought how much easier things would be from now on. The following day I made a truly amazing discovery, but I am getting ahead of myself!

Walashi set about finding a woman for Andrés and came across two mature women willing to have a new experience. She arranged for alternate nights and for us to get the details the following morning. On the first night, when one of them had gone to where he was sleeping, she had some difficulty making him understand what she wanted. She was amazed by the amount of hair on his body: chest, legs, arms and around his penis. In addition, he was clueless about love and women.

She thought perhaps it was his first time or that the women where he came from were satisfied with very little. They would have to teach him how to go about it... I could not help reflecting on how shy these strangers were about their own bodies and how much the sight of someone naked upset them. Small wonder they wore such uncomfortable clothes.

The following morning, we went down to the sea to bathe, as we did every day. Andrés did not want to undress. When he finally got round to it, we were able to see the hair on his body, just as the woman had reported. We refrained from looking at him too much, not to make him self-conscious. Instead, I asked his name, to which he answered 'Andrés', and he proceeded to draw some symbols in the sand with a stick. At first, I did not know what he was doing until he began pronouncing the sounds of the symbols. So, this was what Master Tarminaki was referring to when he gave me the task of learning their symbols to paint ideas. I was very excited but I tried not to show it while I delved further. Walashi saw my excitement and came over to watch. I said a word I had learnt and Andrés wrote it in the sand. Then, to see what happened, I pronounced the name Walashi, articulating it twice, before he wrote it in the sand as well. I said two more words in Caribe and he did the same. This was amazing! The symbols represented the sounds of the words in any language. A whole new world of possibilities had opened up. The sand was not exactly ideal but it would have to do until we found an alternative. I tried to make him understand that I wanted him to teach me what he had been doing. I doubt it took this intelligent young man very long to realize that he had found a way to survive amongst us. Furthermore, he had the incentive to teach us with enthusiasm! I say 'us', because Walashi wanted to learn along with me, which I thought was a good idea. In this way, more than one person would learn the new language, and, besides, we could practise together.

The next step was deciding what to do with Andrés; in other words, where he should live while carrying out his task. We would be staying on with the Guajiro for another moon or so before returning to the Sierra. I did not want to take him up to the Shikwakala Nunjué, which anyway was closed to strangers. It would not be appropriate for him to see how we lived, nor our paths. After all, Andrés was the enemy. At present, he was trapped and docile amongst us but unforeseen circumstances could change everything. I was not prepared to take that risk; something would come up.

The days that followed were ones of uninterrupted learning. During the day we acquired new vocabulary and learnt the sounds of the symbols, the 'alphabet' as he called it, and I discovered that numbers also had symbols. He taught us their concept of numbering the years, and according to him the year was 1517. Walashi and I worked out we were probably born around 1477. I was completely engrossed, while Walashi was more relaxed and less demanding of Andrés. Nevertheless, by the end of the day, even I could see he was tired and frustrated by not having something more suitable to write on. By night, he was engaged in his own very different form of learning, much more enjoyable, and the women described his progress. There were now other women going to visit him out of curiosity. We could see he was definitely more at ease in Walashi's presence.

A few days later, we were able to have small conversations using a limited vocabulary. He told us there were no women among them because their big chief did not allow them to come from the other side of the sea; the few women over here were with their chiefs. They were only allowed to have sexual relations to have children, otherwise it was forbidden by their 'religion'. It was not clear what he meant, by whom or why this was forbidden. When he talked further about his customs and religion, I was completely at a loss. It was all very interesting but I was disappointed that I was not learning faster.

After Walashi and I made love at night, we talked about many things and we tried to have conversations in Spanish (apparently the name of their language). On one occasion, she told me not to press Andrés so much in my urgency to learn, as the poor man was exhausted. Henceforth, I tried to be less demanding and he did seem more relaxed. There was one thing of which I was sure. I had to empty my mind and not compare one language with the other, otherwise I would never learn to speak like one of them. I had to cease translating into Chibcha or Caribe. Fortunately, I possess a facility with languages; apart from Chibcha, I spoke several Caribe dialects. In addition, whilst in Rapa, An Yupami had taught me to speak his language. Walashi too, appeared to have an amazing ability and often it was she who corrected me.

One moon later, we were able to have more interesting conversations. In this way, we found out how Andrés had arrived among the Guajiro. He was not a sailor but a clerk on a ship that was exploring a handful of barren islands located a few days, navigating north-east of the land of the Guajiro. The men were short on food and they sailed closer to the coast, seeking sea turtles that emerge at night to lay their eggs. One night, in need of a change, he volunteered to go ashore in a small boat with several of the men. They searched the beach in darkness and, inadvertently, he wandered away from the others. He had no idea what happened but when he got back, he saw the body of one of the men lying in the sand, slain by a poison dart. The rest of the men had gone, probably without realizing he was not with them or they presumed he was dead. For the rest of that night and half of the following day, he hid in the same place, hoping they would return for him. But he saw no ship on the horizon and by then he was desperate for water. He walked along the beach until he came across footprints leading inland, which he followed all the way to the Guajiro village. That is how he came to be there.

What he told us explained many things about the different behaviour of these strangers. Not all were warriors: some were sailors or merchants, others had similar occupations to his. They wrote down everything that took place and recorded the quantity of 'treasure' that was acquired. Not all the Sué knew how to read and write, only the chiefs and men like him. He told me that gold was valuable because it was made into coins that were used to purchase anything they wanted. The more gold a person had, the more powerful he was. An illness they brought with them, called a 'common cold', had killed most of the Caribe on the Islands; allegedly, because 'it prevented them from breathing properly', or so it was said. Now the Sué needed to find more people to enslave – *en naboria** was the term Andrés used.

Their 'religion' (beliefs) was imposed by friars. They tried to inculcate it among the Caribe by pouring water on their heads. Andrés thought the '*Indians*',[†] as they called us, simply acquiesced so they would be left alone and only pretended to be 'converted'. They used 'paper' and 'books' to write in and these were made expressly for this purpose. The symbols or 'letters' were written using a quill and ink. This I did understand because we use quills and different coloured dyes to decorate the body, blankets and other objects. I reported every bit of new information to Master Tarminaki.

It was all very interesting, but it was time to return to the Sierra. I informed Andrés one morning and he was crestfallen. He was enjoying the women's nightly visits and was apparently performing very well; the women were also satisfied. I told him he had no alternative but to leave with us. Luckily, he felt safe with Walashi and myself and set about bidding farewell to his new friends. On the day we left, a large group had even gathered to see him off!

We took the same route back along the beach and all the way the three of us spoke in Spanish. We asked him questions about anything that came into our heads and his answers led to more unknown facts and further questions. Fortunately, young Andrés was good-natured and replied readily without hiding anything. He considered we were his

---

* Unpaid servants

† Columbus originally thought he had discovered a new route to the Indies

friends and tried to please us in every way. Likewise, we saw him as a friend, which was only natural after the time we had spent together. We were lucky that Andrés was not only an educated man, willing to teach us, but he also had the ability to do so; I would not otherwise have wasted my time with him. I could see he was trying to find better ways to teach us, though nonetheless we were able to read and understand what he wrote in the sand. We were somewhat irritated by the attention he attracted from the inhabitants of the villages where we stopped to get provisions. Although this was to be expected, it distracted us from our objective. By the time we reached the foot of the Sierra, we were having long agreeable conversations and my knowledge of the Sué, or rather the Spaniards, had advanced considerably.

All the way I kept asking myself what I was going to do with him. Finally, I came up with the answer. I would take him to Guachaca, a Toucan village not too far up the Sierra; this way I would not be violating the rule we had made. Luckily for Andrés, he was travelling with me because any other way, he would not have stood a chance. I saw the hatred in the eyes of the Caribe and the Taira when they first encountered him. But they were restrained and respectful in my presence, other-wise... poor Andrés. Walashi, in her kind, straightforward way, without me realizing it, persuaded everyone of Andrés's importance. She was quite remarkable and the more time I spent with her, the more highly I valued her. One day, without beating about the bush, she told me she was with child. Then calmly, she carried on with what she was doing. Walashi was forty and it was usual for our women to bear children before they were twenty. She had the strong, firm body of someone who does a lot of physical activity and few could match her knowledge of the female body. It reassured me to think she would have no problem with her pregnancy or birth, and as I put my arms around her, I said, 'In my heart, I was hoping this would happen and that's why I have been so insistent!'

The first person we informed in Spanish was Andrés, and the three of us had a little celebration. He told us that on these occasions, the Spaniards would drink a toast with wine. We drank water under the stars and without uttering another word, lay down on the sand and gazed up at the sky. Several shooting stars crossed the expanse, which we saw as a good omen. The next day, we set off again in good spirits.

Andrés's concern was that when we left the beach, we would not have anything to write on. We tried other surfaces, among them clay, but erasing was difficult and it dried too quickly. It was possible to write using the charcoal of a burnt log but we had no surface to write on. It was unsatisfactory and one day without giving it too much thought and more as a sign of his frustration, he lightly said, 'If only we could obtain some ink and paper from Cuba.'

His words made me think of the Spanish settlement in Zalab's territory. I did not say anything but that night I sent a message via the jaguar and spoke to Zalab in the World of the Spirits. Andrés had told me that the scribes and the monks possess leather bags containing blank sheets of paper, ink and quills. Zalab had been into the settlement many times at night to speak to Panquiaco and he knew exactly what I was referring to. He would try to get hold of one.

In the meantime, the three of us went up to stay in Guachaca, where Zhiwé, Mina's mother, lived. Andrés was not welcome. I had to assemble the entire village to explain, in no uncertain terms, that this was a matter for the Mamas to learn about the Sué. I told them their cooperation was essential to carry out our task and make Andrés feel at ease. They calmed down and a few days later, the Mama Rigawiyún arrived with Nua to lend further support. Walashi and I were thrilled to see my son, now a fully grown man of twenty-five, strong and full of the wisdom that living with a Mama had instilled in him. It was certainly a special occasion for his grandmother, Zhiwé, who had not seen him for several years. They met the amiable young Andrés, who was frightened by his new surroundings. With their help I made him feel more at home.

The issue now was that as he spoke no Chibcha and his Caribe vocabulary was more suited to his encounters with women, Walashi and I were the only ones who could talk to him and be his interpreters. That is how I had wanted it to be initially, but now I saw the limitations. We decided to occupy a secluded hut on the edge of the village where we could have some privacy. This would also allow Andrés to learn our language on his own, providing it did not interfere with our lessons. I thought it a good idea that the Mama Rigawiyún and Nuaxtashi learn along with us so that more than two people could speak Spanish. It began this way but since Walashi and I were more advanced, we had to divide Andrés's lessons; he was no longer available only to us. Still, I thought we had made a great deal of progress but we needed to improve our accents, which according to Andrés would sound strange to a Spaniard. We still had the ongoing constraint of not having anything other than dust on which to write even the simplest of things.

Everything continued in this manner for two more moons until one day a messenger arrived with a present from the Shaman Kaku of the Emberá. It was the scribe's bag that Zalab had procured from the Spaniards. We were very excited and now our problem was solved. This was further confirmation that Serankwa was with us and our endeavours. The bag even had a board that the scribes put on their knees to write on when they do not have the appropriate piece of furniture. We now set about learning to write, which I must confess was exceedingly hard. Andrés said it was a skill better acquired as a child. Our writing improved as time went on and Walashi's was artistic as well, much to Andrés's delight. Since the amount of paper was limited, we decided that it should only be used when more advanced, as was the case with Walashi and myself. The other two, in the meantime, would continue to learn to read and write in the dust.

On receiving the leather bag, I examined its contents, and apart from the tools we needed, my attention was drawn to two sheets of paper with writing on them. One afternoon, I showed one of them to Andrés.

'It's a letter from a certain Sebastian Davila to his brother, Martin Alonso, who it appears lives in Cuba; though his second name is not specified, it's probably Davila, the same as his brother. The letter was ready to be sent on the next ship when it somehow went astray!' There was a touch of complicity in his smile as he said this.

This letter was the first text I had ever read. I was fascinated by the idea that one could express thoughts that someone else in another place could read and re-read as often as they wished. Now I understood what Master Tarminaki meant, when fifteen years ago, he told me I would be 'the Messenger of the Future'. He wanted me to write about our world so that, like the letter from one brother to another, someone else could read what I had written, even after my death. In this way, ideas are preserved so that in the future others can know and understand how we think now. Sitting in his small arbour in the forest, this man, as old as the trees and wiser than any other living being, had grasped the significance of the written word. I could hardly wait to speak to him. I let him know via the jaguar and that night in the World of the Spirits, I told him I understood the enormity of what he wanted me to do. He simply smiled, and at that moment I understood his true merit to all mankind. I humbly expressed my deepest admiration.

The letter served not only as a reading exercise but also as an example of how to write. According to Andrés, it was written in excellent Spanish with good spelling that the writer had obviously learnt from educated people.

I will now tell you the content of the letter. The author was venting his anger about the problems in the city they called Santa Maria la Antigua del Darien. Apparently, a delegation, which included a governor, a bishop and his assistants, had arrived without bringing any provisions. Rain and floods had destroyed major crops in the area and they were reduced to eating the pigs and the horses. Life was difficult enough and to add to their problems, the 'Indians' were now rebelling.

Many had escaped, which made getting supplies even harder. The writer was infuriated by the delegates who had arrived on ships that had already left. They were giving everyone orders, consuming the scarce food and not helping in any way. If the situation continued, he and many of his friends would find a way of leaving the city.

The second written sheet of paper referred to a consignment of 'valuable articles' Sebastian was supposedly sending his brother, Martin Alonso, in a sealed chest on the next ship. It consisted of a bag with fifteen pearls, eighteen gold bars, several silver objects and a few polished coral necklaces. The writer asked his brother to look after the treasure for both of them, to be discreet about it and give the captain of the ship a considerable sum of money to ensure his silence.

I informed Zalab about all of this as an interesting insight into the mind of the settlers. It was certainly an unexpected way of finding out how these strangers thought and what motivated them. Later, in my discussions with the Mama Rigawiyún and Nua, we reflected on how vital it was to know the enemy and make no mistakes when fighting them.

Now that we had all this new knowledge, we asked Andrés if he could explain the behaviour of the Sué. Nua was still shocked by the way in which the Sué had stripped the valuables from their dead companions following the atrocity they had committed against us in Turbaco. Andrés seemed to think there was nothing unusual about this, though he said they could, at least, have buried the bodies. Many of the soldiers were mercenaries, hired in Cuba, with no bonds of brotherhood or friendship between them; each one was out for himself. The men probably considered it a waste to leave valuable objects lying around for someone else to take. Andrés went on to say that accumulated riches passed from parents to children and this was how families became powerful.

Simultaneously, Andrés was undergoing an important transformation. He said he felt more at ease amongst us than with his own people, especially with the women! It appears that before the Guajiras, he had only been with a woman once, when he had to pay whom he called a 'loose woman'. This had happened in a port in Spain shortly before coming over to what they referred to as the 'New World'. Now he had fallen in love with a young girl who was currently the only one. He was happy, relaxed and no longer ashamed of not wearing clothes. Our people had finally accepted him and he had made friends while learning Chibcha, which he was doing when we gave him time off from teaching us.

He went down to the River every day to bathe with our people. He told us that the Spaniards only bathed when they had to, for example when they got muddy. Usually, they only washed their hands and their faces briefly in a bowl. It was considered a danger to the heath, to wash away their 'natural body oils'!

Only time would tell the true value of having Andrés amongst us, and his new-found loyalty was still untested. Walashi, who day by day was getting bigger and more beautiful, questioned him about the illnesses that had decimated the population of the Caribe in the Islands. Andrés was unable to enlighten her very much on this subject. He said it was commonplace to have 'colds' especially in 'winter', which was when their weather was cold. The nose became 'congested', the lungs filled with mucous and the person had a sore throat and a temperature. It was spread by the sick person's breath or sneezing. This was all unknown to us, except for the temperature. The other illness which Andrés did think was dreadful was called 'smallpox'. Personally, he did not know anyone who had had it, but it was said that the people who survived had scars all over their faces and bodies. In Cuba, he was told the story of a sailor with smallpox, who with a captain by the name of Cortés, had travelled to the land of the Maya in Yucatan. 'The infection' had spread there and wiped out the entire population of that nation. There was no known cure and it was contagious, though not as easily caught as a 'cold'. He had heard that it took a few days before it was apparent that a person was 'infected' and in the meantime he could 'infect' others. What happened to the Maya frightened us. We were descended from them many generations ago and it is terrifying to think that something like that could happen to us! Andrés said the Spaniards thought we 'Indians' were weak because we died from these illnesses.

We were all silent, wrapped in our own thoughts after this conversation and we retired for the night. The following day, Walashi informed me she was going home. I think the horror of what she had heard and the new life in her womb, made her want to be as far as possible from Andrés. I did not question her decision, although it was obvious that Andrés did not have any of these illnesses. She must have felt the need to prepare her 'nest'.

It was 1519 by their calculations and I had been thus occupied for two years. I now had the feeling that I had abandoned my other obligations. Walashi's departure left an enormous emptiness, making me realize that I needed to go back to my mountains. Andrés would stay behind with Nua and the Mama Rigawiyún.

CHAPTER SIXTEEN

went back down to the sea and was about to set off along the beach towards the estuary of the River Yuma, when an ocelot informed me that Zalab wanted to speak to me. That night, alone on the beach, he informed me that they had finally defeated the enemy in his area. He had finally managed to convince Panquiaco to assemble a large army and they had ambushed a troop of over one hundred, many with horses. The Sué, who had gone looking for 'their Indians' (disappeared into the night), had fallen into a well-planned ambush and they had all been eliminated. Those left in the settlement were so traumatized, they embarked in great haste and not even one remained. A few days prior to this defeat, the two more experienced captains, Balboa and Pizarro, in the middle of a long-running dispute, had left the settlement to seek the help of the Governor Pedrarias to find a solution. But the Governor had Pizarro arrest Balboa, who was accused of treason and summarily executed. The settlement had been left in inexperienced hands, which somewhat accounted for the defeat. When we announced the news there was a general rejoicing. It was possible to vanquish the enemy. This was the message that had to be spread to all. They had defeated us on the Islands, now it was our turn to retaliate on the mainland. For the present, it was the Caribe who were stemming the invaders; but it was not the end, they would evidently make further attempts.

Zalab had managed to get hold of a large quantity of paper and books that he was sending me. Walashi and I were making a great deal of progress in Spanish, which according to Andrés was as good as his. Moreover, we could read and write it, which was more than many Spaniards could do. I was still feeling jubilant when An Yupami informed me that the Inca Nation – Tahuantinsuyo – had been invaded by one of the men Zalab had defeated in Darien, Francisco Pizarro. The news was not good and it got even worse. The armies of the Inca were being progressively defeated by the advancing *conquistadores.** From far up north, we heard of the destruction of the Aztec Nation by the Spaniards. It was not comparable to the resistance the Caribe were putting up, which was proving so successful. These were indeed difficult times.

I was reunited with Nisa, who had been waiting among her own people on the River and watching the estuary for me. The first days were rather difficult after being with Walashi for so long. They knew of each other, this I was always clear about, but they were so different and I had become accustomed to Walashi. Nisa, being an intelligent woman, gave me time to adapt.

---

* Conquerors

I returned to my duties on the estuary of the River and we had a few peaceful years, in spite of the terrible stories that continued to emerge from Tahuantinsuyo and the Aztecs. Then we heard that a large army of Spaniards had landed in a bay near Bonda, where they had established a settlement. Their captain was now a certain Rodrigo de Bastidas.

The year was 1524 by their calculations. I had no alternative but to go back to the Sierra, though I would not be doing so alone: I would be taking Nisa with me. We both knew I would be removing her from her environment and her people but I did not want to leave her behind. Having surveyed the area with the jaguar, I realized I might have to stay in the Sierra for a long time. I was not being pessimistic; this was different. The invaders were here to stay or at the very least endeavour to do so.

I had been practising my Spanish with the Mama Rigawiyún in the World of the Spirits, as well as with Walashi, Andrés and Nua; the Mama and I wrote to each other on a regular basis. We were all consolidating our knowledge of the language and Andrés was more than satisfied.

On the return journey, I had chosen to walk along the beach where we were continuously warned of the danger by the lookouts. Nevertheless, I considered that the sooner we got to our destination, the more rapidly we could work out a plan of action. Everything was new to Nisa and I sensed her nervousness. Even so, she was great company, and on the way, I taught her some useful basic Spanish. She was thoroughly intrigued by the Sierra, which we could see in the distance. As we drew nearer, she kept plying me with questions but I thought she could observe everything for herself when we got there. There were places we did not have a beach to walk on. The sea washed up against the rocks and we had to take one of the numerous busy inland routes; only now the travellers were scarce and going in the opposite direction. They warned us of Sué men with dogs, searching for Indians; nonetheless, we had to carry on. We walked through abandoned villages, where crops had been destroyed to stop them falling into Sué hands; a necessary procedure but so very sad. As we got closer to the enemy, I felt a great pain invading my spirit. In this, Nisa and Master Tarminaki were a great comfort to me. Then, inevitably, we came face to face with the enemy.

A group of about fifteen Sué soldiers with horses and two dogs were resting by the side of a small stream in the forest. Having picked up their smell, it gave us a chance to hide and observe them. The dogs detected our presence because they were suddenly alert and sniffing. Clearly, these animals gave the enemy a considerable edge over us. They were not only guard dogs, they were also dangerous when attacking. I resolved to get hold of some, for our advantage. Right now, we had a problem: the dogs were fully roused and the men were standing up in a threatening manner to see what was provoking them.

We gathered some stones for our slings and Nisa also had a cerbatana with which she was very good. We made full use of our skills as Fishermen of the River, to make ourselves invisible among the trees. The dogs were confused but still seemed to sense us, then I realized we were not alone, and it was probably not our scent they were picking up at all. There was a jaguar hovering in a tree not far from where we were. Although the dogs had picked up its scent, what I found interesting was that they were trained not to attack unless given the order. I immediately saw the jaguar's predicament. Even if it was out of the reach of the dogs, it was within distance of the men's weapons and they had long-range crossbows. I was not about to let the jaguar become a victim.

Using gestures, I pointed out the situation to Nisa and we cautiously circled the men. The Sué were obviously aware that something was amiss, for they were brandishing their swords in all directions. I had to eliminate their advantage, namely the two dogs, and we could do this with a dart from Nisa's cerbatana and a stone from my sling. We had to remain at a distance to maximise our chances. I was counting on the fact that the Sué had no idea what was happening despite sensing a danger. I could but hope that Nisa had understood. I need not have worried, for just then I felt her breath close to my cheek. We each targeted a dog and I came out from the bushes to use my sling. The men were still looking in the other direction and did not think to look left, until both dogs fell simultaneously. I saw the men's anger, and as experienced soldiers they now knew where the attack was coming from. They turned and a few ran in our direction, though there was not much they could do without their dogs, since they were unable to see us. I could have touched two of them by stretching out my arm but they were blind in the face of our ability. Thoroughly disconcerted, they regrouped, took to their horses, and rode off in great haste, leaving the bodies of their dogs behind. We waited a bit before going over to where they were lying. I hoped the dog I had struck was only stunned, which turned out to be the case.

The other one had not survived Nisa's poisoned dart. Perhaps the jaguar would find a use for it once we removed the dart!

Over the following days, we looked after the dog that had a big bruise on the side of its head. He accepted us with the surprising loyalty sick animals give to those who heal them. We have dogs in Quicagua, only they are small and skinny and do not bark; very different from these large, noisy ones. I knew I could not turn it against the Sué but it was good company and it kept us alerted. It was loyal and obedient, and it would be useful to improve the breed of our own dogs. As the days went by, it became attached to Nisa in a very touching way. The Fishermen of the River do not keep animals and the novelty made Nisa lavish attention on the dog as if it were a child. The dog, in turn, returned the affection in greater measure.

Without further incident, we arrived in Zhiwé's village among the Toucan which we call Guachaca. Our dog was greeted with dismay and certainly it now had a dilemma: before we were the prey, now we were its masters. At first, it did not find the learning process easy. More than one person got a fright and a few got a bite but, in the end, the dog learnt its lesson.

Nisa had an emotional reunion with Nuaxtashi, who was now a robust, mature, thirty-five-year-old man. The Mama Rigawiyún informed me that the Grand Master had asked Nua to go to Rapa; which he was preparing to do. As we had been instructed to make no mention of this name, we said he was going to spend some time with the Muisca and then the Yalcón as part of his apprenticeship. I was very proud of this honour, especially now that so few were going. Shamans were at present being trained in places near their own nations.

If they did go to Rapa, it was for brief periods and in great secrecy. There is nothing comparable to being an actual disciple of the Grand Master. Before Nua left, we spent our last days together conversing and my heart was full of love.

However, these were different times. We were at war and this was the focus of all conversations and activities. The enemy were now arriving with black men and women, who they regarded as slaves and treated badly. The women accounted for about one third and they were used to reproduce more slaves; even the Sué had them as bed companions. The new arrivals had also transported a number of animals that, according to Andrés, was a sure indication they were here to stay. This was our first encounter with cattle, pigs, chickens and goats. Nisa and I decided to go along with Andrés and the dog to have a look at the settlement. I wanted Andrés to provide us with as much information as possible about these people: how they were organized, their different devices, their habits, weapons, ships and religion.

Andrés had become quite the Tairona and now had several children. His wife regularly removed the hair on his body and he himself did so daily from his face. When I first met him, I thought he might turn out to be a valuable friend and I was not wrong. Without his knowledge of the Sué, we would never have been able to put up such an effective resistance.

The enemy's settlement was on one side of a bay, where I saw several of their ships. It was surrounded by a simple palisade made of wood that afforded no protection against attacks, including fire that was evident in some places. They had cleared the sparse vegetation that existed in the semi-arid surroundings and now they had to go to the foot of the Sierra in search of wood, where they were always ambushed. Some assaults were successful, a few less so, but the settlers were no longer enthusiastic about leaving the settlement. We watched them at our leisure from where we stood on the side of a hill. Their sentries could surely see us but they probably thought we were bait and did not come after us. Andrés explained everything concerning their buildings, the way in which they organized their settlements and anything else we asked him. Much of this he had already told me, but to view it all made it that much easier to understand.

Everything was a novelty to Nisa: she felt as if she were living in some sort of fantasy world. Even the way of life and the customs of the Taira and the Caribe, with whom she could at least communicate because they spoke the same language, were strange and new to her. Her innate curiosity led her to propose that we get hold of a few of the settlers' animals. This had not occurred to anyone else and we thought it a good idea, which would also contribute to further weakening their self-sufficiency. Thus, the Caribe carried out raids and obtained some of the animals which Andrés showed us how to feed and look after. While making these incursions, we realized we could count on the black people's lack of enthusiasm to participate in the defence of the settlement. It did however mean they were punished and that led to their frequent escapes. They were well-received by us, though they provoked a great deal of curiosity.

At this time, the settlement had approximately seven hundred Sué men, a few women and about four hundred black slaves. Their governor was an old man by the name of Rodrigo de Bastidas. Shortly after our arrival, we witnessed an uprising of the two existing camps. One was of the conquistadores, who sought their fortune, and the other, the colonists who wanted to settle on land given to them by *encomiendas*.* The Governor, one of the latter, was mortally wounded by a certain Juan de Villafuerte, who, with the help of his supporters, fled by land because he could not do so by sea. Fearlessly, he headed for the Sierra and was rapidly captured by a handful of Caribe. We were close by and as the Caribe knew that Andrés and I spoke his language, they promptly brought him to us for interrogation. The Mama Rigawiyún, Andrés and I met the man in a clearing of the forest at the foot of the Sierra. Andrés was to prove his value yet again. After studying the man carefully without getting too close, he was extremely agitated as he turned to me and said, 'This man has a cold.'

Andrés had noticed the man's nose was red and that he wiped it on the sleeve of his shirt, after sneezing a couple of times. With no hesitation, Andrés shot him with a poisoned arrow and did not allow us to approach him. But it was already too late for our brothers the Caribe…

The outbreak was of epidemic proportions and it reached the entire population of the area surrounding the Sierra and further. Fortunately, the Taira were spared because the Shikwakala Nunjué was closed. It was the first of many epidemics with which the Sué conquered Quicagua, our known world. In all fairness to the Spaniards, I am not saying

_____

* Ownership of land and Indians granted to an individual or *encomenderos*

it was deliberate. Rather it was something they did not take into account nor did they grasp the wider implications. All we could do was watch helplessly from a distance. The death toll was dreadful and the survival rate, one in ten, was appalling.

Our people were already on the alert, having been warned by Andrés when he first arrived in the Sierra. This is where my mother Zhi'nita, our venerable old healer, now seventy years of age, played her part and managed to protect us from this illness. She had a theory that the body develops its own defences against an illness; the more the body endures, the stronger it becomes. At a great personal risk, she collected samples of the horrible phlegm that some Caribe survivors had and after drying it she obtained a powdery substance that contained 'the illness'. Next, she applied it to a wound she had made on her own shoulder. The following day she developed a fever that lasted several days, that she endured in isolation, but she lived through her experiment.

A few days later, she informed us she was going to expose herself directly, by looking after the sick in one of the infected villages. She survived this effort as well. As a result, she called together all the Taira and the Caribe healers who were alive and, without getting too close, advised them to do as she had done. Her experience provoked all sorts of responses, from astonishment to fear and scepticism. But because she was such a revered healer, with the support of Zhiwé, Walashi and Mixia Caita, she persuaded them in the end. The next step was to assist each other in applying 'the illness' to a self-inflicted wound. The effect was different in each one: for some it was very serious and sadly one died from the fever.

For the remaining, the result was as expected and they set about visiting the villages to treat as many as they could. Today, we know her vision and experience prevented the illness from spreading in the Shikwakala Nunjué and the Cataca Nation. Many years before, the Grand Master Tarminaki had told me this would happen.

What followed was a huge effort on the part of the Caribe to minimize the devastating effect it had on them. All the survivors, men, women and children, regrouped in an endeavour to form new families because so many of them had lost members of their own. There was no other way but to form new relationships. All the new families gathered in Bonda and Pocigueica and continued to be the bastions of the Caribe defence. The survivors were a mixture of Gaira, Mocana and Guajiro, who making a brave effort, isolated themselves from their nations in an attempt to contain the illness.

We spread the false story that the dead Spaniard, Juan de Villafuerte, was helping us in our continuing attacks. This further increased the division between those who wished to conquer the interior and the followers of Bastidas who wanted to settle and colonize the area where they were. The badly wounded Bastidas had found refuge on the Island of the Cuba. The commander, Palomino, who was possibly one of the most vicious of the conquistadores, was preparing an assault inland, on our Sierra. We organized the defence and a few moons later, we were able to resist and defeat them when they attacked Guachaca. We all took part in this battle, including Andrés, who was now a valued Taira warrior. The Sué could not work out where the relentless attacks were coming from: day and night, with no rest or respite. Aluna Jaba, our major ally, made it rain incessantly for four days and turned their expedition into a nightmare: they slipped and slithered, had accidents with their horses and drowned in the fast currents. Among others, their commander Palomino was himself a victim while fleeing across one of the swollen rivers flowing down from the Sierra. Throughout, we attacked them unremittingly with our poisoned arrows, darts, lances and the crossbows, of which we now had several. The assaults came from the trees but the rain prevented the enemy from seeing us. Very reduced in number, they managed to reach the village where we had our only casualty, a young man who fell while trying to escape and was slain with three arrows from a crossbow. They tried to set fire to the village but even in this they failed because it was too wet. Our defence was so fierce that they made no further expeditions into the Sierra, which was not the case in other places. Instead, they concentrated their efforts on the lowlands surrounding the Sierra. But this was not the beginning of the invasion of the whole of Quicagua.

An Yupami informed us of the fall of his nephew, the Inca Atahualpa, who had been brutally executed by the conquistador Pizarro. Greed for gold continued to drive the invaders insane. In the meantime, a major Spanish expedition had gone east round the Shikwakala Nunjué and attacked my relatives, the Wiwa, who sought refuge in the Sierra. They plundered every village they found and reached the River Yuma by way of the valley of the chief of the Upar. There, they came to a halt and returned using the same route.

They had found a route into the interior...

The gold they brought back further heightened their voracity. The new governor, Pedro de Vadillo, who had been on the expedition, was caught stealing the share of the gold he was supposed to send his king. He was arrested by his own men and replaced by Garcia de Lerma, who, trying to colonize, distributed our land among his men by the system they called 'encomiendas'. The war intensified and we attacked them continuously, to such an extent that they were forced to stay inside their palisade and endure hunger. This situation lasted for years, during which time we did not allow them to colonize as they wished. Their only settlement was this city they called Santa Marta.

Nisa had adapted well to living in the Sierra and accompanied me when I went into Santa Marta. My daughter with Walashi grew into an enchanting young woman. Following in her mother's and grandmother's footsteps, she was training to be a healer. Her name was Yama, the word for 'beautiful doe' in Guajiro, the land where she was conceived. Nuaxtashi remained in Rapa and the Taira learned to live in a constant state of war. The difference was that now we had infiltrated their settlement. We had men and women who kept us informed of everything that happened in the city. They chose to live in servitude for this purpose, pretending to be converted to the Spaniards' religion and way of life. This led to the next stage of my relationship with the Sué.

Over the years, I had continued to perfect my Spanish to such a degree that I spoke and wrote it as well as Andrés did. In this way, I was able to go in and out of Santa Marta without any hindrance. The guards were far from imagining the old Indian (I deliberately made myself look older than my fifty years) who spoke their language so well, was in fact their enemy. They presumed I was a servant, something I did not refute, allowing me the freedom to become conversant with their way of life. Meanwhile, Master Tarminaki told me to go ahead with the writing of our history for the future. This happened to coincide with the arrival of the bishop, Brother Tomás Ortiz.

By now, I had become a master of deception. Everyone thought I worked for someone else. With the help of our men and women and the connivance of the black slaves, I was thoroughly at home in the city. My success consisted in never giving explanations and in letting everyone assume whatever they wanted, which I then partially agreed with. I became an everyday figure in the city, a bit simple, or so they thought, but I was one of them. They did not plan an expedition or an attack in which I was not involved, to make it fail or at the least more arduous. All our people helped in the contamination of the water and the food stores; animals went missing or died inexplicably; weapons disappeared and there were frequent fires. With the arrival of the new bishop, I had access to as much paper and ink as I wanted, and I was allocated a small room removed from everyone where I could work undisturbed. The Bishop thought I was a scribe for the Dominicans, who thought I was a servant who had arrived with the Bishop. I did not agree with or deny either of these versions. In due course, I struck up a friendship with a friar, Brother Domingo Esquivel, who turned out to be very useful. The following years were dedicated to the writing of my narrative up to this point. However, Serankwa had other plans and they were not in our favour.

The siege of the city was so effective that it prevented them from making Santa Marta a viable settlement. Consequently, in the year 1533, a captain by the name of Pedro de Heredia led an expedition by sea, as he could not do so by land, to establish a new colony in the Bay of the Turbaco: the same bay where we had had our victory against the Sué and where they had burnt our village to the ground. Only this time, the Calamarí and the Turbaco were so decimated by the illness that they were unable to put up the necessary resistance. The Sué were thus able to settle successfully and many of the colonists migrated from Santa Marta to the new city they called Cartagena de Indias.

The many outbreaks of 'the cold' did so much harm that the founding of the city of Cartagena was the ultimate defeat. We were unable to avert the invasion of the Sué into our known world, Quicagua. The Caribe who had presented such a formidable obstacle were not defeated by weapons or battles but by the illnesses these men brought. We had no defence against them, save for some isolated successes, such as my mother's achievements at the beginning.

Now the captain Pedro de Heredia constantly made expeditions to plunder the nearby villages, leading to the discovery of the Sinú burial grounds. The Sinú have an ancient tradition of making gold artefacts that they exchange with other nations. Most of the gold ornaments that we Taira possess were crafted by the Sinú goldsmiths. They had such an abundance of this metal that they honoured their dead by burying them with quantities of gold objects. The pillaging of the villages and the burial grounds unopposed by the Sinú went out of control.

The amount of gold attracted more conquistadores and more colonists. We were unable to prevent Cartagena from turning into a strong, wealthy city. Apart from a few trivial attempts on our part to attack the expeditions, we had no successes whatsoever. The Sinú were vanquished by the illnesses, almost without ever encountering the enemy or understanding what was happening. By the time the Sué appeared in their lands, there were only a few remaining to put up a feeble resistance. Master Tarminaki had warned us this would happen. Nevertheless, we harboured the hope that we could stop them or at the very least limit their advance.

Now we needed to reinforce our efforts to maintain the balance of Aluna Jaba, because these new men were like termites. They had no consideration for the forests or the animals. More precisely, they went on dreadful hunts, burnt down the forests and razed everything to plant their crops. It was the beginning of 'the Era of Chaos, Disease and Death' the Grand Master had warned us about so many years previously.

I never imagined it could be so bitter!

CHAPTER SEVENTEEN

stayed on in the city of Santa Marta for two more years, until Serankwa decided it was sufficient and I was found out. But I am again getting ahead of myself.

I spent the days in a room in the communal area between the Palace of the Bishop and the Monastery of the Dominicans. In those days they were adjacent and in the centre of the city. The people of the city called them 'Dominicanos', which apparently means 'Dogs of the Lord', which I found rather strange. Anyhow, I made the illustrations for their books on the so-called 'New World'. I discovered that I not only had this ability, which was highly appreciated by them, but that I thoroughly enjoyed it as well. But more importantly, I could get on with writing my narrative without their knowledge. I told them my name was Tobias and said absolutely nothing about my apparent 'conversion'. Rather, I pretended I was not very bright and this gave me a certain amount of freedom, such as not having to attend their religious ceremonies. They were content in the belief that the only thing I could do was draw.

Since the Spaniards thought we 'Indians' were inferior, they could not for a moment imagine we could be smarter. This was unthinkable, which made them even more gullible and naive. But we did not delude ourselves; they were a dangerous enemy.

Brother Domingo Esquivel was a talkative, inoffensive man, who prepared my meals and kept me informed of life outside the monastery. Through him I heard about the disagreements between the Governor and the Bishop, the Bishop and the Dominicans, and the conquistadores and the colonists. There was unease among the friars because of the way our people were being enslaved. I learnt that their king had given orders to the contrary, but with him so far away, few followed his instructions. Even so, many Spaniards did not like the fact that the powerful did not follow orders and it was a continuing source of friction and debate.

On the other hand, they had no problem with the suffering they inflicted on the black people. They seemed to think that because of the colour of their skin, they were not only destined to be slaves but that they felt no pain and had no feelings. We found this astonishing because, to us, they were men and women like any other. Even the children the Spaniards had with the black women were slaves. The horses and the dogs received better treatment than these unfortunate people. From early on, I decided they would be our allies.

But let us return for one moment to Brother Domingo, who was at the bottom of the hierarchy in the monastery, followed by the Indians and last, the black people. I had my own status, as they thought all I could do was draw. I had told the Brother that I needed to work in solitude as I was easily frightened and then unable to work. This was the story he told everyone in the monastery and in the palace of the Bishop. All my assignments came through Brother Domingo and this was all that was expected of me.

My people knew who I was and as the weeks went by the black slaves began to deduce it as well, though no one was aware of my real mission. I was somewhat disconcerted by the way in which the black people reacted in my presence. They were clearly afraid of me, and some of their women even fainted when I entered one of their dwellings. Apparently in the land they came from, for whatever reason, the Shamans had this effect on them.

I lived in a small hut at the foot of the secluded vegetable garden that Brother Domingo tended as one of his duties. Nisa kept me company there, without anyone knowing. The Spaniards, in particular the friars, were wary of women. Nearly every night, as a jaguar I visited my territory in the estuary of the River Yuma and our neighbourhood. On these occasions, Nisa watched over my body, assisted by anyone of our people who lived nearby, and even some of the black men and women. The black slaves frequently saw the jaguar, which only compounded their fears. It was not ideal, but I did not know of any way to change their perception of me. Nisa made efforts to reassure them and eventually they ceased to be openly terrified, though they never entirely lost their fear in my presence.

We left the settlement on a regular basis and went in search of my brother, the Mama Rigawiyún. It lifted our spirits after having to live among the Sué and we were able to keep the Mama up to date with what was happening. I spent time with my family, saw my daughter Yama and made plans. I told Brother Domingo I was visiting a sick relative and disappeared without further justification. On one occasion the Brother Superior angrily rebuked me for leaving without permission and threatened to have me whipped. I tried to calm him down by using every argument I could think of: Christian love, my faithfulness to them, and I even invoked the favour my drawings found with the Bishop. In the end, I presume he reasoned that since I had not escaped, it was pointless to pursue the matter.

I was frequently in touch with my Master Tarminaki, who informed me that he had instructed the Mama Rigawiyún to find a place to conceal the manuscript. We discussed this when we met and he told me that one of our people, a carpenter, was making a box out of *guayacan*.* The box would then be treated with bitter palm oil and the extract of a poisonous fruit the Spaniards called *manzanilla*† or little apple. This fruit bears a close resemblance, though in a smaller version, to an appetizing fruit found in their land; this mistake had taken the life of more than one hungry misinformed person! The wood was to be soaked several times in the mixture and allowed to dry out in between coatings. The box would be able to resist almost anything, with two exceptions: dampness and fire. To resolve these issues, we concluded that the safest place for the manuscript would be in the cathedral at present under construction. The next question was, where in the building. After days of

---

* A hardwood native to the Americas

† Camomile

observation and evaluation, two of our people who were working there, suggested under the floor, but partially under a wall so that any future renovation would not uncover it. Wisely, they led the architect friar in charge of the construction to reach what he thought was his own conclusion: to make the level of the floor inside somewhat higher than that of the ground outside. This would afford protection from damage caused by the natural humidity of the ground. At night and with great care, in an isolated place they prepared a small space made of bricks, where it would be protected from heat in case of a fire in the cathedral.

I carried on with my writing while all this was being done, and not even I knew of the exact location in the cathedral. It was not clear how long the manuscript would lie hidden, though no doubt Master Tarminaki had already decided and given the relevant orders, as well as instructions for its safekeeping.

Cartagena's prosperity on the one hand and the poverty, disease and hunger endured by Santa Marta on the other, led to continuous quarrelling and ill-feeling among the Spaniards in this city. Between the years of 1535 and 1536, they had four different governors, until in the end one of them, Pedro Fernandez de Lugo, established his leadership over the conquistadores. Trying to emulate the success of Cartagena he organized two large new expeditions: one by land, consisting of six hundred men, horses, dogs and 'porters', chosen by us; the other by sea that would go in search of a way onto the River Yuma. This one was made up of eight brigantines and about three hundred men. The two expeditions would meet up at the estuary of the River Upar, already known to those who took part in the previous expedition in 1529. Their biggest challenge was to discover the way onto the River Yuma. This, they thought they had solved when they 'found' some Mocana guides that I myself provided. Here, I was taking a big risk, but I had no other choice, otherwise they would have compelled one of ours, using torture and who knows what other barbaric means. The 'guides' had been told to lead them through the most arduous and constricted of branches, while the Mocana still in the area and the Cataca would harass them constantly.

In the year 1536, when all preparations were made, the expedition set off by land led by the conquistador Gonzalo Jiménez de Quesada. They were fully aware that they would be going through hostile land and, to elude any attacks by the Tairona, they avoided going too close to the Sierra. Even so, together with the Caribe we harassed them constantly, though, very astutely, they used the porters as shields. Five days later, the 'guides' went missing with a considerable amount of their supplies!

Despite this substantial loss, they did not give up and continued the expedition for several more months. But the jungle conditions, the sicknesses and the lack of provisions all took their toll. Only half of the men that had originally set out arrived at the meeting point. We were unable to stop these conquistadores but we were more successful with the ones that set off a few days later, in the brigantines under the command of Diego de Urbina. The difficulties they encountered on the River, the river fevers and our relentless attacks forced them to give up and turn back with only three ships and less than seventy men.

But greed, the driving force behind their tenacity, led them to organize a new expedition with six brigantines and no guides, as they now had doubts about our people. This expedition did manage to meet up with the one that had gone by land months previously, but both groups were in a pitiful state. The one that arrived by the River – decimated, totally disheartened and reduced to three ships – on reaching the meeting point found that Quesada was not there. Quesada and his men, tired of waiting and in spite of the state they were in, had decided to press on. They forced their way through the jungle and numerous mosquito- and caiman-infested swamps, harassed by the Talaiga, the Chimila and the Chiriguaní. It was Quesada's good fortune that the men on the three ships chose to persevere and found him besieged by the Cacique Tamalameque in the land of the Muisca. However, if this gave them a temporary respite, the two expeditions were unable to merge due to their rivalries. Further along they would split up and the vessels went back with no glory whatsoever.

At the same time as all this was happening and Jawi was sending me regular accounts of the events, I began to feel a growing hostility towards us in Santa Marta. At night we were helping the black slaves to escape. They were guided to the Gran Cienaga, where we handed them over to the Cataca, who took them to various places along the River Yuma. They set themselves up in small communities and tried to live as they had done in the land where they came from. Few of us knew where these new locations were.

The governor, Fernandez de Lugo, had hoped that his expeditions would bring him many riches, but he was disappointed.

There was no sign of these, and a previous governor was doing his utmost to depose him. This man, called Anton Bezos, finally succeeded when the three brigantines, all that was left of the expedition, returned with no treasure of any value. Quesada had acquired quantities of gold and emeralds but did not dispatch them back to Santa Marta. Instead, he sent some bits of *tumbago*, 'poor man's gold'.* With no further news from his expedition, the city sank into despair and insolvency. The inhabitants were also suffering from hunger. Because of us, they could not grow or produce food in the 'encomiendas', as we did not even let the 'encomenderos' leave the city. Even their defence was in the hands of a few disheartened soldiers, the more experienced ones having gone with Quesada's expedition. We intensified the siege and the only access was by sea.

The continuous migration to Cartagena, which was a thriving Spanish city, further restricted the development of Santa Marta. Although we could have forced the invaders out, the weakened state of the Caribe after the 'common cold' epidemic, followed by others, had seriously compromised our efforts, and the Taira were dispersed all over the Sierra. Although the first outbreak of the epidemic had been averted, the subsequent ones were devastating. Unfortunately, my mother's treatment had only been effective that first time. The communities had scattered in the hope that by avoiding contact the illness could be contained. This the Spaniards did not know. We only had sufficient numbers to show some measure of strength when we

---

* Alloy of gold and copper indigenous people used to make their artefacts

attacked anyone who ventured out. We would never have been able to prevent or repel a serious confrontation.

Sadly, on a personal note, I was apprised of the death of my mother at a very advanced age.

The prevailing mood of pessimism and failure felt by the city, the constant escapes of the black slaves, the shortage of food and the siege, all contributed to the increasing antagonism towards us. We began to suffer insults, ill-treatment and beatings for no apparent reason until eventually our people began to escape whenever possible. To make matters even worse, one day, the Bishop called all the inhabitants of Santa Marta together to announce with 'great joy' the arrival of one of the institutions of their religion called 'The Holy Office of the Inquisition'.

Everyone listened in total silence. The Spaniards knew exactly what it meant, and they gave it a joyless reception which, I noticed, included the friars. Neither our people nor the black slaves had any idea what it was about. We were introduced to an obese man with devilish eyes, who, standing in front of us, was putting on a show of meekness for the sake of the Bishop. The Inquisitor with his two assistants observed us impassively, trying to give an impression of benevolence. They were friars of the same order as the ones already here, but that is where any similarity ended. What was more, the community did not understand why they were here at all, given that the king had given orders for us Indians to be protected.

I think I understand the human spirit well and until then I had never encountered such evilness, save for perhaps that one felon, Go-Naka, with whom Jawi and I had that incident in my youth all those years ago. These men had the malevolent aura that envelops those who inflict suffering on others. The spirits of the countless people who have died at their hands are pointing accusingly at them; such men have no conscience. They presume to act in the name of goodness but they are demons. They even had their own guards who only answered to them: twelve soldiers in full armour, with plumes in their helmets and spotless weapons. The method 'The Holy Inquisition' used was to torture and put to death the Indians accused of not accepting 'their religion'. This was to terrorize everyone else into submission. In reality, this was the purpose of their existence. Even the Spaniards themselves were targeted as well as the black slaves. Though in the case of the latter, as they were not considered to be human, they were 'baptized' and made to attend their masses. The Inquisitor treated the Bishop and the Governor with deference, but I have no doubt that all concerned knew full well that he was higher than them. The effect of this hypocritical humility was to sow even more fear amongst the population. I decided on that first day that I was going to be a major obstacle to their work and to do everything in my power to protect my people and the black slaves who remained in the city.

From the day of their arrival everything changed. The Spaniards disavowed the Indian and black women, with whom many were living, and hid their mixed-race children. Everybody went to mass every day and I advised our people to do likewise, myself included. The Spanish women began to feign a religious fervour they had never had. I swiftly made sure our women, among them my beloved Nisa, left the city. There remained only the ones the Sué had brought with them from the Islands. This alarmed the Spaniards and they began to wonder who was really giving orders in the city. The Inquisition that had commenced with a low profile, simply watching and obtaining information, stepped up and questions were asked more openly. From the very beginning, they focused on the story of Juan de Villafuerte (the man who had done us so much irrevocable harm with his 'cold'). The Spaniards and, of course, the Holy Inquisition thought only one of their own, someone allied with their devil, could have organized the resistance and the siege of the city so effectively. The fact that it had been us was, according to them, totally out of the question since we were incapable of such feats. In the Inquisition's eyes, this could only mean someone inside the city had allies who were also servants of the devil. It was therefore the duty of every Christian to find the culprits of this affront to God… I genuinely believed the story would keep them busy for a long time, as it was pure fiction. I could never have imagined their methods were such that they would turn a myth by force into a mortal reality.

The first thing the Inquisitors did was to search until they found anyone who had even the remotest connection to Juan de Villafuerte. Several hapless individuals were brought to the convent simply because they had a falling-out with someone or for any other absurd reason. On the first occasion, they were questioned with veiled threats of torture to search for weaknesses and allowed to return to their homes. In this way, pieces of information were gathered and used to identify some innocent person whose only fault was, say, to have lived with one of our women as a 'concubine'. Then just before dawn when it was still dark, the Inquisition soldiers arrived at the house of the poor wretch who was to be interrogated and 'purified by pain'. For weeks, I heard the screams, groans and crying of these men, who were being made to confess their allegiance to Juan de Villafuerte and the devil. If they did not confess, the tortures intensified and became increasingly crueller, until the man died; though it was more usual in the throes of pain to acknowledge guilt. But it did not stop there, and what happened next was even more diabolical. Amid continuing tortures, they were made to denounce an accomplice. Faced with this, someone innocent was named, who in turn was apprehended and the procedure began all over again. The unfortunate person who had 'confessed' to everything was then burnt at the stake, where the flames purged him of 'his sins' and 'God forgave him'. This carousel of death continued for several weeks, until it finally involved one of our own. By then, there were few of our people left in the semi-deserted city, from which many of the Spaniards had also fled before it was their turn. There reigned an atmosphere of terror, incriminations and public executions. The man concerned was a Gaira who looked after the pigs in the convent. I was not going to allow this to happen.

A very frightened Brother Domingo, who kept me informed of everything, came to tell me that someone being tortured had denounced the Indian Sebastian. That night, when a squad of four soldiers from the Holy Inquisition appeared at his doorstep, a jaguar attacked and killed one of them, mortally wounded the second and the other two fled for their lives. The Gaira also disappeared in all haste from the city. The next morning all the inhabitants of the city were summoned to the public square where they were informed that there was now concrete proof of the presence of the devil. Two of 'the Soldiers of the Lord' had been attacked and killed that very morning.

'What more proof do we need, to demonstrate the presence of the devil,' said the Inquisitor, full of holy wrath… and everyone crossed themselves and there was fear and some ladies even fainted!

It was time to take preventive measures. That day, I suspended the writing of the manuscript and it was concealed. I would finish it later and the Mama Rigawiyún would then hide it for good. I had to remove anything that might be incriminating, including a dagger imbued in our poison that would be rather difficult to explain! I was about to rid myself of it when at the last minute, I changed my mind and secured it to the underside of my worktable instead.

The problem now facing the Inquisitor was that his chain of denunciations had been broken. He would have to resort to his 'enquiries' again until he found something else to hold on to. Given that I was out of sight, I assumed I had gone unnoticed. But in the city, there were certain sailors who it was said, bore a grudge against 'an Indian' (they were not sure which one), who had provided them with guides for their first expedition inland. These guides, having turned out to be 'treacherous', had deserted and the sailors blamed them for the failure of the expedition. The Holy Inquisition rapidly picked up the scent of this story which put them on a new line of enquiry.

One morning, the Inquisitor arrived in my room, with his assistant.

'Holy Mother Mary,' he said on entering.

'Conceived without sin,' I humbly replied.

The assistant settled at my worktable with a smile and an air of delicacy, whilst preparing to note down all questions and answers. The Inquisitor spoke very slowly, using his overly pious tone.

'Brother Tobias, the friars have spoken of your beautiful illustrations in their books.'

'The friars kind; I humble servant of the Lord.'

'If you do not mind me asking, how did you learn to speak our language? The friars say you already spoke it when you first arrived.'

'I servant of Don Sebastian Davila in Santa Maria La Antigua del Darien, then the Cuba; he return to Spain, he leave me with friars; I learn with him; good man, good man...'

I was treading on dangerous ground for that was the name of the writer of the letter in the bag Zalab had obtained for us. The defeat of Santa Maria La Antigua del Darien had not been well-received by the Spaniards. Furthermore, I did not know if the person I was referring to was reputable, or even if they knew him. I felt I had awoken his curiosity but it was too late to go back. I needed to play my role of being a 'bit simple', very carefully.

'Santa Maria La Antigua del Darien... Yes, yes, we had to abandon that city. But you, Brother Tobias, why were you there?'

'Don Sebastian good man, he help me; I baptised, I love the Lord.'

'Yes, yes, Brother Tobias, but what were you doing there?'

'I draw, I draw, Don Sebastian teach me, he good man.'

'Brother Tobias, you do not seem to understood me, were you born there?'

'The jungle very big, I afraid, I small; Don Sebastian, make me pray, very good.'

'Yes, yes, the jungle is very frightening… Mm, so you lived in Cuba… How long were you there?'

'Seasick, I seasick in ship, sick for long time. Don Sebastian, he look after me. Don Martin cross, he punish me. Don Sebastian bring me to friars. They very good.'

My nonsense was exasperating the Inquisitor!

'Brother Tobias, you are not answering my questions. We could continue this elsewhere, but… I like your room… Yes indeed, it has plenty of light. The Lord teaches us to be charitable, but we must protect the Faith from our enemies.'

'I make pretty drawings in books. His Eminence, he like them, the friars too.'

'Now, tell me about this Indian woman who lives with you in your little house in the orchard, because… you do live with a woman, do you not?'

Now, I knew for sure this man was not fishing; he knew exactly what he was after.

'She bring me food; I hungry!'

'Brother Tobias, you know the Sacraments; you must know that fornication is a very grave sin.'

'She bring me food.'

'Where is she now? We have searched for her everywhere. For all we know, she's a witch who comes into the monastery. That is forbidden for women in any case, but she has disappeared along with the other Indian women.'

'She bring me food.'

'You have apparently not received communion since you have been here. When was the last time you confessed your sins?'

'I draw.'

'Two years ago, when the expeditions set out to propagate the Faith in this godforsaken land… was it not you who provided guides who turned out to be servants of Juan de Villafuerte?'

'I work here. I make pretty drawings; the friars happy.'

'Brother Tobias, are you not some sort of Indian chief, in the service of Juan de Villafuerte?'

'I make pretty pictures for books; his Eminence happy.'

At that moment, I realized there was no way out and I was weighing up my chances of escaping. Despite my age, I could probably take on both of them. One was obese and had trouble moving, and the other was a friar with no apparent physical activity. I doubted he was strong. What I did not know was whether there were soldiers outside the door with orders to apprehend me. They were waiting for me to speak when suddenly Brother Domingo bustled into the room with my meal on a tray. His entrance was unexpected and it gave me the chance to see that there were no soldiers outside. What is more, if there had been, they would not have allowed the friar to enter.

'Brother Domingo, you are interrupting the work of the Lord,' shouted the irate Inquisitor.

Brother Domingo jumped in fright and abandoned the room, muttering excuses but leaving the door slightly ajar. Now I had a way out and I was reassured.

'Brother Tobias, is there not something you wish to share with me? Put yourself at the mercy of the Holy Inquisition. Tell us of the pact you have with Juan de Villafuerte or the devil himself, for they are one and same!'

'I love the Lord, I draw, I no understand, I no understand!'

'I am going to send my assistant, Brother Gonzalo, to prepare a place where in all comfort, you can confess all you know about Juan de Villafuerte and how long you have worked for him.'

All this time, the hypocritical smile had not left the Inquisitor's face while he addressed me as if I were an idiot. Little did he know!

The assistant stood up from my worktable, bowing in a show of respect, and smiling sweetly, left the room. They should learn never to underestimate anyone! Whilst I mumbled incoherently, bending over in mock contrition, I removed the dagger from under my table and plunged it to the hilt into the fat chest of that diabolical man. With his eyes full of pain and fear, he only had time to hear my last words, said in perfect Spanish:

'I am the Mama Kwishbagwi of the Tairona; your life and your evil deeds end here. You are the most wicked man I have ever encountered in my life; go find the devil waiting for you.'

He was dead. I stepped out into the corridor, trying to look composed, not knowing what I was going to find, though, in fact, it was empty. At the end of the corridor, on the right, a door was closing, probably behind the assistant, Brother Gonzalo. I went in the opposite direction, fully aware that it did not lead to the floor below or to an exit but instead to a little chapel with a window that looked out onto the roof of the stables. Easing myself down to the ground, I calmly made my way to the large front door, which, strangely, was unbolted.

I emerged into the street, calculating that the assistant and the soldiers would shortly be arriving in my room, where they would find the body of the Inquisitor and trigger the alarm. I turned to look back at the monastery and saw Brother Domingo waving goodbye to me. He then went back inside and closed the heavy door behind him. This friar, my friend, had consciously facilitated my flight; he had even left the front door unlocked. I do not think he expected me to kill the Inquisitor, but he had helped me and this I would never forget.

Once in the street, it was easy to hide from view in a city I knew well. I traversed the alleyways and streets where there were people about. When the alarm was raised, I was already bolting over the palisade to hide in the scarce vegetation on the other side. Unfortunately, I was seen by a sentry and a short while later, six men on horseback with two dogs came after me. The men were not an issue; I could hide, but the dogs were altogether another story. The semi-arid terrain was uphill and although I was fit and healthy, my fifty-nine years were catching up on me. I ran towards one of the streams that provides the city with water to try and put the dogs off my scent. Unfortunately, I did not think there were any Caribe warriors in the area, contrary to what the Spaniards thought; this was an illusion we had created. Instead of coming after me directly, the men were looking about in all directions, afraid of being ambushed. The dogs did not have the same concern.

To kill an Inquisitor was the worst crime that could be committed. If even in their hearts, the people were overjoyed and relieved, they could not display this in public; dismay and indignation had to be shown. I could expect no mercy; rather, a horrible death awaited me. It was out of the question to be caught.

The stream had very little water, certainly not enough to fool the dogs. I took off all my clothes and leaving them in a pile on the bank, I ran to the highest point. There, standing on a rock, armed with my faithful sling, I prepared to slay the dogs. From where I was placed, I could certainly eliminate both of them. However, I was out in the open and a target for the fast arrows from the men's crossbows. I had very little time to deal with the dogs and conceal myself. Luckily, dogs always run ahead and in this case the men on horseback were holding back, full of apprehension. When the dogs reached my clothes, they paused to sniff and tear at them. Serankwa was on my side and this gave me the time I needed. I had no desire to kill them but I had no alternative. When the first dog fell, the other one saw me and letting go of my clothes, came at me. But I was ready with the second stone and the dog collapsed scarcely twenty feet from where I was. The men saw me poised on the rock and the dead dogs lying on the ground. As they could see no weapons, they must have assumed there were more of us around. They paused, full of uncertainty.

'You are surrounded; go in peace,' I shouted.

Silence. Then nervously, they lowered their weapons and slowly withdrew. Once at a safe distance, they spurred their horses and galloped back to the city in all haste. Surprised at my good fortune, I climbed off the rock and went to see if either of the dogs was alive, but they were both dead. I was very lucky to have hit the second one at all. If it had come any closer, I would not have been able to aim my sling.

I sat down in an effort to calm my body, my spirit and my mind. I thanked Serankwa for having protected me all this time and for having assisted me on this day. I remained thus for a long while. Then, I looked for the last time at the clothes I had worn as a servant of the Spaniards. Now, once again, I was back to what I had always been, the Mama Kwishbagwi of the Tairona, the name I had identified myself with to that evil man in the last moments of his life. I noticed a group of Caribe warriors nearby, silently watching in amazement, having witnessed all that had happened. I realized then, that the Spaniards must have seen them as well and had wisely decided to leave me alone.

I was invaded by a feeling of elation and a sense of freedom after nine long years of living among the Sué<en> and I had all but accomplished my mission.

CHAPTER EIGHTEEN

isa and I returned to the River. I was no longer needed on the Shikwakala Nunjué. The Jarlekja of the Sierra had the situation under control and the Mama Inkimaku would be watching over the decimated Caribe. There were a lot of challenges that I now had to address on the River. Over the years, I had tried to supervise this area but most of the effort had fallen on Jawi, now an exceedingly old man of one hundred, with somewhat limited physical abilities. During the first two moons, Nisa and I found it difficult adapting to life back on the River. But we adjusted and eventually regained the strength in our arms, chests and backs and were able to resume the routine that had been such a part of our lives. Luckily the River Fishermen had been spared the 'common cold' epidemics because of their way of life and were delighted to have the Mamakwish and Nisa back among them.

One afternoon, a few moons later, a hawk informed me that the Grand Master Tarminaki wished to see me. I found an empty platform and after eating sparingly, I lay down and freed my spirit to go in search of my Master, who I found easily. He was already with the spirits of many of my Shaman brothers. He told us he would not be in the land of the living for much longer. Accordingly, he issued instructions to each one of us present, which included An Yupami, Zalab, Zyo (Quemuenchatocha), Sagesagipa, Berich, Jawi and Nuaxtashi. Further along, I will tell you about each one of them, but for now I will concentrate on the Grand Master. We all listened for the last time to his words of wisdom as he left us three missions.

The First: He drew our attention to the new Grand Master Chubaquín who was replacing him, our Master Tarminaki, the wisest of all men living in our world. Most of us knew very little about the new Grand Master since he had lived in Rapa as a hermit. Notwithstanding, we had no doubts about his capabilities. Master Tarminaki would not have chosen someone in whom he did not have complete confidence, and we all declared our support. Jawi remembered him well as Chubakin had been one of his pupils. Together with Master Tarminaki, they were all from the old generation. Jawi remembered him well since Chubaquín had been one his pupils in the long-gone days of Rapa. It was Jawi who told us of the extraordinary mental powers of the new Grand Master that we would discover in the years to come.

The Second: Our efforts to resist the invaders over the last few years had to be taken to the next level. The Master thought we were forgetting Aluna Jaba, and this she would not allow. The Sué were invading us from all directions and, save for the Shikwakala Nunjué, we were not having any success in driving them away. The illnesses were decimating us and the immediacy of what was happening was distracting us from the essential. This was unacceptable, especially as he believed a new era was approaching: 'The Assault on Mother Earth'.

The Third: The search for new Shamans. We were not to underestimate anyone having this gift, even among the black men or the Sué; the future would reveal who were suitable. Whilst the indigenous communities everywhere continued to be at the forefront of the protection of Aluna Jaba, we were to seek those who could take on this responsibility in the future.

With my heart full of sadness, I heard him say he was departing on a final flight with the hawk, across his beloved plains in the east, where he had spent his childhood, there to seek out the flat-top mountains where the Gods dwell and his people are cleansed by cascading waterfalls. During my life-time, I have encountered men who are wise and good, men who have great mental powers and men who have a complete vision of the world, but he encompassed everything. It was my good fortune to have known him and to have had him as my guide for so many years.

The Grand Master Chubaquín let it be known that my son Nuaxtashi would be the next Shaman of the River Yuma. He would accompany Jawi for as long as the latter remained amongst us. The estuary of the River, now that the Sué had discovered all the entry routes, no longer had the same importance as when Master Tarminaki entrusted it to me. Master Chubaquín's decision gave me great joy. To have Jawi and my son with me was the best thing that could happen to me in these exceedingly difficult times. The three of us would establish which particular areas we would each take care of. That night on the solitary platform, the three of us agreed to meet up in Talaiga territory. Nuaxtashi was about to leave Rapa and Jawi was in Opón territory. It appeared that the Spaniard, Quesada, had gone up into the mountains to the land of the Muisca with the seventy-two remaining men out of the nine hundred from the two original expeditions.

It took Nisa and me three moons to go upriver to the meeting point. What a pleasure it was to be a part of that peaceful life again. On the way we rested with families of the Fishermen of the River, catching up with the lives from which we had been so disconnected during the previous years. We made love in the tranquillity of the same place we had done so for the first time some forty-three years before, with her endearing cousin Apixa. We offered her this act in remembrance of her spirit. We knew she had accepted it when, on awaking the next morning, we were delighted by the presence of a pair of parrots. Subsequently, they flew off to go about their lives and we were left with a smile on our faces for the rest of the day.

Nisa was euphoric as she came across family and previous friends. I got faces and names muddled up, but she had not forgotten a single one. What is more, on the occasions that we approached an occupied platform, she started calling out names before we even got there. What we did find different from before was that few men and women of our age were still alive. The tough way of life on the River and the fevers did not allow these people to grow old. The adults we now encountered were the children of those we had known as children or adolescents.

We finally reached the Talaiga, who, in spite of their mysterious and secretive ways, greeted us cordially. We expressed our wish to stay on a small, isolated beach and they obliged without further ado. We were told the Talaiga Shaman of the River was nearby and they would bring him to us when he was ready. I was not quite sure what this meant until two days later, when Jawi arrived in his cayuco, rowed by two Talaigas. I realized then that he could no longer row himself. He got out very slowly, gesturing that he did not wish to be assisted, and we embraced with profound affection. I was so overwhelmed by the pleasure of seeing him again that I did not hold back my tears. Later, Nisa told us how the rowers, moved and embarrassed, after witnessing such a display of affection by two Shamans, had tactfully retired to the forest. When I put my arms around his now slight, frail body, I remembered when he was strong and his muscles were as hard as wood. Nisa approached Jawi and bowed as is customary, but he lifted her up and embraced her, saying in his gentle voice, 'Anyone who cares for my son like you do, is as beloved to me as he is himself.'

He knew all about Nisa, though he had only seen her briefly during the two days of our reunion when I returned from Rapa thirty years before. We settled down to spend the night and await the arrival of Nuaxtashi, who was on the far side of the Talaiga territory. Jawi had seen him while flying with his eagle, which meant that it would be a few more days before we were all together. Usually, Jawi communicates silently but that night, he proudly announced: 'I have not been alone these last few years, "my arms" have been those of a charming man, who wears a golden hummingbird around his neck.'

This was indeed gratifying and even more so because it was a son of mine who had watched over him. I was excited to think that soon I would meet this son, now a grown man. Jawi and I spent the following days reinforcing our special relationship. He was not very active, but he enjoyed listening to Nisa chattering away like a parrot, as she usually does, while he watched us getting on with our daily routines. The two Talaiga were never far, keeping at a discreet distance, not wanting to be seen observing us. I knew they were attentive in case we needed anything. Nisa would go looking for them, to leave Jawi and me alone, and in due course she struck up a friendship with these taciturn warriors. They provided the food that Nisa brought us, though Jawi did not eat very much (as is often the case with the aged).

A few days later a River Fisherman joined us. Jawi called me over and introduced him to me as my son Parripar and 'his arms' for the last ten years. This was another of those exhilarating moments because my last memory of him was as an adolescent and he had now turned into a serious, mature man. He knew who I was, but save for the respect he owed me as a Shaman, he had no idea how to approach me. I was somewhat nervous myself. Luckily Nisa, in her usual way, welcomed him with a display of emotion and pointed out the bonds that we all had in common: Jawi was my adoptive father; Parripar was my son; she was a friend and distant relative of his mother; she had known him as a boy; he was Jawi's aide and his brother Nuaxtashi would be arriving shortly... We all relaxed and that was the beginning of a relationship that deepened as the days went by. Nisa was so good at taking charge of any situation and connecting everyone in the known world!

Parripar was a kind, polite, talkative man who had the

straightforward ways of the Fishermen of the River. He had a sincere affection for Jawi and was ever mindful of his needs. Over three days, he told us about their lives for the last few years. Recently, Jawi and he had shadowed Quesada's men until they went up into the *cordillera** by way of the River of the Opón.

I will now tell you about him. I clearly remember Parripar's mother, who was like a graceful gazelle, small and slender with enormous eyes and a lovely smile. She was made pregnant by a Shaman, who, fascinated by her beauty and her diminutive size, was stirred, as were all who saw her, into wanting to protect her. I was that Shaman, only I was not one then. She was the daughter of the sister of the husband of Nisa's youngest sister... The River Fishermen were well known for their ability to remember everyone's family connections.

Parripar grew up with his mother, his grandparents and innumerable relatives. They were one of the families that liked to get about in large groups. In this way, they travelled in five cayucos on the west branch of the River, between the territory of the Talaiga and the estuary of the River Yuma. Parripar's mother usually met up with her friends Apixa and Nisa during the large gatherings that the Fishermen held. There, they exchanged stories, arranged marriages and renewed friendships. The last time they all met up, she had found Nisa sad and disheartened after the tragedy of losing her daughter, her beloved cousin and her niece, her uncle and aunt and other relatives. When Parripar turned thirteen he met his father, the Shaman of the River, who was on his way back to assist the

---

* Mountain range

other Shaman, Jawi, who in those days was already elderly. His father gave Parripar's mother a golden hummingbird she was to pass on to her son when he came of age. The hummingbird would help him to find his way in life and bring him the good fortune necessary to succeed in whatever he chose.

Three years later, the river fever struck and over half of the happy family he had grown up with perished. He and his mother survived along with a little girl, his sister, also fathered by the Shaman. When he reached adulthood, his mother presented him with the little hummingbird that he had worn about his neck ever since. At the next large gathering of the families, Parripar chose a pretty young girl from a family south of the River to be his wife. It was love at first sight for both of them. They spent the rest of the reunion alone together, putting up with the well-meaning jokes that others make about newly-weds. She bore him five children, one after the other, but died giving birth to their sixth child. He was so devastated that he did not take another wife and decided instead to bring up the five children himself. The two boys and the three girls, along with his mother and his sister, survived the successive river fevers and grew up protected by the River Gods.

The years went by and he became one of the chiefs among the Fishermen, consulted by everyone and dealing with the difficulties that present themselves in all communities. In the case of the Fishermen, the setbacks were usually related to the care of the orphaned children whom all wanted to look after but not everyone could assume. Parripar's family was one of the more prosperous, having survived many fevers and thus guaranteeing the continuity of the family. One by one nearly all his children and his sister were married and in due course he turned into a patriarch of the River. At the time of his mother's death, he had several grandchildren and his one remaining son had almost reached the age to take a wife. One night, he was tactfully approached by the Shaman of the River. Jawi, in his thoughtful, considerate manner, asked if he would assist him since age no longer allowed him to fend for himself. Without a moment's hesitation he accepted, overwhelmed that the Shaman had asked him.

He had fulfilled the last wishes of his beloved wife. His children and his sister were the heads of numerous families, successfully managing their lives on the arduous River. His youngest son kept him company during the first year with Jawi. The son eventually met the love of his life and went to live with the family of one of the girl's older sisters. The youth of the River, because of their way of life, tend to procreate at an even younger age than their contemporaries in other nations. Anyway, even when Parripar was with the Shaman of the River, he managed to see his family on a regular basis.

One of Jawi's new duties was to organise the resistance to the Sué should they appear; something that inevitably happened. But Jawi was not a man of war nor was he capable of even being aggressive. At the most he could be a lookout, our 'eyes' on the River, and this was all we could ask of him. Parripar was not a belligerent man either; it is not in the nature of the Fishermen. They are very effective at observing what happens around them. Day or night, there is not an incident that takes place involving humans, animals or in the forest that they do not notice; that is their strength.

Jawi with the eagle and Parripar with his strength and his powers of observation followed the brigantines of the Second Sué Expedition. They kept the warriors of the other nations informed about its progress.

On one occasion, however, they did in fact participate in an act of war. One afternoon, several large Chiriguaní canoes attacked four of the Sué brigantines. One of these, though damaged, was still firing its cannon that was inflicting serious casualties on the Chiriguaní. The other three undamaged brigantines did not have or were not operating their cannons. Instead, they were defending themselves with muskets and crossbows, with a limited range. The Chiriguaní realized it was useless to continue the attack and run the risk of being annihilated by the superior weapons of the enemy. As the warriors retreated, the cannon on the fourth ship sank two of their canoes, killing many of the warriors. Fortunately, the sun was setting and the Sué ceased firing for lack of visibility.

Jawi and Parripar were watching the events from a short distance. They noticed three features regarding the Sué. Firstly, their total ignorance where the River was concerned; they repeatedly ran aground whenever the water was low. Secondly, the fourth ship, that must have hit a sand bank, was damaged. It was being bailed out continuously, added to which the wood was most likely rotten. Thirdly, the other three vessels showed no inclination to come to the assistance of the stricken one, apart from taking a few of its men on board, hence only a skeleton crew was left. Even so, the cannon was still a formidable weapon.

The Sué usually anchored at night for fear of running aground, hitting a tree trunk or the riverbank in the dark.

That night the fourth brigantine had not done so, possibly attempting to catch up with the other three. When, finally, it stopped, it was still at a considerable distance from the others. Jawi and Parripar had the idea that a large tree trunk would put it out of action permanently. During the course of the night, with the assistance of some Churiguaní warriors, they dislodged an enormous trunk that was half buried in the sand. It so happened that it had a jagged point on one its extremities; quite possibly from where it had split while still standing. Near dawn, when the watch tends to be relaxed, the warriors attacked the ship from the opposite side to where the Sué would have expected. A few of the strongest rowers positioned the trunk between two of their canoes and drove it with great force into the rotten wood of the brigantine. The ship capsized in the midst of the darkness and the cries of the Sué. When daylight came all that was visible was the mast and the intrusive trunk jutting out from the water and no sign of survivors. The three remaining vessels raised their anchors and departed in great haste. It was these three brigantines that eventually met up with Quesada and subsequently returned, thoroughly demoralized, to Santa Marta. Jawi and Parripar had not participated in the venture but they had directed it. It was one year later that they came to find us.

When at last Nuaxtashi arrived in a Talaiga canoe, it was a very emotional moment for all of us. He had become a tall, strong man of forty-five, with the imposing presence of a Shaman, which commanded the respect of everyone he encountered. Nisa and Nua had a close relationship going back many years to when he was a boy. He was my son with

Mina and my love for him knew no bounds. At this point, he was to encounter a brother he did not even know about. In addition, he was meeting the legend that was Jawi, who he would be replacing when the time came. I will not dwell on the significance of this reunion. I will, however, say how much it redefined and consolidated our bonds as a family.

There were many matters we had to discuss, starting with the issue of the runaway black men and women. At present, they had two settlements but more were planned for the future, though not on the main River where they were too visible. They had to be established in the remote, now unpopulated areas once belonging to the communities annihilated by the epidemics. In this way, they would be hidden from the Spaniards, who were furious about losing their slaves. The value of these was calculated in gold, which was what they prized most. It was settled that Jawi and Nuaxtashi would watch over the area of the River between the territory of the Talaiga and that of the rapids, in the land of the Colima. From there all the way to the estuary would be my responsibility.

Since Parripar and Nua wished to spend time getting to know each other, it was decided that they would remain together with Jawi. The smile on Jawi's face showed how pleased he was to have my two sons with him; this I concluded as if he were telling me. Nisa saw to it that the Talaiga caciques were summoned, to be informed of our decision. They duly arrived the following day and listened with respect to what we had to say, since we would all be travelling through their territories on a regular basis. Now we had to bid each other farewell and we parted with sadness.

News of the events happening elsewhere followed us, and we heard that Quesada had reached Cundur-Curi-Marca and the Zipa Tisquesusa and Sagesagipa had organized the resistance. Seeing that the Sué were looking for treasure, the two of them had asked for nine volunteers to conceal it. These nine men would consequently be buried with it, to act as guardians for all eternity. In this way, only the Zipa and the Shaman Sagesagipa would know where the gold was. This was not because it had any value to them but rather to persuade the Sué to go and look for their treasure elsewhere. All these two martyrs achieved was a slow, horrible death in the midst of daily tortures that went on for months. In the end, they died without revealing their secret, much to the rage and frustration of the Spaniards. Quesada had no intention of leaving either. The existing rivalry between the Zaques had worked to his advantage. The favourable conditions he now found himself in, led to his staying on and founding the settlement of Santa Fé de Bogotá.

Berich reported that a number of somewhat different Sué with hair the colour of gold had been fiercely attacked by the Yuco who had killed their leader. The survivors were heading north to the land of the Muisca, by way of the eastern plains but following the cordillera. The Grand Master Chubaquín told us of another group of Sué who had passed not far from Rapa, coming from the south, the nation of the Inca. They were making their way north, also to the land of the Muisca. The legend of the ritual of the Zipa, who bathed in the sacred lake covered in gold, had awoken the unimaginable greed of the Sué.

The next victim of their insatiability was my friend and brother the Zaque Quemuenchatocha, who, while trying to resist the Sué, suffered terrible losses, among them his beautiful Temple of the Sun that was burnt to the ground. He himself was tortured to death without giving in to their demands. This put an end to the resistance of the Muisca. Save for a few small unsuccessful uprisings, they also fell, victims of the illnesses. Isolated as I was, the only thing I could do from afar was make offerings for their spirits to rest with those of our other brothers in the next life.

These were troubled times and it would have been easy to allow despair and pessimism to fill my spirit. Jawi's wisdom and insight greatly assisted me. He encouraged me to persevere and carry out the orders of the Grand Master Tarminaki and then those of the Grand Master Chubaquín. When we were on our Journeys of the Spirit, he quietly pointed to the riverbanks, where the magnificent forests covered Aluna Jaba like a blanket. He showed me the many animals going about their daily activities and the macaws that gave us so much pleasure. He made me look at the abundant rivers, the lakes and the streams that are so essential to our Great River Yuma and necessary to all animals. He reminded me that An Yupami in the Inca Nation had successfully concealed their last hideout, Machu Piqchu, from the Sué. Zalab was also succeeding in preventing them from reaching Darien. He showed me that Serankwa was present in everything. I was able to go back to the River, to Nisa, with my spirits restored and my mind full of all that had to be done to take care of Aluna Jaba.

About a year after our reunion with my sons, Jawi and I were together in the World of the Spirits, when he said to me: 'Son, I am leaving this world but I am going to another one that is undoubtedly better. There, I will join our esteemed brothers and I will wait for you, the person I have loved most in this world. Honour your work; carry it out with love and dedication; do not allow yourself to become discouraged.'

There was nothing more he could possibly have said.

Later, Nisa, who somehow knew what had taken place, cradled me like a child while I wept for all the memories I had of him. The next morning, I went ahead with my tasks with the renewed sense of purpose that this old man had imbued in me.

I heard from Nuaxtashi that the 'common cold' and an illness the Spaniards call 'the measles' had decimated the mysterious Talaiga. The Spaniards established a new settlement called Mompox on their land, on the eastern side of the River.

I have now reached the end of my narrative, fulfilling the wishes of my Master Tarminaki. Future generations will know our version of what took place in our world, Quicagua, and the attempts we made to protect it. A Mocana messenger is standing by, ready to take the last three chapters of the manuscript to the Mama Rigawiyún. It will be concealed where agreed and it will be safe. The messenger will be protected by the jaguar to ensure its safe arrival in my beloved Shikwakala Nunjué.

I am also sending a letter of gratitude to my friend Brother Domingo Estivel, together with a little green stone I found one day on a riverbank and which reminds me of him.

A black man, recently escaped from Santa Marta, told me that after the death of that terrible man the Inquisitor, the Inquisition had, by orders of the king, returned to Spain. They have all my sympathy.

The River Yuma, 1541

EPILOGUE

The Tairona resistance continued for about one hundred years, until a peaceful agreement was reached with the Governor Lope de Orozco in 1576. But the Spaniards had already settled on most of the lowland surrounding the sierra. Five hundred years later, the indigenous communities that still exist as such, have had to adapt in order to protect themselves from the modern world. The changes have been many; some positive, others less so. The authority of the Catholic Church and its impact on their way of life, customs and beliefs have only had a negative effect. They have lost their autonomy, along with the erosion of their lands, which further highlights their plight.

Rapa is today known as the Archaeological Park of San Agustín and continues to be protected by the Spirits of the Kasouggui. There are countless Mamas and Shamans who continue to watch over what is left of the forests, the rivers and the mountains. If we observe carefully, we will see them at their judicious work. The indigenous communities everywhere are at the forefront of the care of nature. But these are difficult times for Aluna Jaba; she is not pleased. The termite men are advancing on every side and consuming everything they find, while giving nothing in return. If we listen carefully, we will hear what she is saying: 'The balance has been lost.'

The Proofreader

GLOSSARY

alpargatas: espadrilles made from vegetable fibre; sometimes tied round the ankle

Aluna Jaba: Mother Earth

Andrés Arias: captured Spaniard; Kuktu's Spanish teacher

An Yupami: an Inca and Kuktu's teacher in Rapa

Apixa: one of Kuktu's 'Parrots'

arepa: a corn patty

Aru Maku: Wiwa musician; Kuktu's father

Arwa-Viku: force of life and light from **Aluna Jaba**

ayawasca: a psychoactive infusion prepared from the *Banisteriopsis caapi* vine and yahé or other DMT-producing plant

babilla: small alligator

Berich: Zalab's teacher in Rapa

caiman: South American crocodile; smaller than an alligator

Calamarí: Caribe nation in Bay of Cartagena area and estuary of River Yuma

Cataca: Caribe nation in the Gran Cienaga

cayuco: dugout canoe

ceiba: type of tree with pods containing cotton-like threads; sometimes known as a Cotton Tree

cerbatana: blowpipe

cienaga: wetland

coati: small ring-tailed mammal with a long snout

Colima: Chibcha nation in region of the rapids of River Yuma

Conquistador: Spanish conqueror

cordillera: mountain range

cubio: root plant, cone shaped with bitter taste; used for cooking

chicha: alcoholic drink made from fermented corn/maize

Chiriguaní: Caribe nation in eastern plains of the Lower River Yuma

chontaduro: species of palm native to tropical forests

Chubaquín: Tarminaki's successor as Grand Master of Rapa

Domingo Esquivel: Dominican friar; friend of Kuktu

Emberá: Caribe nation of the Darien

encomienda: land and Indians granted to an individual or **encomendero**

en naboria: unpaid servant

envuelto: maize/corn wrap

frailejon: shrub found in highlands of Colombia, Venezuela and Ecuador

Gaira: Caribe nation at foot of the sierra by the sea and north of Gran Cienaga

Go-Naka: villain; kidnapped people to work illicitly extracting emeralds

Guahibo: nomad nation on plains of River Orinox (Orinoco)

Guajiro: Caribe nation of Guajira Peninsula and Gulf of Venezuela

guama: sweet fruit in long pods from Guam tree

guayacan: hardwood native of the Americas

Guka: Zalab's mother; named in honour of a palm from hot lands

Hiwi: nomad nation on eastern plains of River Orinox and the Roraima region

Indian: name used by Spaniards to refer to the indigenous peoples; Columbus initially thought he had discovered a new route to the East Indies; now an offensive term

Jarlekja: grand meeting of Mamas

Jawi: Talaiga Shaman of the River; Kuktu's teacher; a seashell

Juan de Villafuerte: Rival of governor of Santa Marta; transmitted a common cold to the Caribe people; killed by Andrés Arias

Kasouggui Spirits: **Jate Kalawia** present in the mountains; and **Jate Kalashé** present in the trees and vegetation; control equilibrium in forests; certain trees sacred and declared as such by Kasouggui Spirits

Kuktu: the narrator; Shaman Zu; Brother Tobias to friars

maloca: large communal hut

Mama: replace 'shamen': term used to describe a Shaman in Sierra Nevada

Mama Inkimaku: Guardian of the Sacred Lakes and Glaciers

Mama Kwishbagwi: Guardian of the Forests; title later given to Kuktu

Mama Rigawiyún: Tairona Mama of the Jaguar Clan; Nuaxtashi's teacher

mamoncillo: small round green acid fruit

manatee: herbivorous marine mammal; 'a sea cow'

manzanilla: camomile

marañones: yellow and red fruit with nutty taste; 'cashew fruit'

Mina: Kuktu's beloved; Nuaxtashi's mother; Zhiwé's daughter

Mixia Caita: Muisca friend of Kuktu; a healer

Mocana: Caribe nation in region of the estuary of River Yuma

mochila: traditional bag of sisal cotton or wool made by the indigenous people of northern Colombia

Muisca: Chibcha nation in region of central highlands: Cundu-Curi-Marca

Muzo: Chibcha nation in the emerald region between River Yuma and Cundur-Curi-Marca; miners of the emeralds

Nasa: Chibcha nation of the Upper Yuma; guardians of Rapa in south and east

Nisa: Kuktu's companion; a river woman

Nuaxtashi: son of Mina and Kuktu; named after sacred stone used as protection against fierce animals

Opón: Caribe nation in the Middle Yuma

Panche: Chibcha nation bordering Muisca in central highlands

Panquiaco: Cacique of Darien; befriended Spaniards; later change of heart

Parripar: Kuktu's son; Jawi's assistant

peccary: aggressive pig-like animal

Pijáo: Chibcha nation bordering Muisca in central highlands

poor man's gold: an alloy of gold and copper known as **tumbago**

poporo: small gourd in which seashells are ground with coca leaves

Quemuenchatocha: Shaman Zyo; pupil of Am Yupami in Rapa; later Muisca Zaque put to death by Quesada

River Yuma: today known as the River Magdalena

ruana: poncho

Sagesagipa: Shaman and Muisca cacique put to death by Quesada

sand stove: small insulated area of sand and stones for cooking

Serankwa: force that controls the Universe

Shikwakala Nunjué: the Heart of the World; mountain range inhabited by the Tairona; today known as Sierra Nevada of Santa Marta

Sué: the White Birds; Spaniards

Tahuantinsuyo: Inca nation

Taira: Tairona

Talaiga: Caribe nation in region of delta of the Lower Yuma

Tamo: Crossed the cienaga to the river with Kuktu

Tarminaki: Grand Master of Rapa

totuma: a gourd-like fruit used as container for liquids

turba: potatoes

Turbaco: Caribe nation in region of the Bay of Cartagena

ulukukwi: poisonous snake

Walashi: childhood friend and companion of Kuktu; a Hummingbird Clan healer; mother of Yama

Wiwa: Caribe nation in region south-east of Sierra

Xante: Kuktu's Muisca friend

Yalcón: Chibcha nation in region of the Upper Yuma; guardians of Rapa

Yama: daughter of Kuktu and Walashi; named after a doe (in Guajiro)

yuluca: state of harmony and equilibrium of the spirit

Zalab: Kuktu's childhood friend; later the Shaman Kaku

Zhatukúa: Journey of the Spirit

Zhi'nita: Healer of the Hummingbird Clan; Kuktu's mother; named after a beautiful seashell

Zhiwé: Healer of the Toucan Clan; Mina's mother; Nuaxtashi's grandmother

Printed by BoD™in Norderstedt, Germany

9 781915 036025